Praise for *The Night of the Rambler*

• Selected by the *Airship* as a 1
• Finalist for the Premio Casa de las Américas 2014

"Colorful detours into native lore . . . strike grace notes that echo Márquez. Readers . . . will be rewarded with the little-known tale of how the underdog country demanded its own place in the 20th century." —*Publishers Weekly*

"With tremendous humanity and humor, the novel articulates these themes through the power of the relationships and the urgency each character demonstrates in this quest for self-determination." —*Caribbean Writer*

"Revolution and historic change—words that can remain detached concepts unless we can somehow connect them with their human face and the lives behind them. This is what Kobbé achieves in marvelous style and depth—weaving a Caribbean tapestry of places, wider events, the individuals shaped by them, and how they ultimately come together to shape events themselves in the times leading to a revolution on Anguilla in 1967." —*MACO*

"However unusual this revolution is, it is a prelude to Anguilla's eventual divorce from St. Kitts and Nevis, before becoming a separate British territory; its unconventional LOL factor could diversify an elective college course on revolutions with something bloody peaceful." —*New Pages*

"This is a book about revolution and the underdog, about a small, isolated island fighting for recognition, opportunity and justice; it is a compelling tale about a curious historical episode, but also a vital look at priorities, perspective and the right to live in dignity, issues that, much like Anguilla's rebellion of 1967, are all too easily forgotten." —*Island Review*

"*The Night of the Rambler* is revolutionary, a reliquary, an impressionist tale of men who are by turns melancholy, raging, and often comic, their voices unique to this place and given a singular story." —Susan Straight, author of *Between Heaven and Here*

"This is a fine novel, a surprising novel, perhaps the first true novel I have read about the nature of revolutions. *The Night of the Rambler* raises all sorts of questions about what revolutions want, how revolutions fail, and why revolutions are necessary—challenging all the while how history remembers them."
—Percival Everett, author of *Erasure*

"*The Night of the Rambler* is exceptional. Riveting, deeply thoughtful, and constantly inventive, Montague Kobbé's novel is part literary thriller, part revolutionary study, part epic historical narrative. Altogether, it makes for one profound read."
—Joe Meno, author of *Marvel and a Wonder*

ON THE WAY BACK

MONTAGUE KOBBÉ

AKASHIC
BOOKS

Published by Akashic Books
©2016 Montague Kobbé

ISBN-13: 978-1-61775-441-8
Library of Congress Control Number: 2015947209

Akashic Books
Twitter: @AkashicBooks
Facebook: AkashicBooks
E-mail: info@akashicbooks.com
Website: www.akashicbooks.com

To Adrian, for all those games we played so many years ago. Here's the result.

A Marisol. Tu favorita, al fin.

At Antón we couldn't get into the church to see the miraculous Christ. The church was locked and no one seemed to know where the priest was. "Never mind" said Chuchu. "On the way back." It was the second time he had used the phrase and suddenly in my mind it became the title of a novel which, alas, I was never to write.

. . . Captain Wong, the miraculous Christ, the Haunted House, all were promised on the way back . . . In my book the promised return would never be fulfilled—there would be no going back for the chief character.

—Graham Greene, *Getting to Know the General*

In the tropics one must before everything keep calm.

—Joseph Conrad, *Heart of Darkness*

PART I

I

I am the Dragon. My real name belongs to my father, Nathaniel Jones. We both bear the exact same name, the exact same curse. There isn't even a distinguishing *Jr.* between us. One night, many generations ago, during a family reunion somewhere in rural Illinois, one of the Jones women called out for Junior. At that point, father, grandfather, and son simultaneously got up from the table to attend to the call. That night, it was decided that no other Jones would ever use the qualifying annex behind his proper name. Fifty years later, the second son of the youngest of the Joneses present in that family reunion filled out the forms that acknowledged the legitimacy of a baby born from a young German woman with sparkly blue eyes, calling him Nathaniel Jones. Not Nathaniel Jones V. Not Nathaniel Jones, Jr.—partly because he, the father, was himself not called Nathaniel, but Horace—simply Nathaniel Jones.

As soon as I heard that stupid tale, at the age of eight, I, Dragon Jones, first and only son of such Nathaniel, refused to follow the unimaginative tradition of the family that abandoned my father long before the blueprints of my being could be sketched in the ducts of his testes. It was then that I acquired the identity of a man who would forever be taken for a Welsh peasant. I, Dragon Jones, am *not* Welsh. In fact, I'm half-German—twice: my father, half-American, really

German, met my mother, half-German, really Australian, in
the place where I was born: the Federal Republic of West
Germany. When my family discovered the fact that a country
with soaring economic growth doesn't necessarily provide
the entirety of its inhabitants with economic well-being,
they decided to move to a place where they could put to use
their Teutonic American and thick Australian accents. The
closest one was England. I don't feel identified with any of
these countries, none of those nationalities seem to apply to
me. However, given that very few people in England know
either my real name or the bizarre dimension of my true
story, very few people in England believe me when I say that
I am unequivocally *not* Welsh. (After all, is there anything
more Welsh than *Dragon Jones*?) Nevertheless, in due time,
I learned that it was better to be what I was not, than to be
what people wouldn't believe I was, so I embraced the motto
rather Welsh than German (if only marginally) and stopped
asserting what it was that I wasn't.

Though I have tried my best to disentangle myself from
Nathaniel's name, I still share his curse. Fate and Nathaniel
have brought me to this flat islet with the shape of a snake on
the northern edge of the Caribbean. Anguilla is a recondite
destination: sixteen miles long, three wide, little vegetation,
and no history. But Anguilla is also surrounded by an enormous coral reef. Take that fact and combine it with the effect
of the tides and a large, large dose of time, and you will be
left with the most beautiful beaches in the world. *In the world*.

It was seeking beauty, comfort, and seclusion during Easter over one year ago, that Nathe stumbled upon the un-
attractive name of Anguilla. He was considering returning
to the Seychelles until the moment when he opened Hotel
Anguilla's website. From then on, there was no turning back.
Had he not randomly landed on that page, he might have

gone to the Seychelles. Had he not come to Anguilla, he would have never met Sheila Rawlingson. Had he not met Sheila Rawlingson, he never would have married again.

Sheila Rawlingson is my father's wife. Sheila Rawlingson is half Nathaniel's age. Sheila Rawlingson might well be the reason why I'm here. Nathaniel met Sheila on the second week of his two-week vacation during Easter, over one year ago. After a short period of courting and a large amount of controversy, Nathaniel and Sheila married. Their long honeymoon was followed by a decision to return to the homeland of their love, perhaps to appease the clamor raised by their private wedding. It was at some point after their return that Nathaniel came up with the extravagant idea of setting up a commercial airline based on Anguilla to feed the rest of the Leeward Islands, to connect with European destinations, and to link with the most important of the Windward Islands. Sheila told him he was crazy; I had to read the e-mail he sent me twice, to make sure he wasn't joking. But Nathaniel is tenacious to the point of stubbornness and his persistence has made me travel to an island of which I had barely heard before to form a partnership with a woman I had never met. Sheila Rawlingson is a gorgeous woman: she is exuberant, beautiful, elegant. I, the Dragon, have a secret to tell you: I'm in love with Sheila Rawlingson, my father's wife, our business partner.

▌▌

T*he plane will arrive at seven thirty in the evening, please have me picked up at the airport.* Four weeks of uncomfortable silence came to an end with the short, polite phone call Dragon Jones paid his father and business partner on the eve of May 7, one year and one month after Nathaniel's departure for his two-week Easter holiday. Nathaniel Jones had already resolved not to have his son picked up at the airport, but to go fetch him personally. Consequently he waited, alone, in the emptied hallway of Clayton J. Lloyd International Airport as the ATR 42 that carried Dragon Jones from V.C. Bird International Airport in Antigua to the northernmost of the Leeward Islands landed on Anguilla later that evening, two hours behind schedule. *Welcome to your new home.* The embrace that ensued cut through the bile that, like an ocean, had lodged itself between the two during the preceding weeks.

Despite the jetlag, the fatigue, Dragon Jones immediately expressed his approval of the house Nathaniel had rented for him on the western quarter of the island, far enough from his own home in East End to avoid the friction that comes with overexposure. Dragon's two-bedroom house was perfectly located for him to enjoy and assess the bores and privileges of the lifestyle of the obscenely rich in Anguilla without having to be isolated in the fantasy-island exclusivity offered by Viceroy, by Cap Juluca, or by any other upmarket hotels of the kind. Nathaniel wanted his son and business partner to have a taste of the very best Anguilla had to offer—the existing brand, the development potential—but he also wanted—needed—him to formulate his own version of the possible pitfalls, of the risks of failure faced by any venture in this place. If this plan was to work, it was going to have to stand up to the entirely different perspectives, motivations, and ultimately objections he and his son would raise against it. Convincing Dragon of going ahead with the venture was the least of Nathaniel's problems: what he needed most was for him to develop his own arguments *against* the investment—and the West, as islanders called it, with its half-derelict mega-developments and its preposterously underused professional golf course, provided the perfect environment for him to produce just that.

During a spell of little sense and much indulgence, Dragon basked in the sun and experienced firsthand the unique splendor this obscure island had to offer: he embraced the chance to putt (on his own) in a golf course with a view to the turquoise sea and to the rundown skeleton of a failed real estate project that once upon a time had reputedly cost a certain Mr. Tinkerman his place in the *Forbes* list of billionaires; he rejoiced at the sight of his white skin tanning under the scorching tropical sun; he found in the solitude of a deserted beach the forgetful solace that allowed him to distance himself from the misgivings that had followed him on his excursion, and then he was able to enjoy his rum punch, piña colada, or cuba libre as he gazed into the sun every evening—just before six o'clock—when it sank into the ocean to bring the day to a peaceful end. Unlike his father, Dragon did not need to fall in love with anyone to fall in love with Anguilla.

Nathaniel Jones allowed Dagon to revel for a full week in the amnesia that the island had brought to his senses. In the meantime, he redoubled his effort to have everything in place before the defining day when the two men who constituted the board of directors—the high command—of Jones Investments would get together to discuss the feasibility, practicality, even the desirability

of entangling in the most ambitious of fantasies: establishing a
local commercial airline to serve the Leeward Islands and the rest
of the north Caribbean.

When Dragon Jones showed up on the morning of Thursday
May 15 at Nathaniel's East End quarters with a briefcase full of
numbers and a notepad full of questions, his skepticism had already been besieged by the staggering beauty, by the inebriating
peacefulness of Anguilla. Nevertheless, the enthusiasm instilled in
him by a week of fantasy in never-never land could not remove (at
least not totally) the anxiety he felt at being swept into an enterprise whose main driving force was clearly the latest of Nathaniel's whims. *We cannot jeopardize the financial health of Jones Investments
on the basis of a caprice. We will need at least three aircrafts, plus licensing,
plus staff, plus rent. Local financing is out of the question, and any backing
we might get will depend directly on Jones Investments acting as guarantor.
We'll need to commit at least one million dollars of hard cash before we can
even dream of getting started.*

Nathaniel knew Dragon's first card would be sense, so his
response was almost automatic: *Suppose we manage to get independent means of funding the project, suppose we can manage to keep control
of the airline without having to put in the capital to set it up.* Nathaniel's
face lit up with the sort of rush gamblers get from wagering large
amounts of money on a dark horse, the kind of kick that can only
come from a fresh, unchartered challenge. His eyes hid behind a
studied wince—a look of ambition and concentration replicated
by his mouth, jaw slightly askew, the lips parted just enough to
allow the top end of his lower teeth to show, glint almost, in expectation. Nathaniel, you could tell, was drawn to excitement, to
risk: everything Jones Investments had always stood against.

Dragon could see exactly where Nathaniel was going but he
stopped himself short of interrupting him. *This is the perfect opportunity to embark on an activity that combines your interests and mine. We'll
be developing a real business, a very human affair, but we'll have to depend*

on other people's confidence, on the commitment we can extract from them. He listened attentively, gave away nothing at all, while Nathaniel, *The idea is to concentrate the company's attention—not necessarily its funds—on one ambitious undertaking.* Dragon's reason was engaged in an internal duel between the unnatural sympathy he felt toward this adventure and the prevalent sensation that *it simply cannot work.*

All I'm proposing is we take a risk that in the worst of cases might involve you spending a year of your life in this franchise of hell. Nathaniel noticed his son's resilience giving way, and pulled the final trick—the one that, he knew, would tip the balance in his favor—out of his hat. *I have a name that you'll like: Dragon Wings.* Dragon's eyes gleamed with the fire of approval at the sound of his own name soaring through the skies, and Nathaniel saw immediately that he had sealed his first, the easiest, of what would need to be a long sequence of victories, if Dragon Wings was ever to become a reality.

Nathaniel and Dragon Jones spent all of Thursday morning and most of the afternoon negotiating, devising, calculating the pros and cons of such a risky enterprise. No matter how you looked at it, this was madness. But Nathaniel was determined to see his insanity through and Dragon was more inclined to back the venture than he ever thought he would be. *With one condition: we will not inject any funds from Jones Investments into the development of this airline. That is where we draw the line.*

Deal!

III

So one Sunday evening, about ten days after first getting to Anguilla, I meet Sheila. A long Thursday of negotiations had caused some friction between Nathaniel and me. Somehow, I had almost wanted to be convinced about this project and at the same time I resented the fact that I was being forced into a plan solely conceived, I was sure, for my father to enjoy the earthly pleasures offered by his wife. Much of this he disguised in schemes, strategies, calculations, but deep down inside both of us knew what this was about—and I wasn't amused, though I didn't mind that much either.

At least that's what I thought. At least so I told myself.

We agreed, almost tacitly, to give each other some space, to take a small break from business dealings, to let time settle the old dust we had lifted from each other's skins. In short, we decided to take Friday off. *Come join us for dinner on Saturday night.* Saturday night was not a good night but I would have said no to his first invite no matter what, simply out of principle, to get one back on him—even the smallest of paybacks—just to tick him off. *Sorry, I already have plans for Saturday.* So it's Sunday night when I'm first confronted with Sheila Rawlingson's gracious figure criss-crossing her way down the catwalk that is the dining floor of the Straw Hat, a charming restaurant by the beach. The scene is enthralling,

she is divine—beautiful, elegant. Nothing can go wrong this
Sunday evening: dinner is a blast, Nathe is in great spirits,
Sheila is delightful, and me, I just wonder why in the world I
ever had any doubts concerning the success of our partnership.

After such a promising first impression, the meeting Nathaniel has arranged with Deianira Walker, his lawyer, for
Tuesday becomes little more than a formality: shake hands,
take seats, *This is my advisor, pleased to meet you, here are
the papers*, read through provisions, sign at the bottom. And just
like that, in the blink of an eye, Dragon Wings comes to exist.

Formalities continue in the guise of getting an office.
Nathe has been speaking to a slimy character by the name
of Jermaine Dwyer—short skinny legs, stomach bloated to the
size of a boiler, the kind of body that makes an extreme sport
of tying the laces of your shoes. He owns a small building on
the road leading to the airport, which Nathe thinks is perfect
as a venue, but Sheila protests relentlessly against the idea.
Uncle Glen does have an empty space in de Business Center.
The Business Center is a trendy commercial complex where
all the major local businesses (all twelve of them) have an
outlet. Sheila's getting excited. The prestige, the location, the
opportunities. *I goan speak wit' Uncle Glen straight away.* I
can't quite understand Nathe's obvious satisfaction as Sheila
unclips her mobile phone from the top of her trousers—skin
tight, curled over her buttocks—and walks away to make her
call.

Two hours later we convene on a roundabout opposite
the government buildings. From a large red van emerges the
gigantic body of a clumsy man. Glenallen Rawlingson must
be in his sixties but to tell by the blank look in his eyes he
could be the same age as any of the students at Demerara
High School—the school next to what might become our office. His prominent nose, his dark skin (darker than the aver-

age Anguillan), his bulging eyes (made seem whiter by the darkness of his skin), his flat, inward-folded lips—all combine to cloud the expression on his face with a veil of uncertainty. His stride is self-assured, if slow, his voice, ungraspable, both near and far at the same time. He weighs well over two hundred pounds and towers upward at least six feet high. My awe must be evident because Glenallen lets escape a boisterous guffaw as soon as we are introduced. As he leads the way on our short walk to the Business Center, I can't help wondering what kind of genetic affinity might exist between this enormous man and Sheila's delicate beauty.

The office is a small room on the first floor of the building. The large window on the far wall faces northward, as does the road, which means there is absolutely no breeze (the wind in Anguilla always blows from the east), but all the dust from the street still manages to crawl up inside. The room feels stuffy even when completely empty but Sheila is obsessed with the idea of having a place—*Dis is perfect, you know!*—in *the* business complex of the island. *How much de rent goan be?* Glenallen is facing away from Sheila as she speaks to him; he doesn't turn around, he doesn't even flinch—he just lifts his left arm gently and with a sleight of hand, *For you, is free.* Nathe isn't happy. *If we don't pay, we don't take it.* His white linen trousers seem to glide on the stagnant atmosphere until he stops two feet away from Glenallen. *Five hundred.* From across the room, Sheila can still only see Glenallen's swollen neck and the back of his shaved head. Nathe stands motionless, just two feet away from him, observing every crevice in his face. I simply stare, amazed and confused, at the awkwardness of the transaction. *Deal!* Hands are shaken and pledges exchanged but the threatening smell that presided over our meeting follows us on our way to our respective cars.

Two weeks later the local newspaper publishes an article about Nathaniel Jones—"the latest expat entrepreneur to reach Anguilla"—together with a quarter-page advertisement for a full-time secretary/receptionist to work at the Business Center for Dragon Wings. In the meantime, the decoration of the office turns into a makeshift affair: Sheila gets two desks and a filing cabinet from an insurance company that is upgrading their offices; Nathe convinces Saul Newman, the owner the five-star Hotel Anguilla where he stayed originally, to part with a tired Persian rug and an old dark blue two-seat sofa that for years have been the first things you see when you walk into the hotel; a tacky globe, two PCs—with monstrously old-fashioned screens—and a huge map of the Leeward Islands complete the interior of our office.

By the time we are through with the headquarters of Dragon Wings we have a workplace on our hands which oozes anything but luxury: the carpet and the sofa look larger in the crammed space of an office than in the spacious foyer of a luxury hotel; the two desks are slightly different shades of gray than the filing cabinet; the light that floods the room through the vast window is sucked in by the size or the color (or both) of the furniture inside; the desk by the wall opposite the window seems to float under the shaft of electric light that shines on it from the ceiling, covering it with a thick mist. So Nathe decides to bring in six new, comfortable, and expensive desk chairs from Colony Leisure, the colorfully named local interior design specialist. Since that time we have contracted the services of a full-time secretary, we have set up the payroll, opened the office, created a business, but we still haven't received our six chairs. Apparently they will take another four weeks to arrive from the factory, somewhere in Canada or Brazil—it's hard to know. But such is progress in Anguilla, such is life, and there doesn't seem to be much anyone can do about it.

When I first got to Anguilla I was full of doubts and, in all honesty, anger at the waste of time and money this would be. Six weeks later I get the feeling that I understand the Caribbean a bit *less*, not more, day by day, while my knowledge of aviation has been little enhanced by my systematic exploration of "the Bible of the air," as Nathe calls the Eastern Caribbean Civil Aviation Authority (ECCAA) Rules and Regulations. And yet, somehow, we have managed to turn Dragon Wings into something considerably more substantial than just a silly name. Setting up this airline in time to profit from the winter season will be a titanic challenge, no doubt. However, it is a challenge we are eager to face. Dragon Wings will be the first Anguillan airline to run regularly scheduled commercial flights all year round. Dragon Wings is a joint venture between Nathaniel Jones, Sheila Rawlingson, and me. Dragon Wings is a mature man's dream, a young professional's adventure, and a local woman's brave token of love. But Dragon Wings flies my name, is my child. *I am Dragon Wings.*

IV

Nathaniel Jones allowed Dagon to revel for a full week in the amnesia that Anguilla had brought to his senses. For a full week Dragon Jones loitered on pristine white-sand beaches, indulged in the fresh flavors of the culinary gem of the region, and explored the relatively limited options the island's nightlife had to offer after dinner. It was during this time that Dragon ended up, on a quiet Wednesday evening after an overdose of sun, in one of the three establishments that provided entertainment through the otherwise helplessly idle tropical nights. Dragon scanned the premises in search of agreeable company. His happy, tanned face caught the eye of a lonely drinker at the other end of the bar. *SamB, nice to meet you.* An empty public house became the perfect stage for a parade of drunken anecdotes and amusing episodes to blend the souls of two connecting characters. A few hours later they still knew nothing about each other, and yet there was a palpable, inexplicable bond working its way between them. *What does a guy like you do in a place like this, anyway?* He was a pilot for New World Airways. *We operate charter flights to the neighboring islands.* No kidding.

The dose of forgetfulness that Anguilla had instilled in Dragon's mind was not enough to let the most random of coincidences pass by unnoticed. Suddenly, Dragon found in some unfamiliar corner of his brain the instincts of a spy and without alerting SamB to his little secret extracted every bit of information he could gather from his newly made friend. *Oh, I'm just here with my company looking into the feasibility of a business project, but we can't speak much about it yet.* Ignorant of the role he was destined to play in such project, SamB extended an invitation to Dragon Jones to *join us for dinner on Saturday night—it will be a quiet affair, just a few friends out at my place, but we've all been on-island for some time so you might be able to get some tips, who knows.*

That was the cue for Dragon to snap out of his casual oblivion and get back in work mode. Suddenly, the questions that troubled his mind on the long way from Gatwick, England, to St. John's, Antigua, loomed in his consciousness—larger, more pressing than before. These were the questions, the doubts, the objections that Nathaniel Jones faced and was forced to dispel during a long Thursday morning of reservations, negotiations, and compromise that lasted well into the afternoon.

No matter how you looked at it, it was madness. But Dragon felt more inclined to back the venture than he ever thought he would be, and Nathaniel was obsessed with the idea of seeing his insanity through, and the two of them were charmed by the idea of life in the sunshine, so in the end one, just one, condition was agreed upon and a handshake sealed a precarious deal between father and son.

Then came dinner at SamB's with a horde of friends. Then came the blast that was Sunday night, when the foundations of the Sheila Rawlingson cult were laid in Dragon's heart as he simply wondered why he should ever have doubted the success of their partnership. Then came the meeting at Deianira Walker's office, where more hands were shaken, more paperwork signed, and in the blink of an eye Dragon Wings came to exist. Then came Glenallen Rawlingson, the Business Center, six phantom office chairs, and an article in the *Anguillan* newspaper about Nathaniel Jones, the latest expat entrepreneur to reach the island.

But once the relatively simple formalities (nothing was as sim-

ple as it seemed in Anguilla) of registration, location, and decoration were completed, the trio that formed not only the new
Jones family nucleus but also the board of directors of Dragon
Wings was faced with the far more demanding building process
that would occupy the next five months of their lives. The call was
to create an actual, rather than just a hypothetical, airline, but the
greatest difficulty they faced was that all three together could not
rustle up a single day of experience in the aviation business, nor
did anyone on the island have significant knowledge of how to
set up (or run, for that matter) a regular commercial air carrier.
Now that the legal scaffolding was in place, the impending work
seemed as urgent as it was colossal, with every single one of the
crucial elements missing.

Dragon did not have the first clue as to what was elementary,
primordial, or even necessary for a running airline to function.
And Dragon felt ill disposed toward the wasteful implications in
terms of time and effort entailed by the methodical research of
the ins and outs of this new subject he suddenly found himself
tackling. So Dragon decided to follow his instincts and look at the
issue with nothing more than a large dose of common sense. After
all the deliberation Dragon found necessary—not very much—he
concluded that his task should focus on the quest for a chief pilot for Dragon Wings. Routes were still being discussed with the
government and no effort had been made yet to decide what sort
of aircraft would be used, let alone to find the actual machines
available in the region, but Dragon was guided by an inexplicable
impulse to appoint a chief pilot. *It makes sense: we need someone to help
us figure out what we need and how to get it, and I know just the right person.
Don't you worry about it, Nathe, this is one thing we have covered!*

Carried by some sort of nostalgic frenzy, Dragon chose
against the obvious move and instead of turning to the experience
of SamB—*We'll poach him later*—he delved into the distant recesses
of his memory to evoke the presence of an extravagant fellow

who over a decade before had caught his attention with his exotic origin and his unorthodox ways. Filled with expectation and
overcome by an intense resolve, Dragon decided to incorporate
a neglected friend into the current undertaking and convinced
himself that he would be able to do it with a simple phone call.
Despite the fact that Dragon had not seen Arturo Sarmiento in
five years, not spoken to him in months, he harbored more than
a hope—he was dead certain, really—that his old drinking buddy
from the days of university would jump at the chance of joining
the ranks of Dragon Wings. But as so very often is the case, life
had shuffled the cards in the intervening years and Dragon's hand
was found wanting.

V

'm not talking about a girl, Art, I'm talking about a project! My hands are sweating, my ears buzzing, my entire
demeanor has been affected by this unexpectedly long
negotiation. In the distance I catch Nathe's gleaming eye.
His evident anxiety can only be matched by mine, except I've
had the small comfort of draining my internal agony through
relentless talking whereas his only route of escape has been
the short circuit offered by the pattern of the carpet. *That was
not the question, Art.* Nathe's arms cut violently through the
room. Ill at ease in the position of spectator, his frustration
turns into rage. I let out a sigh as I switch the phone from my
left to my right ear. Art's words escape the earpiece loudly, infesting the stagnant air with defeat. We both hear the words.
We both pretend we haven't.

He's out. I can see Nathe containing his anger. I sit, holding my aching head with my thumb and index finger, waiting
for the news to sink in, the ensuing storm to break out. A
few minutes race past us before the silence is shattered. *I
thought you said he would be in, no matter what.* I can hear
the tension stringing together Nathe's words. He doesn't want
to lose his temper but I can already tell he soon will. I still
haven't moved an inch since I landed, defeated, on the blue
couch. Gloom has taken hold of the scene, infecting Nathe's
tired speech as he completes another lap around the ruined

carpet. *What are we going to do?* I'm still recovering from the lost fight, digesting Art's refusal. *What are we going to do?* The room is too crowded as it is to allow silence to filter in, so Nathe rightly chooses to repeat the question over and over again. *What are we going to do?*

The air shakes with his powerful voice and I'm forced back from oblivion. *I don't know, Nathe. I don't know.*

So far, all we have is a business license, a name, and a bunch of promises. Plain facts have never been a trait of Nathe's speech, so the matter-of-factness of his sentence yanks me back from my state of self-deprecating pity. Something clicks inside my mind and suddenly my attitude changes. I jump off the sofa, reinvigorated. Back on my feet, the atmosphere in the room feels different. *Basically, we are fucked.* In the face of extreme adversity we are both, for some mysterious reason, overwhelmed by an unvoiced confidence. *We are fucked.* The repressed smile in Nathe's expression tells me that isn't right.

(ARTURO SARMIENTO)

I

A sullen, dark face cast its sad eyes on the nearly empty free house, sunken in a distant corner over a pile of cushions. Directly opposite the two small black eyes, sitting alone on a table by the window, Dragon Jones got lost in the semantics of putting together in a coherent script all those one-liners that swarmed his mind. Outside, the howling wind punished the flower buds that had blossomed at the end of dormant branches prematurely awoken by an early spasm, a preview, of spring. The music stopped. The empty room, momentarily stripped of sound, became even emptier. Suddenly, the storm outside shifted in the direction of the large window, a shower of ice pellets furiously rapping on the glass. The sad, sullen face acquired a body—short, strong, foreign—walked across the gloomy room, inserted a coin—his last one—in the jukebox. The storm was let inside by the riders of The Doors. The two small black eyes went back to their place in the corner by the cushions. Thunder roaring indoor, hail pummeling the window from the outside, finally succeeded in distracting Dragon from his work.

The small sad eyes, filled with apprehension at the growing shadow of Dragon's approaching figure, showed themselves candidly polite once the initial awkwardness of the situation was overcome by Dragon's generous gesture: a pint. Arturo Sarmiento was a Venezuelan exchange student from the Catholic University of Caracas in the last year of his five-year course in economics.

A combination of circumstances—parental and peer pressure, financial expectations, intellectual aptitude—had guided him through a long, not very straight path, which, after allowing him to pursue his academic interest in the field of sociology and tolerating his desire to test his manual skills as a mechanic, had made him slide right into the slot allocated to him by social determination long before his birth. Arturo had never thought of himself as an economist, but his father was one, as was his older brother, and Art's older sister, while a lawyer, had completed an MBA and worked as a consultant in corporate law. Now, at long last and despite Art's capricious spirit, it seemed as if by the end of the year he too would be worthy of calling himself a Sarmiento, a Sarmiento with a future.

Dragon took an immediate liking to the foreign voice—the accent—that came with that foreign body. He liked the exotic nature of his name, the exotic name of his country. He liked the mature tone of a speech that, unlike his, no longer cracked midsentence. He liked the effect of the seemingly endless amount of knowledge a man only five or six years his senior could display. He liked to think that in five or six years' time he would know as much about the world as Art did right now, just that then Art would *still* know five or six years more than him. But that did not make him jealous, it just made him smile. "There's enough time for time." If he could remember it tomorrow, he would have to add that one to the script. *What I really want to be, though, is a pilot.* Art had the perfect sense of timing characteristic of many South American people—the sense of timing that makes a story flow, that makes a joke work, that Dragon simply lacked. His speech was at times funny, at times serious, always engaging. His cadence followed the rhythm of a silent tune that kept Dragon's mind dancing from sentence to sentence. Every pause seemed to demand a brief gasp, implore for a sequel. The final drops of a second pint swirled at the bottom of the glass as Art firmly planted it on the table. Like a performing jongleur, Art's demeanor complemented his act, contributed to the ultimate objective of a third free drink. *Ah-ah: never accept, my friend, what you cannot later pay for. Sorry! I put my last coin in the machine.* But Art could see Dragon was too captivated to allow him to walk away, so he dropped the mask of politeness and agreed to have another drink. As Dragon walked to the bar, he quickly scanned the provisional profile of the characters in his play, pondered which would best suit the righteous sentence: "Never accept what you cannot later pay for." He would have to create one.

I got bored of business. I never wanted to be a businessman. Art's erratic career as a student bore yet another bracketed pause between the sixth and seventh semester of his degree, when he discovered his passion for the sky. *I quit uni, split from my parents, and went to live with my aunt on the island of Margarita, where I enrolled in an intensive flying course with the air force.* One night, twelve months later, Arturo Sarmiento lay battered, naked, drunk unconscious, hair and eyebrows shaved off his head, in the middle of a field generally intended for the takeoff and landing of the Bell helicopters he was now licensed to pilot, at the end of the traditional military induction ceremony for graduating novices.

Dragon was mesmerized. Every new tale brought a new beer and every pint seemed to run out just before the pregnant climax of each story, which inevitably alluded to yet-undisclosed anecdotes, to more material to unravel, to another drink. The storm receded. The jukebox fell silent. The whole world paused for Art to spin his particular yarn, for Dragon to buy the beer. *I hadn't enrolled as a conscript but as a civilian invitee. I was free to leave the academy, live life.* Yet *life* as a private pilot failed to deliver the emotional fulfillment Art had found devastatingly lacking in academia: one year of hard work turned into little more than three hundred hours of experience and, despite the reputable license that went with them, Art was unable to find stable employment.

Flying for rich people in my country is the best: they give you their Kings, their Cessnas, tell you where they want to go, sit in the passengers' cabin with their friends, and get drunk or fornicate. Art was lost in his memories now, his eyes focused somewhere far distant from that pub, recreating in his mind the scene he wished he could live out time and again forever. *I flew to La Blanquilla, to Los Roques. Believe me, the most beautiful beaches in the world.* He spoke with the conviction of someone who had what he was saying on good authority, which conferred his knowledge with more grounds than if he relied solely on his empirical experience. *One time we went to Los Llanos—the plains. We flew just above the ground, just above the chigüires—I think you call them capybara—the cachicamos—armadillos—the tapirs, mowing the fields with our propellers, scaring the animals—who were unable to see or hear us until we were right on top of their heads—out of their skins.* While he said this, Arturo glided the palm of his open right hand just barely over the back of his left, also open but pointing in a perpendicular direction to the path followed by his imaginary aircraft. *We landed on a finca, had the traditional lunch—spit roast beef—and, after a nap on the chinchorros—woven hammocks—headed back to Caracas. All my boss had wanted was to escape for a few hours with his lover, away from the reach of his wife.* Dragon no longer listened to Art's words. He had been rocketed to the fairyland of Art's dreams. He did not know where all these places were, these islands, he did not know what these animals looked like, what the food tasted like, but he could easily picture himself piloting a small plane in some distant, exotic corner of the world, granting his trusting employers the wish of a safe adventure.

One by one the empty seats that surrounded Arturo Sarmiento's no longer sad or sullen black eyes and Dragon Jones's bloodshot pale blue eyes—just a shadow of his granny's spark—got taken by a growing crowd of raucous students who had left their homes late enough to avoid the afternoon storm. *For the most part, work was sporadic, pay insignificant. I had to return to Caracas, back to my parents' house, to find what little work there was.* Suddenly, Art dropped the pace at which he drank his beer, moderated the pitch of his delivery. *Most of the time I was idle, restless, unemployed. My dad put pressure on me. My enthusiasm diminished. A year ago I stopped flying.* Art was bored of his own life, did not feel like entertaining anyone with it, not even for the hefty fee of a free night of drinking. His voice faded to a murmur, his natural propensity to effusive gesticulation toned down to mimic the sober manner of those around him, his knack for suspenseful storytelling starved of inspiration. *So a year ago I started my seventh semester, and here I am, soon to start my ninth and last.* There was no promise ahead, no justification for another drink, but Dragon was still high on the excitement of his new friend's life, still in the mood to fulfill the potential of a night that had begun during the day with the chance meeting of one of the most mysterious characters he had ever encountered. *Come to the bar, let's raise some hell.*

Dragon's overdraft hit rock bottom that night. By closing time he was lost in the frozen concrete extravaganza that is Leeds University's campus, while Art explored the possibilities of making the fountain behind the Roger Stevens building work on an ice-cold, late-winter evening. Their intoxicated paths met as they entwined their left and right arms around each other's shoulders. Half-slipping, half-skating on the solid ice, they reached the steps that lead to the Edward Boyle Library. They both looked up simultaneously—heads thrown back, spines arched backward—at the imposing flight of stairs towering above them. A slight yelp preceded the explosion of their combined laughter once Art lost his footing, began the skidding backstepping that sent them both—embracing—to the ground. Only the brisk cold of the north could dry the source of their inebriated revelry and force them to look for shelter for the night.

A few weeks later Art loaded a few boxes with his most precious belongings—a Bob Marley flag, a *Star Wars* poster—into the van of a schoolmate who had kindly volunteered to help him move his things from his dorm in Bodington Hall to the shared student flat in Hyde Park which not only happened to have a vacancy but also happened to lodge his best—best*est*—friend: Dragon Jones.

=

The room filthy, messy, the bed undone. Piles of clothes scattered all over the floor. Flies land now on the greasy leftovers of the day's lunch, now on the toppled bottles left behind after Sunday's party. Arturo Sarmiento returns from the kitchen with a half-full glass of milk, sits on the edge of the bed, remains motionless during long, idle seconds. He gets up again, nervous, walks around the room, troubled. One, two, three, four, then round again, down the tired path, across the room, over the dirty linen, the misplaced crockery, the uneaten food. Recurrence endows the trail with no answer, no relief. He reaches the far wall, notices the red and black remains of a flattened mosquito, inspects the splotch with disgust, turns his back to it, resumes the four-step ritual. This time, the journey takes him to the shapeless beanbag before the TV. He drops his inert body on the soft surface, browses through the channels. There isn't much on: Roy Scheider heroically manages to keep his barge afloat in a desperate battle against an oversized shark; in Romania, Rudolfo Marutu has scored his record-breaking twenty-seventh goal in Steaua Bucharest's twelfth consecutive win; in Chile, the heavy snowstorms predicted for the coming week might add to the havoc wreaked by the latest earthquake; local news: police are investigating the disappearance of a journalist in Táchira, near the border with Colombia; the key witness for the prosecution has changed his account in the latest high-profile trial concerning the violation of human rights during the most recent wave of protests in the country; the number of violent deaths recorded in the capital, Caracas, this weekend is of 127, down from 142 the previous week.

Art's zapping comes to an end when, among the mess, the junk, and the filth, his numb senses find peace in the plump tall figure of a second-rate American actress who distills sex with every motion. The story line is poor: struggling young artist meets successful middle-aged dealer who dazzles her with promises, indulges with her in a variety of intensely primitive, passionate pleasures (not to be confused with love), before smacking her with the truth about the modest extent of her talent. Art is amused by the scene of her first physical surrender. She frantically strikes her paintbrush against the large canvas that stands between her and the camera. A horizontal pan reveals the profile of her topless body partially covered by thick lines of bright oil paint, escaping the grip of her torn denim dungarees held at her shoulders by only one of the two straps. In the distance a door discretely slides open as the short square figure of the dealer silently slips into the room. At this point, the unsuspecting painter lifts the tempo of her activity, allowing her large breasts to bounce freely with every stroke, prompting the restrained drops of sweat accumulated at the base of her lean neck to overflow her protruding bones, to run down her chest, along the insides of her breasts. She is startled by his presence. He apologizes, first, then praises the prowess of her painting. She is flattered, if also embarrassed by her nudity. He approaches, stops her as she goes in search of some clothing, (passionately) dries a brazen drop of sweat that heads hurriedly toward her right nipple. His left hand dwells on her wet flesh longer than necessary, their eyes meet, their noses, their lips, their tongues. She is already naked, (primitively) ripping off his jacket, his buttoned jeans, his shirt. The melody of her ecstatic sighing finally lulls Art's tired eyes to a pleasant slumber.

III

know it's four thirty in the morning, Alicia. I need you right now. I want to see you, baby. All women are hysterical. She is not happy about my call but I know how to work her anger. I hold the phone at arm's length, ignoring her reproach but paying attention to the tone of her voice to fill in the gaps with the answers she wants to hear. The TV's still on. The wonderful talent of that American actress has been replaced by the camp voice of a transgender clairvoyant. *I understand, sweetheart, but you could try to understand me too.* That cursed beanbag has tortured my back for hours. I stand up, take three or four steps, feel the pain, trip on a cardboard box with leftover pizza. I need to interrupt her rant, otherwise this call could go on forever. *Okay, baby, I'm on my way.* I hang up the phone before she has the chance to object and leave my house in a hurry.

Caracas is a big city and like all big cities traffic is a nightmare here. Driving in Caracas has always been difficult but for weeks now spontaneous protests have made it almost impossible to get from one place to another. Except for a year when I lived in Margarita, and another when I went to study in England, I have spent my entire life in this hellhole, so I know the city like the back of my hand but sometimes there is simply nothing you can do: if access to certain key roads is cut off, then it's cut off. Caracas is an ugly city, a hard city, a hectic and chaotic city that is not conducive to generous or even sympathetic feelings, but when you spend so much time in the same place you learn to love it, you try to make the most of it. I have my feelings for Caracas, an uncanny form of affection that perhaps makes me qualify as a masochist. Maybe we are all masochists, maybe you have to be to live in Caracas.

At four thirty in the morning Caracas is dead. No, not dead. At four thirty in the morning Caracas lies still, pretending to be dead, for fear of getting killed if caught moving. Because Caracas is one of the most dangerous cities in the world. Life is always on a knife's edge here: the wrong move, and *zap*, you're toasted. Sometimes the wrong move isn't even necessary. Sometimes it's just the knife that moves, and you're still dead, having done nothing. Mind you, Caracas was always dead at four thirty in the morning. This is the one time when the city has always looked drowsy, has always been overcome by silence: there was a time—but not anymore—when at three thirty in the morning Caracas was one big party for the hungry, the lustful, and the drunken to get together one last time before heading home; at five thirty in the morning the roar of school buses would mark the start of the day—of the traffic and the confusion—that would take over once all cool cats had made it back to their respective homes. But then, as now, at four thirty in the morning Caracas lives indoors, in the private quarters of a conquest's home, in the hired mattress of a hired love, in the sweaty frenzy of a nightclub.

These days Caracas lives almost exclusively indoors. Crime has taken care of the *caraqueño's* natural inclination to live life in the streets, as the city has turned into a huge traffic light with green, orange, and red areas. Red areas are off-limits, simply too dangerous to go. Orange areas are borderline—going there is a gamble, and every person must decide whether the prize at stake is worth wagering his or her life. Green areas have long been extinct in Caracas: no one is perfectly safe in this city, no one can rest in the knowledge that nothing will hap-pen. For years, as the murderous red smudge on the imaginary map of the city has grown, devouring the green and orange ar-eas, Caracas's nightlife has migrated to the intimacy of private homes where informal gatherings have come to take the place of the bars and the clubs and the cafés and the restaurants of old. But now even that has been taken away from us. Since the protests started hardly anyone dares leave their home after dark, because if you do you risk running into one of the many spontaneous barricades erected by protesters, checkpoints randomly set up by the authorities, or, if you're really unlucky, units of armed militiamen patrolling the city.

As I take my usual shortcut and drive through the parking lot of the Hotel Eurobuilding to avoid the flyover at the Avenida Río de Janeiro, more out of habit than anything else, I know I am risking my life right now just to get laid. I join the Fran-cisco Fajardo motorway, which cuts through the city from east to west, driving at full speed, watchful of every taillight, every beam in my rearview mirror, every sign of potential danger along the way. But hardly anyone is awake in Caracas yet—the city sleeps, as usual, at four thirty in the morning. At least that much remains the same.

From my home in Chuao to Altamira, on the other side of the river, it takes me six minutes. Hardly long enough to remember those bulging Hollywood breasts, or to fantasize about Alicia's strong, hard muscles. The steep curve traced by Alicia's buttocks must be a blueprint of heaven. Then again, that American tigress did have a mighty pair of ski slopes.

Alicia is wearing her white fine cotton gown. Her dark legs contrast with the pink slippers she likes to wear. She's half asleep. That's the better half of her mood at the moment. I can see the anger in the lines of her face. She's not a beau-tiful woman. I don't think anyone has ever called her beauti-

ful. I never have. She's not. But she's attractive and seductive
and sexy. I can't speak to Alicia, I never could: we were never
friends, just lovers. I'm convinced the role of women in this
world certainly isn't *speaking* to men. Communication between
males and females is a lot more basic than conversation. I
didn't come here, as she seems to think, to talk. *There is so
much I should tell you, Alicia. So much you should know.* But
I know she would not understand, she cannot. *No, of course
I haven't been cheating.* That just goes to show how little she
knows what's going on, how little she knows of my life. She
consoles my silence with a tender embrace.

Her skin smells of recent dreams. Her small head fits the
nook of my shoulder perfectly. Her deep breathing teasingly
rustles the hair on my chest. I reproduce the gentle tickle on
her face with the tips of my fingers. I run my hand along her
ear, her cheek, her fleshy lips, her neckline, her curled, hanging hair, her curved, bony shoulder, her lean, strong arm, bent
over, sheltering the shape of her small, firm, perky breasts
from the reach of my hungry eyes. Her left hand responds to
my stimulation with an equally gentle touch. I've won her over.
I'll get what I came for. Her pouting lips hold a small section
of my skin, then drop it, replace it with another, and another,
and another. Her breathing's still calm. There's no trace of her
tongue. Love and passion flow from different sources in Alicia. I know right now she's acting by the laws of love, not lust.
She would happily stay like this for the rest of the evening, she
would prefer to wake up in my arms in the morning than to
have an orgasm right now. I long for her perverted kiss. I hunger for her bite, her purposely painful scratch. I know tonight I
won't see that side of her but I also know she'll give up every
ounce of power, every bit of her will, to me. *Arturo.* Her whisper
hurts my ears. I cannot see her lips but I sense them shaping
in the shadows the words she knows fill me with fear and an-

ger. *I love you.* My voice should have been louder, coarser. The sarcasm in my words gets lost in the effort to bring myself to say them. Only I understand that, right now, nothing but the opposite is true. I hate you. I hate your passivity. I hate your lack of emotion, your detachment from sex. I hate how easy you make it for me to take your intimacy, what you should cherish most. I hate you, because instead of pushing you aside and walking out of your life forever, I am forced by the taste of your skin, by the warmth of your womb, by the curse of routine, to untie the bow of your gown and renew the bond that so long ago turned old and loose.

Her body pierced to the discolored sofa cushions looks darker than it really is. I press my left hand against her tame back. Her chest gets lost in the creases of the upholstery. Her nipples must be rubbing against the sealed teeth of the cushion cover's zipper. Her hips fly upward like the top of a pyramid, held by the strength of her spread knees. Her whole body bounces with my every thrust. The sofa stops sliding as it hits the far wall. Now nothing can ease the tension of my humanity, pulsing powerfully inside her. The strain of our combined weight is too much on her neck, buried inside one of the armrests. She lifts her body from the sofa with her arms, turns her face over the side of her shoulder to look at me. My eyes shift between her bulging, white, mad cow's eyes, and her two little tan breasts, jolting freely with the aid of gravity. *I want to hurt you. I want to degrade you.* I enjoy that worried look, this conceding posture, your uneasiness. I let my right hand dive into some flesh, I plunge my nails in a mixture of skin, muscle, and tissue, and at last I hear her panting turn into the whining cry of submission. Her hesitant voice takes me to the pinnacle of excitement. I cannot stop anymore, I push harder, I hold her stronger, deeper. Suddenly, in the middle of my ecstasy, I hear the murmur of her plead turn into unrestrained sighing.

Her hands once more drop her body on the slim cushions, her sharp claws land on my thighs, and she fills the room with the loud pitch not of her pain but of her desire. She's been enjoying this as much as I have. I feel tricked, used. I wish I could come out of her. I wish I could leave her lingering in her own debauchery. But I cannot stop anymore, I've gone too far, I need release. I join her wailing and for a few shivering seconds we form a duet of fulfilled pleasure.

Once again she's had the best of me. I land exhausted on her sweaty back. Frustration mounts. I wish this had never happened. *That was great, baby.* The lights are on. She paces around the room, getting ready to start her day. I need sleep but I refuse to give her the satisfaction of witnessing my defeat. I leave the house before her. The city's wide awake as I step outside. The ride back takes ten times longer than two hours ago. As I walk into my apartment, the beanbag seems as tempting as the bed. I'm disappointed not to find her breasts on the TV. There's a documentary about wildlife in the Galapagos Islands, instead. There's still time for a little rest.

IV

Arturo Sarmiento sits, head in hand, on his couch, holding a cold beer, looking concernedly, almost drearily, at nothing. A sporadic sip slowly works down the level of the liquid inside the transparent bottle. It's a warm, humid July evening in the city. What little breeze there is blows softly high above the valley, raising an idle whisper of freshness that makes life at the skirt of the mountain seem particularly sultry, particularly unpleasant. Art perspires almost as much as the bottle in his hand. A tiny puddle of spilled beer, dew, and frustration springs between the sofa and the carpet. Art's house is a random collection of old, mostly meaningless memories: the furniture, almost entirely his parents'—he spent most of his childhood sitting on that couch, eating on that table. The carpet, Alicia's anniversary gift. The hi-fi and the TV, all that remains from his first flat, his one and only attempt to share his life full-time with a woman. He lived with Daniela for a year. After their breakup she took everything, apart from the TV and the hi-fi. *I swear I'll never live with another woman again.*

Alicia walks out of his bedroom into the humid, warm living room. Her dark brown skin—coated in the mirror of her own sweat—gleams through the gaps of her loose midriff, her short shorts. *Don't get so depressed, honey, next year will be better.* She knows there is no relief in her words but she can think of nothing else to do or say to comfort him. Art feels deep resentment mounting

inside, clouding his brain, poisoning the taste in his mouth. He
takes an angry swig, chokes on the sour taste of hatred and warm
beer. No word is spoken. Art has never felt the affinity necessary to
share secrets—feelings—with Alicia. His attraction for her verges
on the animalistic, is rid of all subtleties. Why would it get better?
What would make it change? He has been working in this company
for the past four years, has just been passed over for promotion for
the second time in a row. Another drop of frustration feeds the
puddle on the floor. His new boss is a man three years his junior,
who joined the team eighteen months after him. But Art doesn't
feel like discussing the intricacies of his misery with his partner.
He says nothing at all, nothing about Dragon's call, nothing about
the possibility of flying again, nothing about the prospect of moving to a foreign island, nothing about the prospect of escaping a
place where the streets smell of tear gas and death is your next
door neighbor.

Seeking shelter from the heat and his silence, Alicia picks up
a mop, finds a bucket, wipes the kitchen floor, scrubs the surfaces.
She devotes herself entirely to the self-appointed task of restoring
cleanliness in Arturo's house. The scratching noise of the spring
pad against the cooking hob disturbs him, makes him lift his head.
He sees the silhouette of Alicia's body bending over the cooker,
partially—sideways—facing away from him. He sees the perky
shape of her small tawny breasts bouncing under her skimpy top,
in tune with the rubbing motion of her right arm. She can sense
his gaze upon her, waits expectantly for the cue that will allow
her to do what she so anxiously desires. *Stop cleaning, Alicia, that's
enough.* All he means is what he says. He still wants to play no
part in her life. Alicia reads too much into his words, approaches
readily, swinging her hips sensually, dropping her utensils halfway
down the aisle, replacing them with two fresh bottles of cold beer
and an invigorating dose of lust. She knows Art loves to see a girl
drink beer straight from the bottle. She sits on his lap, whispers

in his ear. He doesn't need to hear her words to understand their meaning. She caresses his chest, bites his ear, digs her fingernails into his skin. He knows the outcome of the evening is inevitable. She strokes him ravenously, immersed in her own desire. He can see their image in the mirror. He looks at himself, straight into his own eyes, as she uses him to satiate her lust. *I like mirrors.* The glass reveals what is otherwise reserved to the touch only, persuades him to join her feast. He grabs her by the thighs, pulls her closer to him. She is already on the verge of ecstasy when his heavy touch, his virile thrust, drive her overboard. He is penetrating her, but it is she, really, who ravishes him. Her tense, arrhythmic shivering hurts him but he shows no sign of pain. She frees him from her grip, kneels before him, licks him clean. He still looks at nothing but the mirror. She meets his eyes through the looking glass as she paces her wide purple tongue up and down the slimy valleys of his masculinity. His expressionless eyes bounce between their own reflection and that of her playful ones. Pleasure mounts: her teeth tease him, her lips rouse him, her hands touch him in the right places. He still makes no sound. For two and a half seconds he finds himself untroubled, almost happy. The couch of Art's childhood—drenched in more than spilled beer, dew, and frustration—serves as a makeshift bed for two exhausted lovers to sleep placidly, serenely, in the company of each other until the morning after.

V

'm furious with that whore. Eduardo knows it, that's why he says nothing. *Say what you have to say.* His driving turns violent, reflecting our shared mood. Still silence. I can see the trace of a smile forming on his face. He finds amusement at my expense, but he will make no comment. *I can't believe she backed out in the end.* There is hardly any traffic: once upon a time, this road would have been teeming with cars but these days hardly anyone ventures out into the Caracas night. That's why the little harlot wouldn't join us in the end, or at least that's what she said. *Say what you have to say.* And still nothing, just the road quickly guiding us through the city. *I have nothing to say.* The smile remains intact, obvious, rude. *Let's go get some hot dogs.* Eduardo slows down, looks out the window, makes a sharp U-turn, and drives in the opposite direction. *No, not this one, man, you know I don't like this one. Let's stop at the one with the green tent.* Even sharper turn to the right, screeching tires, late breaking, approaching headlights. Close call. *Calm down, tiger. It was me who got turned down, not you.* The smile, briefly erased by the moment of tension, returns to his face. This time I fight his silence with more of the same. Not even the radio is on, not even the air conditioner. Five minutes of nothing make for a long gap.

The queue is long but Joao, the hot dog man, is as quick as ever. *Un con todo, por favor. You want one or two? Son tres, doctor.* I hate eating one hot dog while holding another one in my hands. If that means I'll have to queue again for the second one, so be it. *I told you from the start she was a teaser.* I knew this had to come at some point. Just not when I brought it up: it has to be when Eduardo decides is most effective. *On top, Alicia is waiting for you at her place.* I swallow my hot dog in a hurry, find in the queue the perfect excuse not to listen to his moralizing. *Get me a Coke.* A suspect Corolla whizzes past, pulls the brakes, reverses until it's parallel with the hot dog stand. Eduardo's request gets lost in the rackety thumping of the loud speakers. There are four males inside the car, only one jumps out. I haven't seen any of it, only heard the noise that keeps me from catching Eduardo's voice. He calls for me once, twice, but I just can't hear him. I'm still disgusted by the outcome of the night, by Eduardo's comment, lost in my own thoughts, oblivious to the danger of the developing situation. Suddenly, I feel a violent pull from behind. I drop the money in my right hand as I lose my balance. I get thrown into a car, forced into a seat by the slamming door. A large black piece of iron distorts the space around us. *Boom!* I didn't see the lightning, I only heard the sound. It wasn't firecrackers. The car I'm in jolts forward. More tire screeching, slight slide from the back, appropriate correction of the steering wheel. I can see blood. I can still see his blood. Silence.

Eduardo is shaking. He sure isn't drunk anymore. We fly out of Las Mercedes. We're on the motorway, heading somewhere different, not home: we went past Chuao a long time ago. The gap opened by silence becomes so much more piercing when you long for a specific melody to disturb it. No sirens. The guy in front of me in the queue now lies bathed in his own blood, dying for a hot dog. Eduardo lives. So do I. Eduardo drives. I think. I cannot take it anymore. I don't want to take it anymore. *I'm leaving.* My final thought comes out aloud. Eduardo looks at me inquisitive, confused. *I'm out of here, Eduardo. I'm out of this dump.*

PART I
CONTINUED

VI

Maybe I'm being naïve, but for the love of God, I give this guy the chance of a lifetime, the chance to move out of a country that is up in arms, the chance to make his dream come true, and he can only answer, *We ain't at uni chasing after the same girl anymore, Dragon.* I'm not talking about a girl, Art, I'm talking about a project! A massive project, a major enterprise, a fabled fucking fantasy. *Things are not what they used to be, man.* What the hell? What's that supposed to mean? And who the hell is talking about a girl in the first place?

I'd thought one phone call would be enough to solve the first of our practical problems. I'd thought one phone call would reignite a friendship that had once flourished without boundaries, that had emerged spontaneously from precious nothing and had grown as if by magic, until it had turned us—Art and me—inseparable. As it turns out, even the most intense of friendships have a *best before* date, and five years have proven too long to stay inseparable.

Needless to say, the conversation doesn't go the way I'd envisioned, and Arturo is no longer the adventurous character he once was, and suddenly I'm exposed to Nathaniel, in the same room, as I speak to a friend I no longer know, and my agony, my internal struggle against Art, against Nathe, is laid to rest with Art's final words, which escape the earpiece loudly, infesting the stagnant air with defeat.

I'd already arranged to pay SamB back for his hospitality with dinner at my house before speaking to Art, and I'd schemed with Nathe and Sheila to let him into the little secret of our project that night, but in my mind I was absolutely certain that by then the first foundations of Dragon Wings would be reinforced with the presence of an experienced aviation professional. Instead, the couple of days prior to our dinner have been punctuated by a fair amount of disappointment but above all by a growing sense of the urgency of a situation that seems to be getting more critical by the hour.

I'd intended to treat my guests—Nathe and Sheila, SamB and his lady—to a feast of traditional English roast on Saturday evening, but no lamb is to be found on the island, and the beef looks suspect to me, so I've decided to roast three whole chickens and serve them with steamed vegetables, Yorkshire pudding, and apple sauce.

Sheila and Nathe arrive in the middle of the day, well ahead of schedule, and she cannot believe her eyes as the puddings begin to rise in small cupcake containers—the nearest equivalent I could find in the island's shops to a Yorkshire pudding tin. *You cook dat youself?* The glint in her eyes, the curl in her brow, the awe in her face: I'd confess to anything she might accuse me of. Anything at all.

Nathe is watching a football game outside while we busy ourselves in the kitchen for the best part of two hours. Suddenly every recipe, every carrot that needs dicing, every dish that needs washing, turns into a matchmaker, as the touch of her fingers barely brushing mine, the scent of her sweat as the temperature in the kitchen rises, the sound of her laughter with every stupid joke I make, take me farther away from the problems and the disillusion that have been weighing me down over the past two days.

The moon is out in full so there is no need for candles, but on the evening when we were meant to pitch the idea of a regional airline based on Anguilla to the man who might make all the difference to our erratic project, I feel more romantically inclined than is advisable. Under a full display of candles (small, thick, round ones—the kind usually reserved for cemeteries: it seems Anguillans are not particularly fond of candles) it soon becomes bitterly evident that this international crowd (SamB is Zimbabwean, and Jessica—his toy of choice tonight—Vincentian, Sheila has never set foot in England, and Nathaniel, well, Nathaniel is a citizen of the world) couldn't care less about my apple sauce and Yorkshire pudding.

My choice of food proves a rotund failure but all I could have dreamed of getting out of this dinner I got already during its preparation, in the kitchen, sharing precious hours with the most exuberant of women, and my plan was not so much to get SamB's attention with good food but rather to have the board of directors of Dragon Wings sit for the first time around a table with the most reliable pilot on the island on an evening when several glasses of champagne would make toasting partners of first acquaintances.

That's how, suddenly, a matter of acquaintances turns into our first positive resolve to create an actual rather than just a hypothetical airline, when SamB nonchalantly observes that *Simon O'Connor still owns one of his Queen Airs—I see it parked in the hangar every day.* I'm immediately overcome with excitement. *It must be the one that was involved in the accident but at least that means it shouldn't cost you too much money.* Only Sheila is vaguely aware of the details of a scandal that erupted long before Nathe landed on the island. *Ralph McKenzie hit something with the propeller; turns out he'd been drinking, shouldn't have been flying in the first place.* According to SamB, Leyland Airways had had two mechanics at the time but they were only certified by the ECCAA to carry out maintenance, not repair, of the airplanes. *By the time Simon could bring someone from Antigua to make the repairs, he could no longer afford it.* I'm totally oblivious to the fact that the first potential aircraft Dragon Wings might even consider purchasing has been involved in what sounds like a pretty serious accident. I simply do not care. *After the incident Ralph's license was immediately suspended; so was Leyland Airways' air operator's certificate. The investigation lasted nine weeks and Simon had to keep the payroll running. In the end Ralph's license was rescinded for a year and the airline put under probation. No passenger got to charter a Leyland flight ever again. I don't even know whether the Queen Air's certificate of airworthiness was renewed. Ralph's back in the business, though—flying a private Twin Otter over in St. Martin.*

So, where can we go with this thing? Ever the pragmatist, Nathe is typically prosaic about our latest discovery, but if his question has caught me mentally embellishing SamB's story with all sorts of fantasies, I can also see through his cool façade: an innocuous comment, an innocent anecdote, has set the engine of Nathaniel's curiosity in motion. *Once you get it going, it's ideal for the region: St. Barths, St. Martin, Nevis—if you get the permits, even Statia. You won't be allowed to land in Saba, only Winair are licensed to land there, and in all honestly you're better off staying away from that airstrip. I don't know the exact specs of this Queen but most of them sit nine to ten people.* I don't even know anymore why we're only talking about this. *What are we waiting for? Let's get it. Let's go.* But Sheila is there at hand, timely, beautiful, composed, to restore the balance between Nathe's seemingly skeptic curiosity and my overexcited craze. *It sound like we should be having a look—where we find dis Simon O'Connor man?*

VII

The moonlit evening in which social etiquette dictated that SamB should first make the acquaintance of the board of directors of Dragon Wings suddenly became the brightest beam shedding light on the right path for Dragon, Nathaniel, and Sheila to turn their hypothetical airline into a real enterprise. While Sheila spent all her time searching for alternative funding within the island and Nathaniel engaged in the challenging process of clearing the bureaucratic hurdles placed ahead of an official meeting with government representatives to discuss routes, permits, and most importantly, a possible subsidy, Dragon took it upon himself to track down Simon O'Connor and lure him to a dinner table where the rest of the high command of Dragon Wings could join them to discuss the details of the potential transaction that would provide the airline with its first piece of aeronautical equipment.

But Simon O'Connor turned out to be a conspicuous fellow who seemed to spend more time traveling from one place to the next than staying in any of the places to which he traveled, and by the time Dragon made a breakthrough in his thoroughly frustrating detective mission, the full extent of the company's economic precariousness had already made an impression in the mind of all three partners: after three weeks of chasing Simon O'Connor, Dragon Jones finally managed to exchange some words with the man himself, to pen him down for a rendezvous at the restaurant of choice, to begin the negotiation that would eventually liberate him from what for him was, no doubt, nothing more than a problem, and for the new nucleus of the Jones family nothing less than a coup. *No matter what price he names, we cannot afford it.* Nathaniel flipped through a governmental document delivered to him the day before; Sheila considered the last few names on a list of possible investors on the island; dust crawled inside the open window, shimmering as it floated past the ominous shaft of light that invaded the office. Silence. *How are we going to pay for this?* Silence. *How?* Nathaniel hardly took his eyes off the document: *Borrow it from Jones Investments.* Dragon was stunned. *What?* Nathaniel's irresponsiveness fueled Dragon's anxiety. *You can't just take 100,000 US dollars and call it a loan: that is an investment.* Nathaniel momentarily raised his eyes from the yellowed paper and with his powerful voice, *You can, if you replace it within three months.* His stern tone settled on the stagnant atmosphere of the room. Sheila felt obliged to break the uneasy silence: *Not all options have been exhausted, you know, a number of investors kyan be persuaded to join us but dis kyan't all be done in de next couple of weeks.*

Three weeks wasn't soon enough for the meeting with Simon O'Connor, but the date had been set and Simon's unreliable character could not be trusted for rescheduling and the dice already tumbled. So Dragon e-mailed Jones Investments' London office for them to draft a short-term loan agreement and stand by for a transfer of funds from the company's main account into Dragon Wings's account in the Indigenous Bank of Anguilla.

Three cars arriving from three different directions coincided at the exact same time in the parking lot of the Koal Keel, the island's most emblematic restaurant, where over one year before Nathaniel Jones had first dined with Sheila Rawlingson. Simon O'Connor emerged from his stylish Honda with his lawyer. Dragon came alone. Meanwhile, Sheila made the party gasp in awe, her sensual figure delicately hugged by a black dress that hung loosely from her shoulders.

The menus had hardly been collected by the waiter, the wine had not yet been decided upon, never mind poured (Simon only drank club soda with a slice of lemon), when the dry, charmless approach of a hurried businessman harassed an entire family. *I know exactly what you want and why you have taken me here to ask for it, so let's cut to the chase: I want 150,000 US for the plane. If you agree, we can continue with our lovely soirée, otherwise let us save ourselves the time and the energy.*

The price was too high, the attitude was insulting, and the timing was spectacularly ill-conceived; however, Nathaniel, the negotiator, rose to the occasion, took control of the evening. *I would absolutely love to taste that 2003 Chateau de Rothschild.* After an initial, respectful rebuttal—*My friend, we don't even know, yet, whether this plane is suitable for our purposes*—Nathaniel continued to soothe Simon O'Connor's overzealous spirit with a detailed inquiry into the condition of the aircraft, the circumstances of the accident. A long soliloquy that lasted the best part of an hour and took them through the appetizers was finally summarized with the assurance that *you can load this plane with nine people, charge them as much as you want, and take them wherever you want . . . tomorrow, if it pleases you. Everything is within the strictest boundaries of the law: the propeller has been repaired, the plane has been deemed airworthy.*

Dragon seized the opportunity, fired a number of technical questions which made him look more erudite in the art of flying than he really was. Simon seemed surprised to hear Dragon's voice, seemed to have forgotten there were more people at the table than himself and Nathaniel Jones. Startled and not yet recomposed, it was the latter he addressed while answering Dragon's questions. *You buy a young lady in an old dress: the plane was built in '77 but it has no more than five years of active use at most; the engines were replaced in 2002, they have clocked around 5,000 hours each—you can verify*

that in the logbooks if you wish; the body must have around 20,000 hours—a
pittance for a machine of this sort.

The price, which was still too high, was not touched upon
again; the attitude, which had been insulting, progressively turned
more casual, almost amicable; an occasion which had begun with
a dangerously ill-conceived comment slowly took the shape of a
lovely soirée, helped no doubt by the delicacy of a magnificent
meal, by the tact of an astute negotiator, and by the aroma of two
bottles of Bordeaux. By the time the waiter came to collect the
empty plates of the main course, Simon's impenetrable guise allowed for a brief, sharp laugh which fed minor hopes of a cheaper
arrangement.

Before the arrival of dessert, Sheila took over the reins of the
conversation. Her fine, delicate voice contrasted heavily with the
forceful finality of her words. *Come meet us on Monday morning at Mrs.
Walker's office an' you will get a banker's draft for 125,000 US for de plane.*
A long, lingering silence ensued as Simon O'Connor digested the
sour core of Sheila's beauty. *Let's say $140,000 and not another word,*
and as Simon placed the silver spoon he held in his right hand on
the china plate before him, the first success in the creation of a
real airline was sealed, and the future role of each of its founding
partners established.

However, what seemed like a boosting accomplishment one
day was recognized as no more than a minor achievement the
next. The purchase of a plane more readily useful than initially
thought, the purchase, in fact, of the first element of a functional
fleet of aircrafts, was certainly a positive development. But the
price at which it had come was not only financially distressing, it
was also logistically unbalancing: suddenly, the search for cred-
itors and investors would have to give way—without being
disregarded—to the structural development of an organization
capable of operating commercially. So, following the natural hi-
erarchy the group had somehow adopted, Sheila continued to ex-

amine every possible route to provide the enterprise with a healthy monetary foundation, while Dragon busied himself with the more practical matters of operational requirements.

Which is to say that Dragon persevered with his initial instinct to address the shortage of indispensable personnel at Dragon Wings. He had decided against the obvious and turned to an extravagant friend to fill the position of chief pilot at Dragon Wings, partly because of some sort of nostalgic frenzy, partly because he knew it was far too early in the process to try to scout a man who was already flying for a small but successful chartering company. But Arturo Sarmiento had left Dragon with little choice, and a rash impulse compelled him to knock on SamB's door.

Can you afford to pay my salary before you can afford to give me a plane?

A single argument was enough to disarm Dragon's case. Yet, if the prior hope of a boosting accomplishment had been short-lived in the close quarters of the gestating airline, the disappointment triggered by SamB's lack of support never made it to desperation because just as Dragon was forced to look elsewhere for personnel, the news came that Nathaniel had been scheduled to have a meeting with the chief minister to speak about the possibility of the government backing the airline.

Life, improbably, went on.

VIII

The world from atop Sandy Ground looks like an extension of paradise. Even with all the preparations for carnival, with all the excitement about the year's greatest party, this view simply exudes peacefulness. As I drive down the hill that leads to the narrow stretch of land wedged between the deep blue sea—engulfed on either side by the closed angles formed by North and South Hill respectively—and the silver salt pond, parceled by an endless number of small stones lined up in perfectly measured squares, the sun has already begun its race below the thin leaden line of clouds that hangs just above the horizon. Sandy Ground—the umbilical cord of Anguilla—is always calm in the daytime. At night it remains the only bastion of entertainment, but during the day the long white beach is reserved almost exclusively for the affairs of local fishermen and shipping companies operating on the northern and southern ends of the bay respectively.

Everyone must be up at the village already, or getting ready for the opening of what promises to become two weeks of continuous celebration. Whatever the case, I find myself on my own as I sit outside my favorite bar, dipping my bare feet in the soft, cold texture of the virginal sand, sipping my first rum with thirst and delight, holding my sunglasses in my free hand, looking out past the rocking masts of anchored sailboats, past the clear shadow of Sandy Island—right in front of me—into the brazen, living, blazing shape of the blood-orange sun sinking inside the cradle of the blue horizon. The sky burns dramatically with all shades of reds, pinks, and oranges. My eyes—reflecting the glowing flames, I'm sure—ache from watching the sun for so long. I don't want to miss a minute of this show. My sight gets blurry; I start seeing yellow, purple, green floating spots. I shelter my eyes behind the white plastic glass and drink placidly. I shut my eyelids momentarily and enjoy the bitter taste of the booze and the lemon dilating the buds on my tongue, irritating the more sensitive parts of my mouth, burning the top of my throat. I swallow, then open my eyes, gaze at the dying embers of the day with resolution—with scientific interest—ignoring the floaters, the stars popping up on the sky, everything around me. The final orange-yellow cord tucks under the sea. I'm still intensely looking at nothing. The sun is gone. I hold my stare: nothing. I lean back, relax. No afterglow. Again.

I hear Nathe's raucous laughter inside the bar. I can tell by the tone of his voice he isn't alone. I finish my drink quickly before their entrance and wait for a moment. The vigorous grip of his hand on my shoulder contrasts sharply with the tender touch of her kiss on my cheek: he is playing prominent macho, she, sweet intermediary. *We just stopped at the Methodist church on our way down here to watch the sunset.* The confusion of colors and shades has not left the sky, so they both choose to sit on the same bench as me, with our backs to the bar, facing the sea. *You must have noticed the afterglow this time.* I knew this would happen. There is no doubt in my mind there was none, but time has taught me to choose my battles with Nathaniel. The slow shaking of my head is enough to send them into a fit of laughter followed by a dismissal of my seemingly willful blindness. I take it, unperturbed, teased by the tingle of the sand tumbling gently from the top of the heap that Sheila, with the slow motion of her arched foot, has erected between us. The silky clay of her perfect skin brushes an infinite number of grains of minerals to the side; they put pressure on the pile, altering the balance of the whole; as the elements redistribute themselves, the excess crumbles to the base and tickles my leg on its way. Thus—indirectly—Sheila tickles me.

I spoke to the chief minister today. The tone of self-importance has returned to Nathaniel's voice. I'm almost through with my second rum. His beer and her orange soda are still more than half full. The farce of a sunless crepuscule has vanished. Sheila gets up, walks around the table, sits opposite me. Nathaniel follows her. *Was it something I said?* This is business: nobody is amused by the comment. *The Tourist Board is broke, the budget for the year tight. Government is prepared to guarantee no more than 40 percent of our seats.* I'm not in the mood for business anymore. It's been a long day and I just want to join the local crowd and see whether all the hype about this beauty pageant is actually worth it, but I know I'm not allowed to even consider taking an early night out. *We can run the operation on 40 percent.* I feel the scrutiny of Nathaniel's eyes on me. His expression is not only of concern but of deep concentration. He is completely immersed in the figures, the possibilities, feasibility. He knows I'm slightly disconnected, tries to engage me with his commitment. Sheila saves me from his stare. *De people from de Hotel and Tourism Association are prepared to give us deir full support.* The HTA is a powerful private organization that brings together under a single umbrella the main hotels and restaurants on the island, as well as carrying out other activities directly involved in the tourism industry, in order to safeguard their interests. Their support is, of course, one of the necessary conditions for our project to succeed, but I just cannot concentrate on the words Sheila speaks when her lips move with such grace, when her perfect white teeth shine with such splendor, when her voice brings delight regardless of the news it conveys. *What about solid cash?* She's been rambling on about magazines and advertisements and God knows what else. I needed to contribute, to show that I'm still taking part in this discussion, and I wouldn't have been able to comment on what Sheila's just said. Nathe likes my remark; I've fooled him, for the time being. *Dere ain' much available.* His eyes are clouded with dismay. He understands, as I do, that *not much* is being used as an unsubtle euphemism for *none at all*. Sheila looks at me with expectation. Nathe buries his face behind the palms of his hands, holding his head from the top of his forehead with the tip of his fingers. A sigh lingers in the dark air. I don't know which of them let it out. Maybe it was combined. *I need a drink.*

On my return, I find the loving couple analyzing the nature of our problems. Cheap flights for members and guests of the HTA can't be deducted from the 40 percent quota offered by the government, which means it would be more profitable to fly with empty seats than to fly with anything up to 40 percent occupancy if it included passengers from the HTA. Sheila needs relief, seeks it in me, pierces me with her painful gaze. She asks the wrong question: SamB's still sitting on the fence. He fears this might never take off and is not prepared to give up his present job until we can offer him something solid. Sheila's head sinks with disappointment. Nathe drops her hand, stands up, paces around the table. *We need alternatives.* The statement refers to a lot more than simply pilots. We need to get this business going before the beginning of the season. Our absolutely latest starting date is the first of December. What looked like a hectic situation a few weeks ago, as I spoke to Art on the phone, is quickly turning into a desperate one.

What about Ralph? Sheila's timid question is almost a concession of defeat. Nathaniel stops walking, our eyes meet. Sheila waits apprehensively for me to lose my temper, but I don't. Silence is brief but poignant. Looking straight into my eyes, Nathaniel acknowledges him as an option. The final capitulation. I'm furious and frustrated, most of all because the situation has gotten to the point where Ralph can seriously be considered a viable candidate to become our chief pilot. The taste of rum no longer excites my senses. *Ralph destroyed the propeller of the Queen Air in the accident that cost Leyland Airways its license.* They both know how I feel about Ralph but I just want to make it clear that my position hasn't changed. I gulp the last drops of my drink as they discuss when and where to find Ralph. It's taken this much to get me involved in the conversation. As I head up toward the bar, the last thing I hear is, *Better a bad licensed pilot than no pilot at all.* Better for whom? I wonder. We have four and a half months to turn Dragon Wings into an operational airline. We have procured all permits by now, secured concessions from the government, even identified potential routes. All we need are planes and pilots. *Let's keep calm, and things will work out.*

IX

Sheila made her way through the dark deserted beach with short but steady steps. As she reached the wooden platform she brushed the dry sand off her tiny feet with a swift, delicate movement; she slipped her toes into her sandals, waved gently, almost imperceptibly, at the two men sitting on the bench outside the bar, then carried on through her catwalk, criss-crossing her way out of the sight of her admirers. Father and son looked at her tanned slim figure disappearing in the shadows of the night with the same awe, the same satisfaction. *She is gorgeous.* Nathaniel—suddenly detached from the pressing issues that troubled his mind—bathed his lips in the stale foam of bottled Guinness. Dragon mirrored his expression, holding the plastic glass in his right hand with the same casual gesture as his father. Each of them embraced the comment as his own.

The intermission was over as soon as her grainy silhouette turned into a ghost. Pressing issues returned to Nathaniel's mind. What followed was raw business. After a brief exchange that seemed to carry little of consequence, the breaking news: *We have some friends at the HTA.* Dragon swished the rum in his mouth from side to side as he weighed the significance of Nathe's words. *Who did you get that from?* Rumors, gossip, promises form the hardest core of any small society, and Dragon was openly hostile to speculation. *Newman, from Hotel Anguilla, has told me himself that he will back us all the way.*

Before his meeting with the chief minister, Nathaniel had had lunch with Saul Newman, his old acquaintance from Hotel Anguilla. An exquisite meal on the terrace of the hotel reminded Nathe of that *je ne sais quoi* that captivated him on his first stay on the island. Saul's inextinguishable Romeo y Julieta released a thin thread of smoke that curled around his right hand and charged his presence with a distinguished air. *So you're looking for help to set up this airline.* A long drag set alight the burning cylinder between his index and middle fingers, conjured a curtain of smoke that distanced Saul's face from the voice that uttered the words. *At the HTA we can do a little something about that.* Saul's sentence carried a trace of danger, as if an unspoken warning was being issued. But for Nathaniel Jones, the most important thing that very moment was to get all the support he could to turn Dragon Wings into an operational airline in time to profit from the winter season, so as soon as the convenient sum of half a million dollars was agreed between him and Saul Newman, the mystic element of that *je ne sais quoi* he had recalled earlier acquired a very palpable aspect.

All we have to do is set up the airline before the first of December, and we will have resources to keep it afloat for some time, even if it is a grand failure. Nathaniel's intonation came out devoid of its former gloom. Dragon was enlivened by the comment, encouraged by the tone of his voice. He knew that in a place like Anguilla decisions were largely dependant on the whims of an ego trip; he knew that a helping hand in the local game of intrigues was the best ally they could expect; and he also knew that Saul Newman, current president of the HTA, was as good a helping hand as one could get. *What about Godfrey, from the Arawak Cave?* Inevitably, in this maze of personal relations, rivalries often developed into hostile factions that would oppose each other uncompromisingly. *They can sort that out themselves. For the time being we have the HTA's support; their commitment to an operational subsidy would be legally binding for one year so long as we fulfilled our part of the agreement. The money would go into an escrow account as soon as our first flight took off. They would not be able to access it anymore, and it would only become available to us if we declared financial distress—this as a preventive measure to keep us from jumping at the money straight away.*

The thick fake mustache drawn on Nathaniel's face by the foam from a long last tilt of the bottle masked his attentive expression as he gauged the effect of his words in Dragon's eyes. He had kept the news from Sheila in the hope that she might find independent means of funding the enterprise within her family. He had exaggerated its importance to Dragon in a final attempt to get him wholeheartedly committed to the project. *The HTA wants to encourage tourists from Europe to travel directly to the island, avoiding transit through St. Maarten.* Dragon knew the exact meaning of those words: obligatory linking routes to Antigua and St. Kitts, perhaps even St. Lucia. Nathaniel was transferring the focus of the present task from looking for suitable pilots to looking for suitable planes. *All other routes are optional, entirely up to us.* Father and son looked at each other with hopeful eyes. An operational subsidy from the HTA meant a major boost for their airline: the assurance of getting to see at least one more high season filled Dragon with expectations, with genuine aspirations. The visible alteration in Dragon's demeanor gave Nathaniel assurance that he could, finally, count on his son the rest of the long way. *As we stand, if we manage to set up this company, we have a real chance of making it work.*

X

S heila made her way through the dark, deserted beach with short but steady steps. As she reached the wooden platform she brushed the dry sand off her tiny feet and waved gently, almost imperceptibly, at the two men sitting on the bench outside the bar. As soon as she got inside her car she lost her composed expression, tarnished her beauty with the sudden strain of desperation. She kept the teardrops that formed inside her eyes from falling but her vision remained clouded all the way back to her home.

Sheila's eyes were still watery when she arrived, but the short drive had been long enough to restore her nerves, to allow her to regain her composure. As Sheila walked into her and Nathaniel's den of love, she knew that, four and a half months to the day when Dragon Wings would have to launch its maiden flight, the key to the success of the project lay in finding independent means to fund it. Sheila also knew it was her task (appointed or not) to make certain they managed to attract local investors into the venture. So Sheila Rawlingson resolved to spend the long carnival break indoors, putting together an alluring package she would then distribute among the main potential investors on the island for them to consider once the summer celebrations were over.

Sheila knew that it was her duty (appointed or not) to make certain that Dragon Wings managed to obtain local capital to independently fund the project as well as she knew that the success of the enterprise hinged largely on the success of her task, so she spent long hours compiling an exhaustive list of potential local investors she would in due time approach with an offer to join the ranks of Dragon Wings. Nevertheless, Sheila knew perfectly well that it was the name at the top of that list which would make the most dramatic difference in the future fortunes of the airline. The remaining names were more like a balm for the spirit, an insurance policy for her mental health, some safe ground to fall back on, in case Uncle Glen—her primary target, really—failed to show the interest she hoped she would be able to stir in him.

Sheila was aware that in the foreseeable future no credit would be forthcoming from the local banks. The two largest institutions on the island had suffered tremendous losses in the aftermath of the 2008 economic crisis and had ultimately been merged with the Caribbean Central Bank in St. Kitts. The resulting Indigenous Bank of Anguilla was still, one year after its incorporation, trying to find its feet on the treacherous ground of financial markets, struggling to secure enough capital to cope with the toxic debt it had inherited from both precursory institutions, and adapting its strategies to the limiting conditions imposed by the regional authority. In this unpromising context, Sheila completed the forms and presented an application for a million-dollar credit more as a moral obligation than in the hope that anything would come out of it. But at the same time as she put together the company's proposal to the banks, Sheila spent long hours preparing an attractive proposal, carefully crafting a convincing presentation, compiling an exhaustive list of potential local investors who could be persuaded to join forces with the nucleus of the Jones family in the realization of the most ambitious enterprise ever heard of on Anguillan soil. At the top of that list was Glenallen Rawlingson, an influential ingredient in the island's social fabric and one of the five members of the board of directors of the Indigenous Bank of Anguilla.

Sheila knew that at this stage all she could use to lure investors into the company was trust, which in the language of business translates into shares, so her methodical process of selection and approach started when she picked up the phone to call the person whose name was written right at the top of the list. The day when Sheila contacted the man who had once tried to deport her husband from Anguilla, she addressed her uncle, Glenallen Rawlingson, with the distance, the respect, that characterizes business propositions for the first time in her life. But Uncle Glen's initial response was colder than she had expected, and the percentage of shares she offered did not please him, and *you mean we family ain' controllin' dem shares already?* and his reluctance to sell a worthy piece of land for the sake of a shapeless company was obdurate, and by the end of a long conversation Sheila understood why she had spent so many hours compiling a long list of potential local investors to embark with her and the rest of the nucleus of the Jones family in the creation of the first-ever commercial airline to be based in Anguilla.

After the end of a long, frustrating conversation with the man whose name was at the top of her list of potential local investors in Dragon Wings, Sheila gathered her strength, decided to produce thirty copies of the thick folder that contained the proposition to join the airline, spent one whole week plugged into her mobile phone, driving around the island, delivering with hope and determination the documents that she thought would ensure the company's future.

While Sheila went about her self-appointed duty of finding independent means of funding Dragon Wings with solemn dedication, Nathaniel Jones kept from her the good news of an agreement for a subsidy from the Hotel and Tourism Association. He had exaggerated the importance of this development to Dragon—after all, half a million dollars would not keep a commercial airline afloat for very long—in a final attempt to get him fully committed in the process of building an actual, rather than just a hypothet-

ical, airline, but Nathaniel's own involvement in Dragon Wings
was heavily conditioned by his inclination to manipulate people's
expectations, to commercialize potential, to make something out
of nothing. Nathaniel was aware of Dragon's reluctance to get
Jones Investments any more involved in Dragon Wings than it
already was; he was aware of Dragon's disgust at their need to depend on Jones Investments for the purchase of the Queen Air, and
he actually shared such repulsion. But he shared it for different
reasons: Dragon Wings verily combined Dragon and Nathaniel's
interests, but it did so only by virtue of keeping their own resources
out of the enterprise, of enticing external capital—confidence,
trust—into the venture. Nathaniel knew that in case of extreme
need he could persuade Dragon to use further assets from Jones
Investment as collateral for a credit, but he also knew that this
would represent failure in the speculative game of trade and trust
he loved most. So Nathaniel kept the news of his agreement with
the president of the HTA from Sheila to put pressure on her to
find independent means of funding the enterprise either within
her family or in the small circle of influence that was the most
active portion of Anguillan society.

XI

Thirteen sails flutter, neatly lined up side by side along the deepest end of the bay at Sandy Ground. All but two jibs are up and no boats sail across the flat surface of the sea straight ahead, all of them still attached to their provisional moorings on the beach. The starting gunshot should have gone over two hours ago but Anguillan timekeeping can be trusted to be late even for Champion of Champions, the most important race of the calendar. Suddenly, I feel thrilled. It can't be long before they start so I accelerate down the steep hill.

As part of the carnival celebrations, Anguillans devote an entire week to their national sport: sailing. During boat-racing week, large crowds gather on the beach to support their favorite—often their local—boats. But long before the beginning of the race, and again immediately after the silhouettes of the sails lose their sharpness and recede into the distance, the supporters engage in a collective revelry that involves copious amounts of sun, rum, and enthusiasm. Until, that is, the return of the boats four hours later, which is greeted with a roar of confusion, indignation, arrogance, as the ostensible leaders of the race start to emerge closer to the bay. Despite the fact that gauging distances from the shore is almost impossible, or perhaps because of this, claims and counterclaims develop quickly and loudly among the different sets of supporters who boast to each other as soon as the faintest of opportunities arises. Nor are these arguments settled by the outcome of the race. On the contrary, pseudo-technical disputes carry on long after the last of the sailboats has been pulled out of the water, using the rigorous evidence provided by diagrams drawn, wiped, and redrawn on the wet sand or on the sandy surface of the bar to settle the unsettleable, until the time when transit to the evening entertainment at the carnival village becomes appropriate.

Champion of Champions is the main race of the season because only the best boats—those that have finished within the first five positions in the previous races—are entitled to take part in it. Recently, Champion of Champions has been dragged back to coincide with August Monday, the biggest and liveliest party of the year in Anguilla. But August Monday actually starts on the wee hours of Sunday night with J'ouvert—a bouncing procession (people actually *jump* all the way) that heralds the dawn of the big day while it slowly (you can only jump so quickly) makes its way through the streets of The Valley until it reaches the steep slope than leads to Sandy Ground, sometime around noon.

Champion of Champions was scheduled to start at one, but at three it still hasn't begun. If the previous races are anything to go by, it will last until the early hours of the evening, and the celebration will drag until people decide to go to the village to attend what seems to be the overall favorite show of the carnival: the Leeward Islands Calypso Monarch competition. But the true believers, the hard-core sailing fans, have come down today to witness the resolution of the most exciting sailing season since, well, it's hard to tell with any certainty because years are not commonly used in Anguilla to place a situation in its historical context. Instead, landmark events—often tragedies—are used as a frame of reference.

So, it seems like for the first time since Hurricane Lenny, more than two boats have made it to Champion of Champions with possibilities to clinch the title: the new *2Kool*, rebuilt for a second time; *DeRoque*, newly rescued from the bottom of the sea; *Condor*, winner of the Anguilla Regatta—a tough round-the-island competition, the second most prestigious race of the calendar—and *Bumblebee*, all theoretically have a chance to claim the bragging rights that will last through the rest of the winter.

Over the course of the week, *Bumblebee* has become my favorite boat. Apparently it crashed and sank a few years ago and remained sidelined until this season. I've never seen *Bumblebee* win anything: though it's come second eight times in a row, it is yet to win a single race this season. The other day I was speaking to a Dominican friend—that is, a friend from Dominica, not the Dominican Republic—who was explaining to me the local theory for *Bumblebee*'s inability to win: the new shell of the boat was designed and built, plank by plank, by Tyrone "Sharp" Rook, a crazy Rastafarian who claims to have, among many other talents, a natural gift for boat building, a relentless libido that finds no respite even in the simultaneous solace of several tourists, and an uncanny ability to communicate with disembodied spirits. It seems Sharp had a not-so-minor disagreement with Einar Cumberson, the owner of *Bumblebee*, before finishing the job (and here the argument is yet to be settled by popular gossip whether the matter in question concerned Einar's wife, a mutual girlfriend, or the rightful monetary remuneration expected by Sharp). Whatever the case, Sharp was left with little choice other than to leave the work unfinished (and unpaid for) or to accept Einar's terms. He could have deliberately boycotted the potential of his own creation, but artisan ethics and a received tradition of pride kept him

from attempting such cheap tactics. Instead, he made a con-
certed effort to exceed himself and build the most decidedly
unbeatable boat to have sailed the coastline of Anguilla in
the history of time. Then, one night, just past midnight—once
the keel was ready to go, just before it got the first coat of
white paint—his neighbors heard a desperate clamor, a
beastly disorder, arise from his backyard. It was the sleepy
pleadings of the three egg-bearing hens he had snatched
from his corral with one quick motion of his huge right arm.
Sharp walked that night—distilling a trail of rum, sulfur, and
hatred that could be sensed for days—toward his place of
work, at the end of a private dust road, somewhere in South
Hill. When he reached the naked skeleton of his craft, Sharp
loosed the suffocating grip his right hand had over the joined
necks of the three hens and dropped them half-dead on the
floor. Panic-stricken, wounded, and almost asphyxiated, the
desperate animals barely made an attempt—certainly not
an audible one—to save themselves. With a savage, ruthless
motion, Sharp pulled off the heads of each of the hens with
his own hands, while his poisonous breath uttered a curse of
failure to be sealed upon the skull of *Bumblebee* by the warm
sprinkle of innocent blood, by the evil stare of his devilish
eyes, and by his final sacrifice: eating the raw skulls of his
victims.

The fact that the bodies of the three killed hens were only
found after the fifth consecutive second place by *Bumblebee*
this year seems to have raised no suspicion. The additional
fact that after three months the bodies in question were nowhere near the state of putrefaction you would expect them to
be seems to have confirmed rather than challenged the theory of a black magic ritual. *Bumblebee* is forever doomed—
destined—to second place. Thus, considering the current
state of affairs, no one, not even its sailors, thinks my boat is

a rightful contender to the title today: they need to win and hope that the remaining three contestants fail to finish "in the points" (i.e., second to fifth) to complete the triple miracle of turning a donkey boat into a winner, clinching the Boat of the Year Award with only one win over the season, and, most importantly, chasing the haunting spirits of a hoax spell, a certain obeah, that, so far, has been the determining factor in its performance.

The sand is warm on the beach but the white grains are so thin along the southern and western coasts of the island that they seldom get hot enough to burn the soles of your feet. Past the dunes, I reach the bay and head up northward. The final two jibs are up. The tense confusion that precedes the start of every race reigns; all sails glow in the sun, bloated by the wind; the thirteen keels look west at precisely the same acute angle; ashore, two inebriated sympathizers put their drinks aside to hold tight the rope that binds their boat to within five meters of its position on the grid; wayward sailors run from booze stand to booze stand gathering the members of their crew, taking advantage of the opportunity to take a final swig "for the ride," their flamboyant life vests firmly strapped around their waists the only distinguishing element between them and the maddening crowd.

Boom! Somehow the imminent blast manages to catch half the beach by surprise. Only a fraction of the boats aligned sail away. Three or four of them linger impatiently by the shoreline, fighting the impulse of the wind until the entire crew has climbed over the side, until the final bags of ballast have been loaded. I watch mesmerized as this cacophony of shapes and colors moves away from the bay, the boats slowly merging and becoming indistinguishable from one another as the width of this unbounded course shrinks when they approach a buoy drifting out at sea—the vortex of an imaginary funnel, the eye of the needle each of the boats will have to thread before they can turn back and head for the finish line.

Suddenly, the heavy arm of a clearly influenced SamB clenching my throat, toppling me to the ground, brings me back to reality.

XII

Carnival in Anguilla, like in most other English-speaking countries in the Caribbean, has very few religious connotations. The privations of Lent and the excesses that precede it play no role in a celebration that begins almost four months after Easter because it commemorates not the death of Christ but the abolition of slavery in the British Empire. The focal point of Anguilla's carnival is August Monday, the first Monday of the month. The Law of Abolition of Slavery received Royal Assent on Thursday, August 29, 1833, and came to effect on Friday, August 1, 1834. Hence, the significance of the first Monday of the month remains a mystery, but contradictions like that abound in Anguilla: a dry island with little fertile soil where most plantations—tobacco, sugarcane, cotton—failed long before 1834, where consequently the effect of the abolition of slavery was relatively minor, given that most slaves had already been at least partly enfranchised for economic reasons, anyway; an island where independence from the colonial master in 1967 was greeted with a civil insurrection against the central government of St. Kitts, Nevis, and Anguilla—the new state, which threatened to perpetuate and legitimize the neglect the English had brought upon the island though centuries of total disregard by effectively extending colonial powers over Anguilla to St. Kitts, by far the largest and most populous island of the tripartite entity; a civil insurrection—a revolution—that was waged for more than two years, claiming a grand total of absolutely zero lives at all—not one death—and culminating, after twelve more years of political negotiations, in the re-annexation of Anguilla as an autonomous nation with the status of Dependent Territory to the British Crown; a British colony, after all, where sailing is more popular than cricket.

Like cricket, sailing is a summer sport. Not that the weather plays much of a role when it comes to deciding what to do in Anguilla. For the untrained eye of a foreign visitor, summer and winter are notions that do not apply here: the subtle, minor variations that make of Anguilla a much nicer place in December than in June—the change in the direction of the tides and consequently of the temperature of the sea, the slight breeze that picks up in April and dies out in August, the five-degree difference between the warmest day of the summer and the coolest day of the winter—pass by most tourists unnoticed. Strictly speaking, there is only one season in the year that is ruled by the weather: hurricane season. The rest can almost safely be described as a nonseason. Which is why people in Anguilla merely adopt the lingo of the rest of the northern hemisphere, say it is winter when it snows in Massachusetts or in Rome. That, and the fact that during the "winter" the fluctuating population of the island doubles with an invasion of northern tourists, making it the period of abundance when the local population must amass the provisions that will take them through the long, long "summer." There is no time for sailing in the winter. Sailing, like cricket, like carnival, is a summer sport.

But August Monday falls right at the peak of the Anguillan summer, and on August Monday Samuel Bedingford was among the first people to arrive in Sandy Ground, sometime before noon, a good hour prior to the scheduled start of the race. He knew the starting gun would not spew its puff of smoke before two o'clock, and he knew Dragon would not show up on time—he hadn't for the vast majority of the previous races. But Samuel Bedingford could not wait to get down to the bay and partake in the collective revelry, because on this particular occasion, Champion of Champions featured competitors from "the neighboring nations"—i.e., both sides of St. Martin—which guaranteed the presence of a refreshingly foreign crowd among the spectators. When he got to the beach, SamB was immediately struck by the fifteen, twenty motorboats tightly squeezed together, moored on two rows to the north side of the pier in Sandy Ground. His beautiful smile gave away the joy he felt as he approached a stall and ordered the first Cuba Libre of the day, even though the digits of his watch indicated to him that it was still a.m. SamB usually never drank anything alcoholic before noon, but today was a special occasion: today was August Monday; today merited a break from the sobriety—the calmness—that characterized him; today was a day of fun.

The first thing SamB noticed when he arrived in Sandy Ground on August Monday was the invasion of French visitors arrived from St. Martin who, along with fiercely sunburnt skin and funny—camp—intonations, brought to the island their very own sense of maritime fashion: worryingly tight Speedos—often described as "man-hammocks"—were the price to pay for the boon of fluorescent thongs and nipple-covering bras that more often than not slid beyond the subtle bit of skin they were (or not) supposed to cover. SamB was more than happy to pay that price and accommodate the temporary guests with the amount of attention their efforts to impress demanded, joining in on the carefree celebrations for the day.

So it was that on his first wander down the beach, still holding his first drink in his right hand, SamB spotted the rousing sight of an admirer: stunning brown eyes brighter than the sunlit ripples, cowboy hat tilted forward, daring one-piece swimsuit cut in so many places the tan lines on her naked body would resemble a jigsaw puzzle later that night. It was the professional oval-shaped

American football the men of her group were eagerly throwing at each other which told SamB that he would not need to use his deficient French chat-up lines. *Where's that accent from? Australia?* Most Americans were somewhat baffled when they heard the name Zimbabwe, found themselves slightly caught out by the thought of there being any *white* Africans. *SamB. My pleasure.* Samuel Bedingford had acquired the habit of introducing himself as SamB ever since he first got to the island, not because there were any other Sams—As or Cs—with whom he could be confused, but simply because he found it so cool. *Tracey Anne? What a beautiful name.* Tracey Anne was the only Southerner in a group of New Yorkers who all shared one common, constipated American English they called normal. At this rate of normality, Tracey Anne and SamB found immediate affinity in the marked emphasis on the letter *i* in her diction, mirrored in his vocalization of the *a*, in her dragged out *h*, which made his pronunciation sound harsher than it was. An affinity, it must be said, that was reciprocated in the beauty of each other's eyes, in their complementing features, in their mutually flattering company. SamB smiled to himself. Tracey Anne thought he had smiled at her, smiled back. The breathtaking—heavenly—beauty of Sandy Ground, turned quaint for a day, was momentarily enhanced by her perfect charm.

Tracey Anne sat between SamB's plied legs—feet flat on the ground and slightly apart, knees bent upward, serving as support to his embracing arms—surrounded by the rest of a crowd dizzied by the effect of the alcohol in their thirst-quenching cocktails, when the belated gunshot startled spectators and participants alike in decreeing the beginning of the race. The unexpectedly fast progress of the unmoored sailboats, the hectic activity of the delayed starters trying to get on their way before it was too late, contrasted markedly with the prior parsimony, prompted some excitement among a crowd that had almost forgotten why they had come to Sandy Ground that day. Once the bloated sails began to head into the distance, the general evacuation of local motorboats crammed to the rim got going, hyperactive enthusiasts delivering unheard or unheeded advice with the same futility they proffered insults, which despite traveling the seven seas were not even meant to reach anyone beyond their own quarters. Tracey Anne and her friends decided to follow closely the opening half of the race and then head back to the beach once the boats had reached the buoy. One of the football players—the one who looked like a quarterback—went to get some food—barbecue ribs, chicken, fish, johnny cakes, and satay. SamB helped load a few cases of beer into the small boat: two in the cooler under the bench at the back, two in the fridge inside the cabin, and one more simply scattered about. He was lifting the last case, passing it to the wide receiver in the boat, when he recognized Dragon Jones standing on his own on the white sand. *I'll go get my friend. Pick me up on the far side, over there.* SamB's run along the beach was slow and rickety. Dragon could not hear him calling over the drowning melody of the calypso, the jaunty tunes of the soca. The Americans' boat had gone around twice when SamB's clumsy greeting sent Dragon— unaware—tumbling to the ground.

Twelve people on a boat that would comfortably sit eight was nothing short of luxury on a day like this. SamB sat on the bench at the back with Tracey Anne and two other girls. *Dragon, meet Tracey Anne, Stacey, Melinda.* The quarterback and the wide receiver were joined by another raving football player and a pretty blonde behind the helm. *Stanley, John, Joe, Stacey.* Dragon grabbed a beer, joined a group of three on the small triangular deck above the cabin, by the prow: *Joan, Lynne, Joe.* Suddenly, all their names blended into one another and Dragon forgot every single one of them. He smiled. The wide receiver, behind the helm, let out a warning. Four pairs of legs emerged simultaneously from under the railing on the side of the boat almost as soon as the surge of power thrust their heads backward. The scorching sun, ruthless in the shadeless environment of the open sea, dried Dragon's bare chest within seconds, left a thin, pale coat of salt all over his skin. His lips cracked, his throat grew thirsty. The first beer went in a hurry. The wide receiver seemed to enjoy testing the performance of the two 200hp engines as much as anything; SamB took part in the fun, admiring the gracious beauty of Tracey Anne's face, ridded of the long streaks of dark brown hair that covered it before; Dragon and the prow party were slightly less amused by the bobbling and bouncing of the hard surface underneath them. The wide receiver seemed oblivious to the location of the buoy, headed in the opposite direction. Dragon turned around, pointed the skipper in the right direction, and instantly turned into the sailing specialist of the bunch.

The outward sail, aided by a strong westerly wind, was quick and uneventful. The Americans reached the buoy before the first tack, drifted idly as they watched the competitors go past. The wide receiver was replaced by the quarterback behind the helm and two girls joined the crowd at the prow, bringing beers for everyone. Someone opened wide the hatch of the cabin, placed the extra case of beers over some boxes so that it could be reached by the prow party through the opening with little effort. Five boats approached the buoy roughly at the same time. *The Old Oak* went around first, headed back east down the conventional route. *De Vries*, the only boat from Dutch St. Martin, in second, and *2Kool* in fourth, followed it. *Condor*, in third place, and *De Roque*, fifth, both headed south, searching the streaky gusts of the shallow waters, banking on their ability to pull quick tacks along the coastline. *Bumblebee*, accomplished long-sailor that it was, remained the only front runner at sixth to take a sharp turn, travel the longer north path, trying to reach the shore in only one tack. Dragon rejoiced in his newly appointed task as he briefed his friends on the details of sailing tactics. On SamB's request, they drifted by the buoy until *De One*, entangled in an intense fight with the boat from French

St. Martin, came around. It was the only lapse of thirty seconds in the whole day when SamB's eyes were not glued to some portion of Tracey Anne's body.

The quarterback took the opportunity to test the engines himself, chose a roundabout route—via *Bumblebee*'s North Hill path, then *De Roque*'s southern one—to reach the bay. Dragon thought *Bumblebee* had tacked too early, would miss wide of the finish line. But when he asked the more expert SamB about it he got no answer. As Dragon noted *De Vries* opening a gap, he suddenly understood why SamB was disinterested in the race. Dragon switched his attention from the boats to the delightful company. *So, Gwen, is this your first time in Anguilla?* A period of trial and error reacquainted Dragon with the names of his newly made friends and gave him a vague idea of the contrived status of their respective relationships with each other. *The name's Lynne. And no, Martin used to own a house in Sea Rocks, we used to come all the time.*

Who the hell is Martin? Dragon thought to himself. Never mind.

Before Dragon noticed *The Old Oak* losing pace, it dawned on him that he would have to play his cards soon if he did not want to end up alone. Although there were six guys and six girls on that boat, experience had taught him that seldom in such situations do six couples ensue: inevitably there would be at least one frustrated party in this bunch by the end of the night and he desperately wanted to avoid it being him. So he spied Lynne's startling green eyes and the way they drifted past his empty chitchat, past the tiny square windshields by the "bridge" behind him, to focus on the lean figure of the quarterback. *Is that your bloke?* The word *bloke*, Dragon knew, would defuse any awkwardness the question might carry, perhaps even give him an edge by virtue of its exaggerated Englishness to the ear of an American. *Who? John? Noooooh.* The question did not have the desired effect, partly because Lynne's attention was far too fixed on the movements of John, who in turn relentlessly wooed pretty little Stacey, who could not stop giggling to the tune of John's come-on and who also happened to be Martin's sister, who still sat on the prow—legs neatly folded in, hair flowing in the breeze—miserably dreading the blatant infatuation of his one and only meaningful prospect in life, Tracey Anne, with an insolent Zimbabwean intruder.

That's the frustrated one! Encouraged by his find, Dragon embarked on his quest for company for the night. With Stacey's sweet small body already shivering for John, Lynne's jaded eyes burning with jealous rancor, Tracey Anne's smile crawling all over SamB, and an anonymous blonde making out with what was pretty unequivocally her very own wide receiver, the choice was reduced to the two remaining girls on the boat. A gust of wind blew in from the sea as the quarterback slowed down on his approach to the pier. Dragon instinctively turned to get an update on the race, but all he could see were the pale blue eyes of a girl who looked like a mermaid. His job was already done: left arm around her back, right hand pointing over right shoulder, back slightly arched forward, left cheek so close to her right it created static. *That lone boat out north, that's* Bumblebee, *the quickest runner at the moment.* It was all a prank, of course: fluttering jibs, jaunty silhouettes, leaning keels—it all meant nothing to Dragon in the first place, and the boats were far too far to tell, anyway, but to the eager American ears that mattered, it all sounded plausible, possible, wantable. *Sorry, what was your name again?* Jo. Oh, Jo, Joanne, Johanna. Will you make my day tonight?

XIII

My eyes roll open as I'm forced to face the struggle of a brand-new day. What the light of day—banned from my bolt-hole by means of thick velvet curtains (Nathe thinks they belong to a whorehouse)—couldn't achieve, the resilience of my hungry pet has accomplished. A daring spear of sunlight filters in through a crack between the two drapes, landing on a distant foot. It isn't mine. I cease to forget: I'm not alone. I want to remember nothing more. The whirling passage to the living room takes me past an unusual amount of hurdles: too many pairs of shoes scattered on the floor. I don't want to remember. The bag of Cat Chow above the fridge, a medicine kit on the counter. *Sorry, Tiger. Priorities are priorities.* Even aspirin is hard to swallow on this Tuesday morning.

I sit. I sip a cup of something. I stare into nothingness wishing to disappear. Out of a different room emerges SamB. Barefoot and bare-chested, he slowly walks toward me. Today, his face is a smudge. I can't tell whether he's smiling or wincing in pain. His body collapses on the couch, pressing a pile of clothes deep into the upholstery. His left hand battles his own weight to retrieve a pair of (female) pants from under his butt. Stained underpants and sandy jeans entwine in a postmodern sculpture to adorn the silent space between us. I know why he has woken up in my house, but I don't *want* to know. I refuse to remember.

The sun emerges slowly, raising with it the temperature outside. It soon becomes too warm for anyone to sleep and we're joined by our visitors. First, out of my room, Tracey Anne, small brown eyes sheltered behind half-shut lids. She collects her belongings—sandals, top, skirt—as she paces carefully around the house. *There's fresh coffee in the machine.* She covers the pieces of her bodily jigsaw puzzle with an old gray T-shirt of mine from Leeds University which comes down well below the level of the skirt she was wearing the night before. I don't want to remember any of that. Her perfect long legs still look perfect but her rugged mane and croaky voice are more attuned to the general feeling—*my* general feeling, at least—of the day.

Lynne is next. I genuinely can't remember Lynne joining us: a fit of jealousy caused by the painful embarrassment she felt at the dinner table when Stacey asked John to try some of her fish, then proceeded to feed him from her own mouth— lips lingering together suspiciously long—prompted Lynne to join the rest of the girls in their "other" adventure, and to give the gift she had so carefully wrapped for John to a perfect stranger. It turned out SamB was a lot more perfect, or much more of a stranger, than me. Nathe says it's the exoticism of his heritage. I blame it on his accent. I feel uncomfortable as Lynne walks around collecting her and her friend's clothes, and suddenly all I can think of is Sheila Rawlingson. I have cheated on Sheila, the most exuberant woman on the planet. Or at least I have cheated on the idea of Sheila, on the fantasy I have built around my father's wife. I have cheated on my father's wife, who is young enough to be his daughter. I have cheated on my father's daughter. Jesus Christ. I have cheated on my sister, my father's . . . Drop it now, Dragon. Just drop it. *There's fresh coffee in the machine.*

And out comes Jo, jeans buttoned up, top creased and soiled but on. I get up to make more coffee. *Don't worry about me: I need to go.* Is SamB also feeling uncomfortable? Did he also cheat on someone? Is he thinking of my father's wife? Jo's walk is flimsy, her face another smudge. I don't search for a smile. She no longer looks like a mermaid; Lynne's eyes don't have the sparkle of gems; Tracey Anne's beauty fails to entice: no trace can be sensed in the embers of our night of the heat and the passion that made for a wild evening. That is all a part of yesterday, and this is the morning after the night before, and the magic and the spell that drove us through our adventure have somehow disappeared in the space between.

We have our breakfast. *I have to go. Do you want me to drop you off somewhere?* There's a tone of duty in SamB's detached politeness. *Are you interested in a seventeen-seat Trislander, by the way?* My eyes bulge, my brain is startled out of its muted hangover. *I heard there's one going in the Dominican Republic for $150,000.* The girls vanish from my range of vision, the regular weekday morning frame of mind kicks in. *I'll put you in contact with the people. I really have to go now.* A rattling noise disrupts the solemnity of my driveway. The house is a mess, even emptied of the strangers' belongings. Three awkward goodbyes are said on the threshold of my door but SamB's breaking news has replaced my uneasiness with the hope of a hope. A taxi pulls up by my house. SamB has a car. No one has called a cab. The door of my house opens, SamB winks farewell in his usual fashion, the young women stand in line ready to go, yet something prevents the traffic from flowing, the foyer from emptying. Blocking the way, on the other side of the doorway, stands the imposing—small, strong, foreign—frame of a pilot, suited and booted, cap under his left arm, suitcase in his left hand,

right fist clenched and raised, ready to knock on the opened
door: Arturo Sarmiento.

PART II

I

athaniel Jones was born in a small alpine town in southern Bavaria on a cold winter's day several years after the invasion that turned America into the guardian of Western civilization and that left German people with a seemingly inexhaustible moral debt. Nathaniel's mother, Gertrude Schmidt, was a lively member of a prominent local family that had somehow escaped the grip of ideological imposition and had managed to navigate the storm of Nazism without pledging unconditional allegiance to the party. Nevertheless, at the time of the American invasion, Gertrude Schmidt became just another member of that eternally grateful generation of Germans who greeted their invaders with genuine enthusiasm, not just because they—the Americans, the liberators—were the lesser of two evils but because they were, in fact, the most desirable option between two nations so perverse that you would never imagine they could coexist at any point in history.

At the time of the imminent collapse of the National Socialist regime, Gertrude's sparkly blue eyes had barely been alive to the world for seventeen years. As a matter of fact, despite the atrocities of war and the deprivations of defeat, Gertrude's sparkly blue eyes had not seen very much at all before the day she first noticed the long, strong arm of Horace Jones outstretched in her direction, kindly holding a bar of candy in his hand. Gertrude Schmidt did not expect such gesture of sympathy from a man enlisted in

an army which authoritatively prohibited all interaction with the
enemy, and Gertrude Schmidt saw in the generous boon offered
to her by Horace Jones's stiff arm an opportunity to hide, however
briefly, from the ordeal of extreme poverty, so, despite the fact
that Gertrude Schmidt had never been faced with a bar of candy
before, her instinctive reaction was to embrace her benefactor's
sympathy with arms and legs wide open.

Neither had Horace Jones ever experienced anything like the
spark he found in Gertrude Schmidt's blue eyes. He knew he was
breaking direct orders when he followed the path that led to the
source of such spark, when he silently handed Gertrude Schmidt
a Hershey's bar. But once Horace Jones discovered the gentler
side of the master race, he found it impossible to comply with the
rules he'd already broken, so he continued to risk his military career on a regular basis with secret expeditions into the blue spring
of his infatuation, with a constant supply of the simple luxuries
made available to American soldiers by CARE packages: sugar,
coffee, bacon, honey.

Concerned about the consequences of his illegal relationship,
Horace Jones kept it secret long after the end of the nonfraterni-
zation policy, after the lift of the marriage ban. Until one Sunday
afternoon in the summer of 1948, when, amid troubling discussions of denazification and trials of war, Horace Jones pondered
the surreal serenity he had found in the small *gasthaus* where he
had managed to secure a permanent room for his lover. He lay
naked in the thin mattress that constituted luxury for Gertrude
Schmidt, when he noticed the last remains of the twilight shining
through the window over her stretched stomach. She lay, beautiful, on her side, facing the window, away from him. He looked
on and saw, beyond the tracks of her ribs, beyond the dip of her
waist, the convex line that sheltered her womb. He put out his
cigarette, gently pulled back her left shoulder with his left hand.
But the immaculate softness of her cheeks was covered in tears, as

Gertrude Schmidt explained that she was five months pregnant. Three years of careful dating in utmost discretion came to an end four months later, when Gertrude's sparkly blue eyes got glued with agony to the plain white ceiling of the infirmary nearest to the casern that housed Horace's regiment.

Nathaniel Jones was born in a German hospital seven miles away from the American casern in which his father was to spend the last six months of his placement. Gertrude's respectable family and Horace's impeccable record worked wonders twisting, bending, shaping the rules of a busy army, in their effort to endow this indecent union with an impossible level of legitimacy. After weeks of laborious networking, Horace and Gertrude Jones were finally allowed to walk out of a church as husband and wife. Thus, a very private, very subdued service succeeded in completing the task begun by a phallic bar of candy years before: maintaining the heritage of a name that for four generations had identified the firstborn male in the Jones family and that had been denied to Horace by a twin toddler who took it to his grave even before he could learn how to say Nathaniel.

But after Nathaniel's birth Horace suddenly found that the brightness behind Gertrude's sparkly blue eyes dimmed, that her firm, white thighs widened, that her soft, round buttocks began to drop flat, and he found himself harboring uncomfortable doubts about his original plan to take his war bride back to Alton, Illinois. So Horace declined an offer to go back to the USA, choosing instead an assignment in Wiesbaden. Yet he also considered it imprudent—unsafe, even—to take his German wife along to a city he didn't know. He was not allowed to live with her inside the casern, or to share a residence with her outside army grounds. So Horace promised he would seek suitable arrangements and call for his wife to join him in Wiesbaden as soon as everything was in order.

* * *

Six years later, as Gertrude held Nathaniel by the hand on their way to his first day of school, all that remained of Horace Jones in her life was a surname, a monthly contribution toward the upbringing of their child, and a postcard sent by Horace six months after his arrival in Wiesbaden. She counted herself among the lucky ones: at least Horace had proved generous, if not loyal.

Nathaniel Jones was raised by his mother in a small alpine town in southern Bavaria. He quickly and naturally learned to speak his native language. At age six he was enrolled in a German Grundschule. After successfully finishing his fourth year Nathaniel was moved to a German Realschule, where the crisis of his teens came and went with no detriment to his academic performance. Urged to outshine the ones who mocked him for his name, who reviled him for his mother's transgression, Nathaniel decided to continue beyond his eleventh year, completed a twelfth and then a thirteenth year in a German gymnasium. Finally, he was admitted to a German university, where at the age of twenty-four he was the youngest student in his class to be awarded a degree in economics.

But regardless of his accomplishment and despite his best efforts, in the eyes of his cohorts Nathaniel Jones remained—had always been—*ein Ami*—an American. The sparkle in Gertrude's eyes had sufficed, if not to uphold the fire of matrimonial commitment in Horace Jones, at least to ensure his recognition of paternal responsibility, legitimated by the gift of his name. A gift that forever alienated Nathaniel Jones from his natural environment, a gift that Nathaniel hated as furiously as he impersonated it, a gift that immediately and irrevocably shaped his life, turning him into what he is now.

‖

Dear Grandpa,

By the time you read this letter I won't be home no more. I'm sorry. Please don't hate me, like everyone else in the family. I never wished to hurt you. I only wanted to live my life. I think, of all people, you might understand.

In the beginning, things were different, you know. When I met Nathaniel, he was just a tourist passing by who caught my eye. The reason I never mentioned him to anyone was because he was no big deal to me. But things got complicated. He extended his stay without telling me nothing, he spent weeks looking for me, his charm intrigued me, his experienced devotion seduced me. When Nathaniel proposed, it was no surprise. We had been spending plenty time together (alone, in his house, away from the gossip). The final extension of his tourist visa was coming to an end and he told me he would apply for a resident visa. The only problem was I still hadn't told no one about my secret relationship. Sure, people knew something was up as soon as I didn't show up for the parties, and left early from work, and didn't pick up my phone. But nobody knew who I was seeing, nobody had a clue. Not even you, Grandpa. I'm sorry. I'm sorry I never trust you enough to tell you. I'm sorry I never warn you in advance. I knew as soon as I told Mom and Dad about this man, I'd be treated like I lose my mind. I knew as soon as anyone knew, my brothers would go to set the record straight. I knew as soon as I spoke up, Uncle Glen would use all his influence in Immigration to make life impossible for Nathaniel. So I stayed quiet while his papers were still in order. And then I stayed quiet while I helped him settle into his new life in Anguilla. And then I stayed quiet after speaking to Father Rasheed (and forcing him to stay quiet too) about our plans for a secret wedding.

But we couldn't go ahead with it. The truth is we were in love. Nathaniel, a white man twice my age, had won me over. That is the truth. But I also love my family . . . very much. Even if Mom won't let me tell her no more. Even if Dad won't speak to me. So, I had to let you know.

Of course it didn't really work out. The Rawlingsons are too proud for something like that to be forgiven. The Rawlingsons are too stubborn to let a white man decide the course of their precious little one's life. You know what followed: Mom's hysteria, Dad's threats, Uncle Glen's attempts to get Nathaniel deported. He almost succeeded too, you know, had it not been for the help of a friend who I won't name. But even in adversity, we seemed to grow closer, better, bigger, Nathaniel and me. And all along I knew that if someone understood my situation, it was you. You, who had left your little island as a young man, in search of a better future, you, who had found your happiness in the arms of a girl (just a child at the time) from another country, you, who had taken your chances, given up on that "better future," and returned home with a forbidden love and a foreign wife.

How I wished to speak to you in those days of anxiety, Grandpa. But how could I? How could I face you and tell you the truth? How could I face you and hide the shame?

How could I ask you to keep my secret? I was afraid. I
couldn't. Until Nathaniel decided to do the rightful thing.
He showed up all dressed up in his suit and tie to ask Dad
for my hand. I ain't never seen little Dewan so upset in
my life. I thought he was going to kill him. I think we all
thought he was going to kill him. Jamaal was so afraid he
forgot the whole thing and concentrated only on calming
Dewan down. Mom went nuts. She ain't been the same
since, either, at least not to me. And Desmond, the trouble-
maker of the family, the oldest boy, the rudest one, he just
sat there listening, watching, quiet. I think he might've
understood, you know. I think he could tell, Grandpa. I
think maybe he knew. I'm two years older than Desmond,
Grandpa. I changed Jamaal's nappies when he was a baby.
Now he has a wife, a business, a house. I cooked lunch
after school for all the children who ain't living at home
no more. I was almost finished with primary school when
Dewan was born. Now Dewan has a child of his own. I
just wanted to live, Grandpa. I'd just got back from school
in Washington, and what was I supposed to do? Go back
home? Work for Dad? Pretend nothing changed? Pretend
I was still the same little girl? I just reached for my freedom, Grandpa. Then I found a man who managed to pin
me down to commitment. And I was happy about it too,
you know . . . funny how things work out . . . But I think
you might understand everything about the irony of life.
You, who left this island full of hope and prospects only
to sail back poorer, older, but yes, happier. And I think
Desmond might've understood. He never said so much.
He still doesn't speak to me. But I saw it in his eyes that
night. I saw a flame go: "Alright, sis. If this what you want,
if this what you think will make you happy, go ahead and
grab it. Make your new life with this man and leave all a

we behind. We'll be alright. And we hope you'll be alright
too."

It's getting late, Grandpa. The rooster's crawling outside and the sun will soon come out. When the sun comes
out, I'll have to stop writing this letter, I'll have to get on
my way. But before, there's so much I want to tell you,
Grandpa, there's so much I want you to know . . .

III

Nathaniel Jones sat outside what had quickly become his favorite bar, dipping his bare feet in the soft texture of the virginal sand, sipping his bottle of beer from the Caribbean that tasted more of lemon than alcohol, facing out, toward the South Hill side of Sandy Ground, eyes hidden behind the shelter of his dark sunglasses, when the slim figure of Sheila Rawlingson made its sudden cameo, swinging her perfect hips as she made her way through the sand, moderating the criss-crossing of her legs as soon as she got to the safe ground of the wooden deck, leaving a gusty trail of sweet perfume as she moved between the spread-out tables (the very last one of which, by the edge of the deck, bordering the sand, was occupied by Nathaniel Jones). Nathaniel's world blacked out for a moment. For a moment, the steep fall in the Brazilian stock market meant nothing. For a moment, the consequences of a tragic decision to launch a new attack on Syria became unimportant. The price of oil: unimportant. Negotiations: unimportant. Business: forgotten.

Nathaniel Jones had come to this golfing paradise on the northern tip of the Caribbean to forget about everything for a little while (a fortnight). For the best part of two weeks, the professionals of entertainment had failed to achieve what a young local woman had managed with a sleight of her hips. Nathaniel Jones had not been able to deposit the burden lingering at the back of his mind either at the golf course or at the tennis court; he had felt no lighter in the depths of his spear-fishing dive than he had in the comfort of his swim with the dolphins; his thoughts had swiftly glided with him as he flew forty feet above the turquoise water of Shoal Bay; they had followed suit as he dived into Little Bay from the top of a fifteen-foot cliff. But now, for one brief moment, Nathaniel Jones's range of vision faded into nothing as the tide of his consciousness lay flat as a bowl of soup whereupon one and only one wave made any sort of (big, huge) impression: the svelte image of a nameless young woman.

Nathaniel Jones sat outside his favorite bar, sipping his bottle of beer, thinking of a way to make contact with this local woman, when he lifted his sunglasses in search of her eyes. *Is the waitress in there?* He grasped his chance. Quick, agile steps brought him to the bar. *If this is good enough for you, it's good enough for me. Can I buy you a drink?* Sheila Rawlingson sat at the bar—peach daiquiri in hand—waiting for her good friend Leslie Anthony to show up. She had not seen Leslie since her return from America and now, she had heard, he was going away the following day to train for a year as a patisserie chef in a hotel in Paris. Leslie had already made plans to have dinner with someone else that night but he could still squeeze in a cocktail with Sheila after work, before dinner. Nathaniel was unaware of Sheila's plans but he could guess she had not just dropped by her local bar for a lonely drink. *We all have someone to meet, sometime. But you'll still need to have dinner some other time.* Nathaniel was not aware of the terms of Sheila's present arrangement, of the chance that awaited him. *Of course you can promise, anyone can promise anything. Whether or not you keep your word is an entirely different matter.* He waited expectantly. She allowed an ounce of hope to seep through her words. *Okay, den, you kyan buy me a drink sometime, but I kyan't promise when.* Nathaniel Jones had no idea how soon sometime would be. Neither did Sheila Rawlingson.

Nathaniel Jones sat on the pier by the beach opposite his favorite bar, dipping his bare feet in the soft, cold sea water, sipping from his bottle of beer, eyes fixed on the establishment where the only wave that disturbed the otherwise quiet tide of his consciousness shared a drink that was becoming worryingly long but that promisingly had not yet led to dinner, when the Afro-Caribbean male who had until then accompanied her made his hurried exit—*alone!* Nathaniel flung his beer into the sea as he hastily fit his wet feet inside his shoes. While he made his way along the pier, one of the ripples produced by the impact of his bottle on the tranquil sea resonated in his brain, raising a shadow of concern for having chucked an empty bottle into what was otherwise an immaculate beach, for having littered in heaven.

Sheila Rawlingson stood in front of the bar, packing her belongings into her purse, when she met the solitary shadow of Nathaniel Jones walking in from the beach. His attempt to look surprised failed so miserably it made them both smile. Sublime. *You did promise.* The promise that turned into a drink went down in a hurry. Nathaniel's appetite was satiated merely by the sight of Sheila's beauty, but his craftiness told him he needed to come up with something quickly if he wanted to enjoy her company any longer. *Why don't you join me for dinner?* Thus it was that a drink that went down in a hurry turned into a banquet in the most expensive restaurant on the island: lobster, crayfish, crab, an abused tablecloth witnessing the details of a culinary extravaganza, a host of bottles of sparkling wine fueling the evening with a sense of adventure, an unlikely couple sitting in a candlelit corner of an exquisite restaurant, contemplating the moon, amusing each other. *I have a couple of days left, why don't you show me the local side of paradise?* And a banquet in the most expensive restaurant on the island turned into a rendezvous in town the following day. The sun, the town, the traffic all conspired to turn a rendezvous into a guided tour of pleasure. But just like the appeal of a treasure hunt lies as much in the process of finding it as in the treasure itself, it was the behavior of his divulger of secrets that mesmerized Na-

thaniel on a day in which indigenous caves, millenary wells, and
desolate beaches could have been replaced by scorching deserts
and swamping wasteland to absolutely no detriment of his mood.
So, where do you go on a Friday night? Let's go dancing. Turn a guided
tour of the hidden treasures of an island paradise into a late-night
jam session at The Velvet in Sandy Ground. Late night, indeed.
Very late and very dark, making palpable a dream he had not yet
dared turn into a fantasy. Dark and fair skin sweat equally in the
enclosed environment of a crowded nightclub. Dark and fair skin
touching, rubbing, sliding, pressing. After a long stint which pre-
dominantly saw Sheila's back reclining against Nathaniel's chest,
Nathaniel's hands exploring the routes delineated between her
arms, four legs slightly bent at the precise same angle delivering short,
tuneful steps, leaving him completely exhausted, gagging for a drink.

Tomorrow ain' no good for me. What followed was automatic. *Nah,
I busy wit' family stuff all night.* The situation merited one more try.
I ain' sure I kyan make it den, eider. A napalm bomb exploded in the
hall of mirrors Nathaniel had built for himself over the last two
days. One by one the reflecting images of a promise turned into
a drink that went down in a hurry, turned into a banquet in the
most expensive restaurant of the island, turned into a rendezvous
in town, turned into a guided tour of the hidden treasures of an
island paradise, turned into a late-night jam session at The Velvet,
shattered into irretrievably small splinters that pierced the dream
Nathaniel had not yet dared turn into a fantasy. *But why?* There
was no answer. *Why?* There was no why. There was only two cars
that took two separate ways, that forced Nathaniel to spend the
last fifty-four hours of his yearly dose of relaxing amnesia alone.
Except he could not. Because Nathaniel had been bitten by the
bug of love, smitten by the arrows of Eros, and he could not conceive of departing the source of his ailment without finding the
antidote. So he stayed behind. He called the airline, put back his
flight (indefinitely), spoke to the hotel manager, prolonged his stay.

IV

Sheila Rawlingson felt Nathaniel Jones's hardened weapon stroke the curve between her buttocks with delight. Seven years of academic life in an American university had not canceled out the art of overt sexuality cultivated in the islands. She smiled as she tilted her body forward, resting hands on knees, pushing her rear backward, keeping time with the music, dreaming to be had. Shut eyes reduced reality to the darkened beating of soca rhythms and the slippery touch of ever-more-adventurous hands. She obeyed the scratch of nails running up the sides of thighs, digging into pelvis, pulling closer, harder; she enjoyed the tender rub of left hand climbing the stairs of one, two, three, four ribs, molding fingers to the perfect shape of perfect breasts; she longed for the thrust of manhood to help her reach the ecstasy of womanhood, when the clumsy trace of an overexcited hand caught her hardened nipple between its index and middle fingers, pricking her out of her fantasy.

She opened her eyes to the full extent of the scene: she had lost control of the situation. She—the expert teaser—had teased herself into desire. But not all was lost. She reclined her back against Nathaniel's chest one more time, felt the panting of his tired breath. For five minutes or so, their dance continued, seemingly unaltered yet somehow devoid of its previous intensity. Nathaniel did not notice: he could only feel the heavy weight of his leaden feet grow heavier with every step. Sheila seized her op-

portunity to save some face—at least for the witnessing crowd, if
not for herself—kept things going for another few minutes before
granting Nathaniel the wish he wished most: a pause and a drink.
From that point onward their night went downhill, but because
beforehand the course of the evening had skyrocketed, because
the chemistry between them had peaked out of sight, Nathaniel
did not notice how much farther from him she now stood at the
bar, he did not notice how she suddenly failed to lean in his direction when he spoke to her, he did not see her eyes bouncing
from eye to nose to wall to feet rather than attentively—almost
voraciously—focusing on his lips. In fact, Nathaniel noticed no
negative signs whatsoever until the moment of her second rejection. *I'm busy wit' family stuff all night.* No but, no why, no hope.
Desperation would have taken hold of him at that moment had
Sheila not stripped the scene of all emotion, forcing two cars with
three empty seats each to head in opposite directions.

Sheila Rawlingson was afraid. Despite the warm evening, her
left hand trembled throughout the entire drive home. Once there,
she sat on her bed, sleepless, restless. She nursed a lone tear inside
her right eye as long as she could hold it, forcing herself not to
blink. She played back in her mind the two days she had spent
with Nathaniel and loathed the thought of having wronged him.
Then she went through her emotions earlier that night on the
dance floor: she had felt horny, yes, but much more than that.
She'd felt secure, comfortable . . . lost. *I shouda just fuck him on de
beach an' go. Dat way he stay dreamin' of me forever. No sir. I shouda never
have a drink wit' him at all, at all.* But to end up like this: embezzled,
bedazzled, disarmed. Vulnerable to the trickery of a man, a *foreign* man, an *old* foreign man, a man who most likely only wanted
to use her and discard her like an old tissue, no matter what he
said, no matter what she did. A man who would sweeten her up
with empty promises only to let her fall back down. Or worse
still, a man who would see her out of his door before she lost the

orgasmic blush on her face. Sheila Rawlingson almost succeeded in turning the liquid gathered inside her right eye into ice cubes, but just before reaching freezing point she was forced to draw her lids over her bloodshot eyes, bursting the thin coat of ice that had kept the tear from running. It was just an instinctive blink, but the unsuccessful effort to keep her feelings at bay had drained her strengths to the point where she couldn't even open her eyelids one more time. Sheila slept peacefully, sitting fully clothed on her bed, until the morning after.

(SHEILA RAWLINGSON)

Before finding herself rediscovering the spaces of her not-so-distant past, Sheila Rawlingson spent seven years at college in America, building up a résumé and a reputation that would open the doors she had willfully left behind—not fully shut, just partly ajar—when she decided to go in search of a yet uncertain but promising future. During those seven years Sheila learned a lot more than could be surmised by the acronyms that accompanied her name on the diplomas she was awarded for her bachelor's degree in international relations and her master's in business administration. Not that her progress had not been monitored by her family during her occasional homecomings. But most of what Sheila had learned was hard to notice in a place like Anguilla: she had left her safe provincial home in South Hill to join a distant portion of her family in a modernized ghetto in the USA, where African Americans lived the sort of privileged life normally associated exclusively with Caucasian Americans. It took Sheila Rawlingson a long time to venture out of the safe quarters of racial brotherhood. Indeed it took years, until one day she felt the need to make the transition. It was not like Sheila had not been in any sort of touch with white people. In fact, most of the people majoring in international relations with her were white. But she had willfully—albeit perhaps unconsciously—excluded this vast majority from her life, mirroring exactly the attitude they adopted toward her: all of Sheila's friends were black; her favorite actor: Jamie Foxx; favorite TV presenter: Tyra Banks; favorite singer: Rihanna. Sheila did not watch MTV, she watched BET. And never, ever did she go to a club where the music was not a selection of R&B, soul, or hip-hop. In short, Sheila's first and long-lasting impression of the States was a dark one.

But it did not take all that long for Sheila to realize that people in the States were not the same as people in Anguilla. The first thing she had to learn, before any politics, before any calculus, was that city talk is a lot more intricate than the words that compose it. Sarcasm, irony, and malice were things with which Sheila had seldom been acquainted. Even hypocrisy was normally restricted to the higher echelons of political life in Anguilla, and the one common feature she had found between the society in which she had grown up and the one she now faced was that you never believed what politicians said in the first place. Disguised side glances, funny smiles, awkward intonations all went by unnoticed by a gullible young woman who not only couldn't understand why anyone would say something they did not mean but who could really not come to terms with the reasons why anyone would not say what was in their minds anyway. While Sheila Rawlingson adapted to the weather, got to know the city, got over her homesickness, and tried to work out how to read the lines that were neither written nor spoken but carefully hinted at by the way the lines that actually *were* spoken were spoken, she realized that the reality, the concerns, the issues that shape the psyche of African Americans are very different to those encountered by a contemporary Anguillan.

So it was that Sheila Rawlingson looked at racial issues in America with the same attention, the same interest, with which she had faced the challenge of city talk before: that is, with the criterion of a foreign observer. Grandpa had lived a life of struggle and privation not because he was the descendent of slaves but because everyone else's life in Anguilla had always been punctuated by poverty. That was not a social but a political problem. No one had ever cared about Anguilla, not because Anguillans were black but because for the English the island was worthless. St. Helenians were not black. Neither were Faulklanders. Yes, African Americans and Afro-Caribbeans shared one (roughly) common origin: one cruel—more than cruel—one unimaginably inhuman passage. The troubled heritage that Sheila could see still affected African Americans was a particular result of the way in which one nation had dealt with a crime that was not exclusively theirs. But there had been no segregation in Anguilla, mainly because there had been nothing to segregate from. And there had been no civil rights movement, because in Anguilla everyone had always had a right to the little there had been. And then, when Anguillans demanded a bit more than that little, when Anguillans demanded their human, not civil, rights, and were denied, they rebelled, and won the war. The American war was still being waged but Sheila did not think she really belonged to either of the sides concerned. There were sympathies, of course. There were more than enough elements to which she could relate on the one hand, despise on the other, so she knew whom she wanted to succeed. But she did not feel like an integral part of the fight.

Thus, when Sheila experienced firsthand the whiteness of America, she already knew there were black as well as white bullies, liars, and reprobates, she already knew she would find the worst of mankind in a white guise, and she knew that ignorance would lurk behind every corner ready to pounce on her at the first chance. But what Sheila was really curious about, what guided her initiative and fueled her adventure, was a persistent wish to discover the extent and nature of white goodness. Sheila was lucky: within a maze of religious fervor and conservative fanaticism, she just happened to fall into the generous hands of one Aristide Day.

Aristide Day was the best American society had to offer. Crisp, lively, and beautiful, he was a philosophy student with a perpetually tilted black beret who at separate times had embraced with equal commitment the substance of fascist and communist ideologies and had insisted on defending their virtues so vociferously that there was virtually no one in campus who did not know who he was. Despite his notoriety, Aristide was a popular fellow. He had managed to shrug aside the recurrent injuries (mostly verbal) caused by his extravagant attire and his uncompromising, though often contradictory, talk by means of a self-mocking confidence and prodigious wit. Over the years, the general fondness for Aristide had grown to such extent that whenever anybody bumped into him they would greet him with an insult just to hear what sort of clever turn of phrase he would pull out of his magic box. Even his friends greeted him with an affront. In fact, no one had ever heard anyone speak a kind word to Aristide. Many good things were said *of* him behind his back, but no one was foolish enough to speak these words to Aristide's face. It was rumored that ever since the first minute of his existence—after he had been held by his feet and slapped on the butt—when his father took him from the doctor's hands and bit his cheek brutally, telling him off for being so ugly, Aristide had never experienced the comfort of a loving sentence.

Aristide embraced this general attitude quite happily and though it would be unfair to say he actively encouraged it, he was fully aware of the reaction his overly long magenta scarf would produce on campus, or the purple and apple-green woolen mittens his grandmother had allegedly knit for him, or the dark green jester's shoes with the wooden sole and the curling tip, or his eulogy for Ezra Pound's artistry in his Italian radio broadcasts, or the deeper meaning of Stalinist constructivism, or the unacknowledged virtues of extreme utilitarianism—virtues, incidentally, completely ignored by Bentham and Mill. Not only was he fully aware of the reaction all of these would produce but, in fact, he deliberately prepared even more outrageous responses to go with the original postulates, with the disjointed outfits, to counteract what he guessed (almost always correctly) would be the popular reception of his persona. Because neither was Aristide's wit as prodigious nor his outward impression as spontaneous as it seemed. The fact was that Aristide was a naturally gifted artist, actor, writer, who had chosen to live the role he had carved out for himself while majoring in the one subject he might manage to fail.

But there was a lot more to Aristide than just his academic stereotype. Talented at almost everything, he was an accomplished musician who could play the piano, the violin, and the saxophone to semiprofessional standards and who claimed he could play the guitar equally well with either hand, although the one time he had been seen strumming with his right hand—admittedly high, or drunk, or both at some party—it had made so little sense that nobody had been able to tell what it was he was supposed to be playing. He later claimed it had been an obscure piece by César Cui, which nobody would have known in the first place. As it turned out, though, César Cui never composed anything for the guitar. And yet, this, like most other arguments, did not faze him.

When Sheila saw the broken lines that marked the boundaries of Aristide's silhouette the day after such party, she filled herself with courage and took a step outside of her cocoon. *Are you alright?* Although far from alright, Aristide was ready to explain what sort of animal had excreted him from its guts that morning; he was prepared to face the disgust his bodily odor might have produced on Sheila Rawlingson; he would have been delighted to answer why he had not saved the rest of the world from the misery of having to deal with the aesthetic calamity that he was that day. However, Aristide Day was not highly versed in the art of denotative conversation—especially not when it concerned his general disposition—and among the myriad comments he thought his appearance might induce that morning, "Are you alright?" was certainly not in the top hundred. Sheila, vulnerable outside her protected environment, interpreted his blank stare and his impenetrable silence as a sign of disdain. She did not apologize for her impertinence but she did turn around and walk away—question unanswered—without hesitation. It took Aristide three days to come up with the appropriate answer, but by the time he was ready to utter it, it was no longer appropriate. Sheila sat under a leafless tree on a sunny autumn day reading a paper by John Rawls when the long, shabby shadow of the guy in the perpetually tilted black beret hid the sun from the white photocopies she held in her hands. *Yes.* A tap on her shoulder accompanied the incongruous greeting. She understood immediately, let him know with a sublime sample of her sweetest smile. Sheila folded the paper she was reading, got up, and headed toward the building, all in one swift, delicate motion. Before leaving Aristide behind, she turned her head in his direction, almost whispering, *You're weird.* Aristide, feeling much more at home with this sort of observation, would have replied had she not cut in with a final, *I've got class.*

The box of chocolates Sheila found in her locker after class opened a door for her into a world of underground creatures who defined themselves according to values and standards that easily transcended the color of their skins. In a subculture where minorities were the norm and the unconventional was to be expected, more was invented than inherited but nobody knew for certain what was true and what was not. So, for example, the only trace of French in Aristide's life was his name and his perpetually tilted black beret, which led to the growing suspicion that it was all an act he had based on the Parisian cabaret artist Aristide Bruant, who had been immortalized in the advertising posters designed by his friend and companion of absinthe escapades, Henri de Toulouse-Lautrec. But neither Benny "Young" Agbyiiong, the Samoan wrestler who spent his nights creating electronic music to enhance the power of his Jamaican dubbing, nor Roger "Moose" Goose, Aristide's doppelgänger, equally quick, equally bright, but simply less off the chart, really cared about the origins of any of their acquired personae. So, when Aristide introduced Sheila to the group of friends he referred to as "the bad seeds," no one asked her where she was from, no one asked her about her parents, no one questioned her accent. All they asked was what she did. *I'm a photographer.* Sheila Rawlingson, halfway through her international relations major, with minors in politics and economics, suddenly became a photographer, because in the subversive scene of Aristide and Co., nobody was what they were but what they wanted to be, and Sheila had developed a passion for photography— particularly aerial—which she wished more than anything (more than business, more than politics) to guide her in her way through adult life.

The magic spell that filled the inside of the liqueur bonbons Aristide had given Sheila as a conciliatory token fed a romantic liaison which turned out to be as intense as it was short-lived. Sheila, however, could not distance herself from "the bad seeds" as easily as she could part with Aristide. Her voyage through the undertow of normality had liberated her from the oppressions of convention and she was not prepared to make such liberation dependent on a particular person. Thus, once Sheila-the-photographer began collaborating in several projects with a number of the seeds, her status in the group was upgraded from a member's companion to that of sympathetic visitor. None of the other of Aristide's friends had ever made the leap. Only Margarita Peña, a Mexican artist who had been brought into the scene by Roger "Moose" Goose while they were dating, had managed successfully to juggle the pressures involved in the development of a character extricated from the links of its sentimental attachments to be part of the world of her ex. When the seeds spoke of Margarita, they did not speak of Moose's girl: they spoke of Margarita. So, while Sheila Rawlingson's circle of friends became more and more reduced because of the large amount of time she spent with the seeds, her relationship with Margarita Peña grew from a mutual interest in the visual realities of life (Margarita's obsession with photo-realism interestingly overlapped with certain aspects of Sheila's otherwise conflicting theory on photographic impressionism) to an intimacy that saw them share the most vivid secrets of the sexual proclivities of the double-headed eagle that silently ruled over the bad seeds: Aristide Day and Moose.

Sheila Rawlingson spent the last three years of her time at the university exploring every little alley of the world that had been opened to her by a box of chocolates. She dealt with the seeds for so long, in the end her kernel turned sour. She saw Aristide's Persian, New Guinean, Alaskan friends come, and offered them the same curious detachment she had gallantly received when she had first met the seeds. She saw them leave, shocked, amused, or scared, and then she tried to disguise the tiny grin of satisfaction she smiled to herself, knowing she might have done the same sometime before, but luckily had not. Luckily, she had stayed a little while longer, and luckily, she had been able to discern beyond the façade of social inadequacy the merits of a bunch of people who had taught her more than any degree ever could.

Sheila Rawlingson spent the last three years of her time at the university absorbing every bit of wisdom the bad seeds could infuse in her, through a journey that saw her touch the sheets of just about every member, permanent or provisional, of her clique. Then, when she thought she knew everything they did, she decided to close the most enlightening chapter of her adult life by sharing her lust with Moose. He proposed a threesome with Margarita. Sheila refused: she wanted him for herself. But one night was not enough for Sheila to learn what Moose had to teach, and one night certainly did not seem enough for him to enjoy the willfulness of someone seemingly fully versed in the mischief of his preference. So Moose and Sheila-the-photographer entertained each other senseless for a season before she decided to part. Sheila wore her cloak, joined her hands for the dean to clasp, signed the record, and reached the little island of her childhood with an MBA to prove that she had turned into a woman.

PART II
CONTINUED

V

. . . After we got married, we spent months and months doing nothing. I could just tell what the world was thinking, I could just hear the gossip running from mouth to mouth, from house to house, talking up the size of my sin, of Nathaniel's corruption, of my family's shame. At first, I didn't care. I was so happy, I honestly didn't care. Nathaniel's son seemed to be arranging his business in Europe, money wasn't no problem, and we were just too busy with each other to worry about nothing else.

So we spent a long while just traveling. We spent our whole honeymoon traveling, it seems. First we went south hoping to stay away from the hurricanes. We stayed in Barbados, Tobago, and the Grenadines most of September and October. After a little while I started to feel homesick and Nathaniel decided we should return to Anguilla. But things weren't the same here either, you know, because I wasn't able to see my family and I wasn't confident enough to visit my friends. I felt even more homesick in Anguilla than away from it, so after one or two weeks we left again, this time to St. Kitts, Nevis, and St. Lucia.

Nathaniel was born in the countryside and he always missed countryside life in the Caribbean so he was always looking for the forest in the islands, for the mountains. I think that's why he loved Nevis so much. Or maybe he just

liked the monkeys. After traveling for about two months
he wanted to go back to Nevis to spend the Christmas
season in one of the luxury hotels. But I really wanted
to come back to see you, Grandpa, so I convinced him to
come back to Anguilla for a while. And we did, but it was
terrible because everywhere we went I could always feel
so many eyes accusing me of treason, of having let my
family down, of abandoning you. Once, I remember, we
went to The Smiley Face for dinner, and Maria, the daughter of Karina and Eustace Brown, she was working as a
waitress there, and though she was waiting our table and
she recognized me (I could tell by the look in her eyes),
she didn't say anything, until she dropped a glass of red
wine on me (on purpose, even if she say it wasn't so), and
even then, she only apologized *once*. We never went back
to The Smiley Face but that didn't mean there were no
other ugly episodes. Once we went to Shoal Bay during
the day and we went to The Sunshine to eat lunch and as
soon as we sat down at our table the music just stopped
and for the rest of the afternoon there was nothing but
silence. There were only a few people there, and it might
have been a coincidence, but I know it wasn't. I could tell
it wasn't. We still went back to The Sunshine another time
and I suppose nothing strange really happened that time,
but you know what I mean. Every time we were out I felt
there was always something strained, always something
not nice waiting to happen.

We did stay in Anguilla for three weeks before I found
the strength to knock on the door of the Rawlingson
home, which was my own door! The holiday season was
over by then and things were returning to normal. Maybe
you were there but I don't know for sure because I wasn't
let inside. Mom opened the door and when she saw me she

didn't say a word. She just slammed the door back shut. And then Dewan opened it again, and all he said was, "Go. Go, sis. Go." And I did and went back home and said nothing about it to Nathaniel.

We were still pretty happy together, Nathaniel and I. But he could tell there was something wrong. His visa would soon run out and he was worried Immigration would give him grief to get a new one, so he said we'd stay until they renewed his visa and then we'd go traveling again. I was afraid they wouldn't renew his visa at all, but all of a sudden it was as if no one cared about him no more. Within a week he got his passport back and we planned another trip in the Caribbean.

Nathaniel spoke French fluently, so this time we took three months to explore Guadeloupe, Martinique, and St. Barths. Nathaniel liked all of them but he liked Martinique most, so we spent more time there than in the other places. It rained a lot in Martinique and maybe that's why I got so depressed. I can't say for sure what it was, but the longer this situation dragged on, the more ungrateful I felt. I think what hurt the worst was not being able to see you, Grandpa. I was missing all of you, but I was missing you the most. Even through all my years in Washington, we always used to have a little chat on the phone. I missed your wisdom, and your love. I missed you more than I ever did miss you in Washington because this time our complete silence made it feel like you were dead, you know, not just far away. Nathaniel said we needed to do something about it, otherwise I'd be sad for the rest of my life. I said it wasn't too bad and it would go with time but deep inside I knew he was right. So he went up to the hotel manager and told him he wanted to leave to Anguilla as soon as possible, so within three days our honeymoon—

which had lasted from September to March—was finished
and we were back home for good.

One or two weeks later Nathaniel came up with this
crazy, stupid idea. I'm sorry to swear in front of you,
Grandpa, but that's what it was, honest to God, and I wish
we had never done it. It spoiled everything, though everything was spoiled already, but at least Nathaniel and
I were sort of happy at the time. We had been traveling a
lot, and we knew how difficult and expensive traveling
between the islands can be, and Nathaniel knew I had a
passion for the sky, for looking at the world from above.
He had seen my pictures, the ones you say look like I have
found the highest mountain to look at the world from, because it's the only place where the world looks like I feel
it should, and he thought they were very good. I was flattered about his enthusiasm (he, a man of the world, having real knowledge about art, calling my work "special"),
but that is where it ended so far as I was concerned. But
who could have guessed he was going to try something all
crazy like that?

Anyway, Dragon Wings, at the beginning at least, was
a mad-mad effort by Nathaniel to reunite me with my family and make me happy: he thought the project would be
big enough to make everyone on the island have the hots
for it; he thought the Rawlingsons would not let pass the
chance of getting involved in something big and exciting
like that; and he knew I was obsessed with the sky. I loved
him even more at the time for even considering such craziness just for my sake. I hate him now for not listening
to my advice, for spoiling everything.

Of course, I dismissed the idea straight away, but his
support gave me the courage to do what I should have
done a long time before. I came home to speak to you all,

and I wouldn't turn around until I had done so. So Mom slammed the door in my face one more time, and Dad said nothing at all, and Desmond sat and listened and watched; and I just couldn't get a sane reaction from no one. And then you came out of your room and looked at me with your sad eyes, and I couldn't help but cry, but I couldn't be seen crying by the rest of the family, so I just turned round once again and ran away, pretending my sadness was anger.

When I got home, Nathaniel wasn't there. I was pleased, because I looked a mess. I had time to calm down and collect myself. But as soon as he returned, Nathaniel could see I wasn't alright. He knew exactly what was wrong and without asking me anything he just told me how he was just coming back from a meeting with Franklin Howell, the Minister of Communications and Infrastructure, about the possibility of creating a local airline. I had just assumed he had forgotten all about his craziness. But that wouldn't have been much like Nathaniel. He spent his time researching and planning, and he convinced himself that the business was good and that he could use it to get me and my family to make peace.

Just to prove him right, I received a call from Uncle Glen some while later. The same man who less than a year before had tried everything in his power to deport Nathaniel from the island was now taking the first step to bring the family closer to us. Of course, Uncle Glen only wanted to speak to Nathaniel, not to me. And he only wanted to do that because of the airline project, nothing else. But that was exactly what Nathaniel had planned from the beginning, and he took advantage of the opportunity not only to keep Uncle Glen interested in the project but to make him speak to the rest of the family on my behalf.

From then on, the doors to my own house were no longer shut to me. Although Dad still didn't speak to me, and Dewan never once showed up while I was there, and Desmond's visits became less and less regular, and Mom, despite being polite, wasn't really caring. At least Jamaal seemed pleased to welcome me back. Even back then I spent more nights at his house than at mine. And then, when trouble finally arrived, I was more comfortable living with him than at home. I stayed with Jamaal and his wife for almost two weeks before you convinced me to move back in here. Many nights I had long conversations with Shaniqua about life and family and all, and she made me feel loved. But, of course, there was you here, who listened, like always, and held my hand to comfort me, even if you didn't agree with what I was doing, and I couldn't resist moving back home, where I could have you near me. And even though it wasn't the same as before, even though I couldn't tell you everything that was on my mind, and I couldn't be really honest with you (partly because I was ashamed, partly because I was afraid), I could still feel your support when you held my hand. And for that, more than anything else at any point of my life, I really thank you . . .

VI

athaniel Jones spent three miserable days in the privacy of his five-star hotel, cursing fate for dealing him a bad hand, nursing short-term memories of happy days, planning the strategy that would determine his actions in the near future, nesting the hope that the stranger who had become the ruler of his fantasies would also be ruing the wretchedness of her own self. Fifty-four hours later, the DeHavilland Dash 8 that had been scheduled to take him to Antigua in the first leg of the long journey that would mark the end of his yearly dose of amnesia departed the Clayton J. Lloyd International Airport with an empty seat.

Nathaniel had learned enough about the island in the previous twelve days to understand that if you wanted to pass by unobserved, your only choice would be to stay at home. He guessed Sheila's intention would be to keep away from his reach until she knew (thought) she would be safe from a chance meeting with him, so, he figured, she would stay at home for the next three days. Nathaniel Jones's decision to spend the last three days of his holiday—the first three days of his permanent move to Anguilla—in self-imposed seclusion appeased his mind by making it appear as if he were sharing the exile he thought he had indirectly imposed on Sheila Rawlingson. Nathaniel Jones's decision to spend the last three days of his holiday in seclusion meant that he was not there when Sheila Rawlingson sat, lonely and dejected, at

the bar of what had become Nathaniel's favorite hot spot on the
night of the first day they had spent apart from each other since
they had met. Nathaniel Jones's decision to lock himself inside
his five-star hotel room and suffer in solitude what he hoped was
a shared agony meant that he was not there when Sheila Rawlingson walked barefoot along the shoreline of what had become
Nathaniel's favorite bay on the second day of their abrupt sepa-
ration. Nathaniel Jones's stupid decision to serve what he merely
imagined was Sheila's sentence to both of them meant he was
not there when Sheila Rawlingson—in the absence of the partner
she sought—swung her perfect hips in synch with a brand-new
stranger who despite being black and young and beautiful was
nowhere near as perfect as the stranger Sheila had taken to The
Velvet just two nights before. Nathaniel Jones's childish decision
to throw a tantrum far larger than Sheila's meant that he was not
at the airport on Monday at twenty past nine when Sheila sat on
the bench behind the check-in counter, ready to drop the tear that
eventually froze up inside her right eye as soon as she realized
that she had in fact been right about the man whom for the past
fifty-four hours she had thought she had mistreated.

When Nathaniel Jones was ready to lift the veil of mourning
he had found necessary to carry around after Sheila's rejection,
Sheila had already entrenched herself in a mist of bitterness and
sorrow that stemmed from her own projection of what she felt
the man who had made such difference to her should feel. Sheila
felt betrayed, fooled, and manipulated by her capacity of discern-
ment, hence she grieved her own stupidity locked in her room for
seven nights, while Nathaniel Jones systematically raided every
joint and den in town, looking for the one he thought he might be
able to love. Sheila felt she had betrayed every principle the bad
seeds had silently taught her, she felt she had manipulated her
own feelings in order to become vulnerable to an old white man,
she felt she had fooled herself not only about her feelings toward

a stranger—whom she could no longer think of as perfect—but also about the feelings of that probably-all-too-common old man toward her. Sheila spent seven days of rage followed by seven nights of disillusionment, while the man who was everything she had once hoped for desperately searched for the only bit of heaven he could not find in paradise.

After a fruitless fortnight laying siege to an invisible castle, Nathaniel Jones approached with short, longing steps what no longer was or wasn't his favorite bar, when from across the room a hazel lightning dissipated the doubt harbored in his heart. Sheila Rawlingson shared a table with three local men. Lunch had already been eaten, the party engaged in the final arrangements before leaving. *Your glasses.* When the eyes of the only two people that mattered in the world locked, an infinite source of happiness revealed itself to both. *She, your glasses!* Hand outstretched, glasses repeatedly tapping Sheila's hand, eyes lost in foreign latitudes. Not a word was spoken. Sheila Rawlingson restrained her smile, blinked, turned away from bliss, headed in the opposite direction. Only she heard the whisper calling from Nathaniel's mouth. She knew exactly what he had said. She did not hesitate: opened the door of the car, got inside, turned the key, drove away.

Nathaniel Jones walked to the last table by the far corner of the deck, sat, taciturn, asked for a beer. By the time the sun set, his beer was still half-full. Come dinnertime he asked for another. He did not eat but it wasn't a particularly busy night so he wasn't disturbed until closing time. His tab came to eight dollars. Nathaniel Jones was there alright when the employees of the place showed up late the following morning to open the restaurant for lunch. He was their first customer, at 10:54 a.m., sixty-six minutes before opening time. He sat at the last table, by the far corner of the deck, had a beer, no lunch. He gazed blankly into the establishment, eyes wide open, mouth cracked dry, skin burned, hand loosely holding a warm plastic cup. Sheila did not show up. He

remained unfazed. As the sun set again the waitress brought him
another beer; he had not finished his first yet, but no human being
could conceive of drinking that stale old broth. *On the house, sir.* A
drink on the house is a drink you cannot refuse, but by dinnertime Nathaniel's second beer of the day was still untouched. *What
would you recommend?* Nathaniel did not taste a thing, didn't even
move the cutlery. *Take it home. Give it to your children, your husband, your
dog.* He had not meant to be insulting or even patronizing, but he
was well beyond thinking—or caring. Three-quarters of a beer
later, the restaurant was empty, ready to shut. Only one table, by
the edge of the deck, could not be put away. The tall, dark figure
of the manager approached Nathaniel, whose eyes, though still
wide open, no longer registered anything. *You wan' stay dere all night?*
Nathaniel might or might not have nodded. *See you in the mahning.*
Another day went by and by now Nathaniel was treated as a piece
of furniture. He barely moved—did not talk at all—and no one
even offered him a beer. He did not care to ask. The sun, risen
from the east, hugged the sky on its way upward until it emerged
from behind the structure of the restaurant, began its slow de-
scent into the water. Nathaniel's lips revealed two visible wounds,
botched up with the clumsy protection of dried blood and saliva.
The maze of bloodshot capillaries in his pale blue eyes attested to
three sleepless nights. The dark rings around his eye sockets were
highlighted by the clashing contrast of the indigo blue with the
bright red of his sunburned skin. The sun shone for four and a
half hours every day on the particular corner of the deck where
Nathaniel Jones had built his nest to wait for Sheila's love, or rage,
or sense, or curiosity to hatch. The sun shone for four hours too
long on the particular corner of the deck where Nathaniel Jones's
tender white skin got scorched beyond pain. Only the coat of half-
grown (over three days) white facial hair disguised the alarming
hue of a complexion that—no matter how long it roasted—would
never tan.

Nathaniel's throat was dry as a desert, his every breath ached. Every instinctive motion of his larynx to generate saliva and slide it down his windpipe carved a trail of agony in his consciousness. His eyes, even now wide open, could hardly see past the itch of wakefulness. His weakened body had resorted to its fat to produce the energy that was not coming from external sources. Blisters crowded his arms and legs, where the relentless sun had punished him most. His muscles stung, his stomach burned. The sun was setting one more time. Reds, yellows, blues mean nothing when the silhouette of your dreams erupts into an otherwise empty scene. Nathaniel's delirious mind found no strength to gather. His knees buckled, his skin burned, his head whirled. *Still waiting?* Did she speak? Was it her? *We need to talk.* No. Of all the things they might have needed to do, talk was certainly not one of them. *Just take me to your place.*

It took three days before Nathaniel could tell where he was. He never knew how he had made it to his hotel room. It took a full week before he could walk on his own. But one full week was enough time to anchor in a cautious, flattered, intrigued mind the seed of a sprout that had gone from fascination to fear to anger and that would finally be given a chance to grow. When Nathaniel heard the knock on the front door of his private villa, he assumed it was another doctor, a nurse, room service. He did not wonder about the unusual time of the day, he did not think it strange not to have had a previous call from reception. He simply walked, bare-chested, in his checkered boxers and loose green robe, to attend to it. The overwhelming feeling, not necessarily joy, he would never be able to describe yet would henceforth cite as the irrefutable proof of his love for Sheila Rawlingson assaulted him not one second before opening his varnished maple-wood front door. Sheila walked inside without being asked, shut the door behind her, made herself at home. He was fidgety, nervous, shocked. She took control: a long kiss appeased Nathaniel's mind, restored balance to the scene. Her first caress of Nathaniel's lips was turned sour by the piercing sting of unhealed gashes all over his mouth. She never knew it—she always thought it was perfect.

VII

For a man of resources like Nathaniel Jones, renting a house in Anguilla was nothing more than a formality. Three weeks after the kiss that sealed the detour in Nathaniel's life, he stood at the front desk of Hotel Anguilla handing Saul Newman the payment for a stay that had been extended from two weeks to two months. Nathaniel had no bags, no luggage, no boxes. Just a cognac attaché case and a Sunday paper (it was Tuesday). Everything else had been duly transported to his new home on the eastern end of the island, where Nathaniel could experience the more local aspect of life. The balance owed came up to well over a year's rent at his new place. Nathaniel paid it with no regrets, a large smile on his face, and a good deal of plans for the future. *After all, what would you not give for a twist in your life?* Saul Newman carefully tilted forward the cigar almost always found between his lips or between his elegantly curled index and middle fingers or in a large round baccarat ashtray, as he exchanged a vigorous handshake that marked the beginning of an eventful friendship with Nathaniel Jones.

Renting a house, buying some furniture, extending his tourist visa were the sort of bureaucratic formalities a man of resources like Nathaniel Jones could easily brush aside. It was the more mundane routine of life in paradise which posed the greater challenge to a man who had spent more than half of his life in the comfort of a metropolis. Thus, when Nathaniel Jones ventured out of his shell of luxury and experienced firsthand the reality of daily transactions in Anguilla, he was faced with a number of facts he already knew but had never up to that point had to deal with directly.

Nathaniel Jones knew that the battle against mosquitoes in a place like this never ended. He also knew that this was a particularly important battle for him to win, given the white proneness of his skin to swell up and bulge around every bite. By the time Nathaniel Jones was ready to give up his hope of having attained a geographical advantage in the shape of the inspired location of his house—on a green, at the top of a hill—he already felt like his body was a minefield which had been stampeded by a herd of mad bulls. Nathaniel's lost battle turned into a plague he could not avoid, not least because all but two of the window screens in his house were damaged. In good old European fashion Nathaniel complained to his landlord. He had not yet understood that his seventeen requests had been ignored when Sheila Rawlingson walked into the house with Jarred Benn, the local window-screen engineer, reputedly one of the richest men on the island. By the time Nathaniel was finally able to sit in a living room around which intact screens were fitted he had so much poison in his blood that even mosquitoes no longer dared approach him.

Nathaniel Jones found it hard to learn to live the simple life that once, as a child of the war in a small alpine town in southern Bavaria, had been all he had known. He was furious to find out during a sleepless night of doubt and self-questioning that he had no hot water to shower with, because his boiler was a large, shallow metal tank placed over the roof of the house, fitted with solar panels that gathered heat during the day and released it in the evening, and the sky had been overcast for the past two days. Nathaniel's fury was put in perspective three weeks later, when he came to grips (the hard way) with the reality that in the islands you don't just run out of hot water, you run out of water altogether. Nathaniel's hair still dripped shampoo, his body scaled with dried soap, when Sheila arrived with a case of drinking water. Nathaniel found it wasteful to use potable water to wash the soap and shampoo off his body since the water delivery company had promised to send a full truckload *in a little while*. On Sheila's insistence he reluctantly poured three bottles over his hair and body, got ready to receive the driver from Alwyn's Fast Water Delivery Service. He had to wait three days until the cistern in his house was replenished, wondering every time he used a bottle of the local Aronel water to rinse his hair whether the delivery truck would arrive that very minute. It didn't. Three days later, when the driver produced the reasons for the delay, Nathaniel did not bother listening: he was learning slowly, but he was learning.

For a man of resources like Nathaniel Jones, adapting to the lifestyle of a place like Anguilla was more a matter of will than of intellect: he had willfully given up the cultural bustle and the opulence of a cosmopolitan city in favor of the peaceful tranquility of a simple life on a near-deserted island. These were the elements that Nathaniel consciously, calmly, tried to rationalize in the moments of utter exasperation that occasionally overcame him during the days and weeks that followed his recovery from the pangs of unrequited love and severe sunstroke. Because neither Nathaniel nor anyone else could have foreseen the degree of tolerance he would have to develop for the slow pace of Caribbean life, or the directly proportional distancing he would suddenly experience from the set of values that until not very long ago had ruled his every action, his simplest expectations.

In Anguilla, his joy at assessing the quality of extravagant winemakers would be heavily tempered by the restricted choice he could find even at Hibernia Restaurant's wine cellar, the island's most sophisticated, all the way out in Island Harbour. And then, of course, most cellars' list would often not correspond with the actual stock in existence, such that even his moderated expec-

tation would sometimes see its wings clipped by the privations of
the province. Neither did neighboring St. Martin, a plentiful hub
in relation to Anguilla, offer much solace in terms of products
from obscure vineyards. So Nathaniel simply pretended not to
care, tried to convince himself that all was fine, that if he could not
complement his meal with the taste of the exact bottle of wine he
wished to have, he could at least enjoy the sunset in the middle of
winter in a pair of shorts and a T-shirt after swimming on his own
in one of the most beautiful beaches in the western hemisphere.
Except it was tough to accept this argument when the object of
his desire was not an unobtainable luxury in a near-deserted island but a simple bottle of Cabernet Sauvignon purchased across
the channel, only to find upon returning a few hours later that the
wine—the whole purpose of the inter-island odyssey—was corked.
Nathaniel's learning curve took him through the process of understanding that minor matters like this were not worth a great
deal of hassle on the islands simply because shit happens. Going
back to St. Martin to complain about a bottle of wine turned sour
would require more time, nerves, and strength than a whole new
case would merit. And then again, there was still the soothing
rumble of the sea, the amber coating of the moon, the intricate
pattern of the stars.

Only that Nathaniel Jones had not stayed in this exasperating
(inefficient) version of paradise for the stars, the moon or the sea.
He had come in order to experience the beauty of the undevel-
oped world; he had appreciated the excesses of artificial exclusivity
far less than he had enjoyed the flamboyance of tropical sunsets,
and even after examining the negative aspects of the basic lifestyle
led by the locals, he had envied it; but ultimately he had stayed
for one and only one pair of svelte legs. Nathaniel Jones forgot
most things—certainly most *bad* things—when he was graced
with the presence of Sheila Rawlingson. And given that Sheila
Rawlingson had adopted the role of guardian to her foreign visi-

tor, he saw her most when bad things happened. Hence, problems that required the assistance of his ever-ready hostess proliferated in number and diminished in urgency: Nathaniel now needed a hand not only dealing with the bugs that swarmed his house but also sorting out the shelves in his kitchen cabinet and finding the right place to store his tennis gear. On the other hand, it mattered very little whether Sheila's solution brought potable relief to the shampoo itching his eyes, or whether she replaced a vintage bottle of Austrian wine with a cheap selection of Australian Shiraz: to Nathaniel, the most ordinary bottle of table wine would taste like the best Châteauneuf-du-Pape if only shared with her.

Slowly, Sheila's visits to Nathaniel's home became more prolonged. Her days were suddenly planned around the times when she would call on the friend that everybody knew she had without knowing exactly who it was. And so, as the time she spent solving minor problems in Nathaniel's house became less strictly defined, the solutions she came up with became progressively more intimate. Until the day, after running back and forth between her place and his for eight weeks, when Sheila found herself spending an entire afternoon at leisure in Nathaniel's house, pretending to be doing something, convincing herself that she was being useful when in fact she was just lounging with the man she most enjoyed being with. She succeeded in fooling herself to the point where, once night fell, she was absolutely exhausted. Nathaniel was delighted to see her small brown eyes drowse in a slumber. He picked her up from the sofa, lay her down on his bed. Sheila Rawlingson slept all night spooned by the protecting body she was meant to protect.

The following morning, Nathaniel woke up long before his guest. He slipped into the trousers he had worn the day before, began to make breakfast. By the time Sheila woke up the table was already set up. *Did you not sleep?* Nathaniel looked tired, his eyes drooping with longing, dark rings crawling around them. A gentle kiss served as prologue to Nathaniel's guidance of her hand but Sheila was dexterous in the art of stripping herself and others. Nathaniel's recurrent dream—fantasy—took the shape of reality. His anxiety turned into tenderness, her drowsiness into affection. The bed banished the frozen fright of hesitation from the two, encouraged their mutual quest for pleasure. Sheila sensed a tide of emotions rise inside her—it was more than desire, it was all she wanted. Her expert ease was stalled by a sudden sense of importance, her swift motions stammered with the clumsiness of nerves. Naked and observed, Sheila was disarmed by more than her nudity. Nathaniel saw the promise of a lustful day replaced with the signs of mature attachment. He endorsed the exchange. The first moment of intimacy between Nathaniel Jones and Sheila Rawlingson was a dilated experience of love. After that, he had to brew more coffee to go with the cold breakfast.

Sheila Rawlingson did not depart Nathaniel's nest of love for a full week. In fact, Sheila Rawlingson did not leave Nathaniel's house until the moment when—seven nights and one day later— he proposed to add a hyphen and a Jones to Sheila Rawlingson's name. On July 28, exactly one hundred days after the promise to have a drink together *sometime*, Nathaniel Jones, right knee on the ground, stuttered, faltered, struggled as he formulated a question that needed no formulation because Sheila Rawlingson knew exactly what this meant. The trail of tears that bathed Sheila's cheeks carved a path of fear as well as joy. Immersed as deeply as Nathaniel in an unusually intense relationship, it had not been beyond her capability of abstraction to imagine the present scene. In her mind's eye she had already accepted Nathaniel's offer. In Sheila's dreams she wore a white dress in front of a crowded church that rejoiced together with her as they saw her give herself to the future. Sheila's dreams always ended abruptly, shortened, thwarted, tempered by the dimension of her present, by the nightmare of silence, secrecy, and lies that for the past hundred days had accompanied a relationship that had made her so happy she now wished it to last forever.

Sheila bathed her cheeks in tears of fear and joy while Nathaniel tortured his aching knees by refusing to stand up until a word escaped the gasping breath of the woman who he already saw as his future wife. In Sheila's dreams she had already accepted Nathaniel's offer but the empty feeling inside her chest, her inability to catch her breath, the incontrollable sensation that she was falling from somewhere really high gave away the fact that this was no dream. This was reality, and reality was necessarily thwarted, hampered, shaped by a number of elements alien— in fact inevitably opposed—to her fairy tale with a white man twice her age. The words that granted Nathaniel Jones's longed-for leave to lift his knee and stretch his leg were not the ones of certainty and acceptance he had hoped for. *I does need some time. Let me t'ink 'bout it.* An understandable if somewhat disappointing end to a perfect week, only tarnished by a speck of doubt.

Sheila Rawlingson departed Nathaniel Jones's nest of love for the first time in seven nights and one day not to go home and speak to her family, not to show signs of life to her friends or siblings, but to seek help, guidance, and support at the doorstep of Father Rasheed, the old priest from South Hill who had baptized her, who had seen her grow into a devout Christian, who had first given her Holy Communion, and who had seen her become an independent member of his congregation after she had willfully confirmed her beliefs. Although Father Rasheed had lost sight of Sheila Rawlingson's development as a person and as a Christian after fate had taken her so far away from her place of birth, she, like the rest of the children he had helped raise, like the rest of his flock, still had a prominent place in his heart.

So when Father Rasheed saw the hasty, anxious steps that delivered a visibly affected Sheila Rawlingson to his doorstep, he was overwhelmed by a mixture of feelings—relief, joy, concern—

which did not allow him to think clearly. Sheila spent a long time explaining the situation before she brought herself to ask Father Rasheed to be an accomplice in her forbidden love, to tie the knot that no mortal could untie before she announced to the world the size of her folly. Father Rasheed advocated patience, communication, confidence. With every word of advice Sheila turned more desperate, more inconsolably lost, and Father Rasheed, softened by age, overwhelmed by emotion, *My choild, I will always stand by your side, you know.* By the end of a visit that lasted hours, Father Rasheed had anchored Sheila's hopes with a promise he had never meant to keep.

Father Rasheed never meant to keep his promise to secretly unite a disparate couple in the name of the Lord, because the name of the Lord is sacred, irrevocable, and true, and anything done in the name of the Lord needs necessarily be done with pride, determination, and faith, and a secret marriage lacked at least two of those qualities. But Father Rasheed did mean to keep his vow not to tell anyone about his confidential interview with Sheila, because Sheila had asked him to, because Sheila had always shown sound judgment, because it was, after all, a family matter, and because family matters are better dealt with by the families in question.

But Sheila's sound judgment was nowhere to be seen when, after a week of absence—meditation—she returned to Nathaniel Jones's East End quarters, bringing with her a conditional yes and a proposition to accept Father Rasheed's help, to marry on the sly. During a week of silence, Nathaniel's home slowly turned from a nest of love to a cuckoo's nest over which he flew over and over and over again, becoming progressively angrier, wearier. Sheila's proposition was not only silly, it was unacceptable because it spelled failure every step of the way. Sheila had not even contemplated the possibility of Nathaniel disagreeing—after all, he had already posed the question and only her answer stood between them and marriage. *If we're going to do this, Sheila, we're going to do it the right way.* If? What if? When had *if* come into the equation? It took Nathaniel Jones the time Sheila Rawlingson needed to regain her composure to wear his dark suit, his red tie, his Italian shoes, his French eau de parfum. *I've had enough of this stupid game. Take me to your parents' house.* Sheila could not find the strength to go against what she knew deep inside was the only sensible solution.

Nathaniel Jones came knocking on the Rawlingsons' door on a Sunday at the beginning of August, in the middle of the largest celebration of the year, asking Sheila's father—in the presence of the rest of the family—for his daughter's hand. The ring on Sheila's third finger was the first source of outrage. Then came the hysterical fit of an old lady in disbelief. Then came the youthful bashfulness of an old man spitting a tirade of threats and insults. Then came the madness of a young man so far beside himself that everyone feared he might kill someone.

One week later, amid the celebrations of carnival and such, Father Rasheed sealed the union of a disparate couple who had shown enough courage, pride, and determination to deserve the blessing of the Lord in a service which, if not secret, was as private as anyone could remember in Anguilla.

VIII

The paperwork for Nathaniel's permanent visa sat on the desk of Akira Hart, Glenallen Rawlingson's second cousin and childhood sweetheart. Akira was well aware of Sheila's outrageous relationship with Nathaniel Jones, of the Rawlingsons' reaction to his intrusion in their family. Just one day before, Glenallen had spoken to Akira, pointing out the importance of this particular application. That conversation had prompted a cascade of orders that had led to the singling out of one seemingly indistinct file in a mountain of documents. The scrutiny of Nathaniel's application was an unnecessary detail: this man was to be denied stay.

Akira Hart sat in her office, behind her desk, rejection stamp in hand, browsing Nathaniel Jones's application just out of curiosity, when the front door was thrown open by the full weight of Gwendolyn Stewart's rotund body. *Afternoon.* Akira was startled out of her prying merely by the rarity of the sight. Her jaw dropped, her eyes lingered in expectation, her pulse accelerated. Akira would have asked Gwendolyn to sit somewhere, had she not been too afraid none of the chairs in her office would fit the size of her unexpected visitor. *You shouda tell me you coming, Auntie Gwen.* The effort to seem natural made her drop the stamp she held in her right hand. She never picked it back up.

Ever since childhood, Gwendolyn had enjoyed the privilege of an imposing presence, a commandeering look. Connor Stewart's firstborn child, she had been appointed the role of matriarch by her father even before she displayed the judiciousness and determination that characterized her from an early age. Connor Stewart was a man of deep convictions and profound faith who only trusted the edicts of God's design above his own judgment. When Connor Stewart's wife Belinda, a plump and grounded woman who at seventeen years of age had all the poise of a grown adult, informed him that her belly was full with baby, he immediately knew she would give birth to the future chief of a family clan that would control all aspects of the island's life. *Better get used to it, woman, dis jus' de first of foive boys I goan give you, you know.* He wasn't joking either, nor was he trying to intimidate Belinda. He was just being as plain and honest as he could be. *Is foive pickney you wan' have? Boy, I hope you figure out how you goan feed dem all, 'cause I ain' goan be no poor-poor modder feeding me choild dust and mud, you hear?* There was no doubt in Connor's mind he would be able to provide for his family of nine, because five was the number of sons he planned to have, and added to them he wanted two daughters, one on either side of their middle son. He never listened when Belinda told him to mind his own business and *let God do God thing and sen' us what he wan', a boy or a girl,* until the day when Belinda went into labor, banning him from the house, telling him to stay away for the day *'cause if I see you too soon after dis I goan cut you head for true.* When Connor came back to his own house in Island Harbour the following day, still smelling of the rum that had helped him through the previous night, the first thing he did was hold his naked baby in his arms and search for the stick between its legs. *Boy, I guess dat mean God make we start from the back.* Adamant that he was right, Connor gave his firstborn a name starting with the seventh letter of the alphabet.

Though not a boy, Gwendolyn was raised from the day she was born to become the boss of a family that did not yet rule the affairs of Anguilla. The total control Gwendolyn held over the Stewarts went disguised by her benevolent disposition toward the well-being of her loved ones, but whenever a given situation called for a strong hand, no one on the island would stand firmer than her. It was perhaps for that reason, out of a combination of fear and respect, that none of her six siblings—five brothers and a sister—had ever dared to challenge her authority.

Under Gwendolyn's guidance the Stewarts had expanded their range of influence from their homely quarters in Island Harbour to a wider, more national network around the island: the Stewarts had been part of the local government since the late 1960s, when Walter, the son of Gwendolyn's oldest brother Fabian, had taken part in the revolution against the central government in St. Kitts; the Stewarts had recognized the potential of the tourism industry as soon as it began to be developed in the mid-1980s, actively participating in a number of projects; the Stewarts had been among the country's most prominent voices advocating for the extension of the airport to make it suitable for jetliners in the 1990s, and had been the most enthusiastic investors in the island's public water works when the company was floated in the early 2000s; the Stewarts were partners in the Indigenous Bank of Anguilla, they were involved in the seriously important business that was the golf course, they were connected to the people in charge of developing a public transport system on the island. In short, Gwendolyn had overseen the process that had watched the Stewarts go from being a relatively prosperous family in the flotsam village of Island Harbour to becoming part of the local aristocracy over the course of not quite fifty years, and yet throughout this long progression her general attitude had remained the same. Thus, Gwendolyn's goodwill—now extended not only to the members of her family but to the friends of her clan—had earned her the nickname of Auntie Gwen. Everybody called Gwendolyn Stewart Auntie Gwen, even people who didn't have the faintest kinship to her or any of the other Stewarts.

But since the days when Gwendolyn Stewart had first earned the name of Auntie Gwen, her hair had turned gray, her eyes had grown smaller, her cheeks had given way to the load of time, her back had hunched, her perky breasts had sagged, her wide stomach had grown wider. These days, Auntie Gwen's overloaded knees struggled to hold the weight of her weathered body; these days, Auntie Gwen's tired ankles clicked and cracked with every step she took, as if giving out a warning of their imminent expiry; these days, Auntie Gwen's hips refused to turn, compromising her freedom of movement. Which all meant that these days, Auntie Gwen seldom abandoned the reclining chair in the backyard of her house just to the northwest of Island Harbour, overlooking the sea.

Nevertheless, on this specific morning Auntie Gwen had received the unexpected and, in plain terms, desperate visit of Tanika Percy, the youngest daughter of her sister's son. Tiny little Tanika had spent many a wasteful night mourning in solitude or evading in bad company the wretchedness of her star for not allowing her to be with Antwan Thompson, the man of her dreams. The fourth son of former Chief Minister Rudolf Thompson, Antwan was madly in love—obsessed, some would say—with Sheila Rawlingson, the single most extraordinary woman he had ever seen and probably the only one who did not pay the least bit of attention to his tireless romancing. However, the ill luck that for so long had darkened Tanika's prospects had suddenly been reverted by the appearance of an old white man who in a matter of weeks had taken full control of Sheila Rawlngson's life. After years of if not chaste at least loyal waiting and courting, Antwan Thompson could not even contemplate the possibility of Sheila choosing an old white foreign man over him, the most eligible young man on the island, the son of one of the most powerful men in the country, so instead he chose to shield his pride behind the widely held opinion that Sheila was *jus' like any odder whore, you know, whoring behind the whiteman money*, and he pretended he had never had any real interest in her in the first place, and he finally buried his ambitions of conquering Sheila Rawlingson so deep that he convinced himself they had never existed. The next best thing, the most readily available alternative to the breathtaking beauty of Sheila Rawlingson, was Tanika Percy, and Auntie Gwen's niece had been more than willing and able to profit from the latest developments, finally capturing the attention of the man who for so long had denied her his favor.

So on this specific morning Tanika Percy had come together with Maria Brown, her best friend from school, to ask Auntie Gwen, her eternal benefactor, to intervene in the minor matter of the deportation of a seemingly indistinct tourist, who in fact was performing an enviable task at ensuring the happiness and stability in her idyllic relationship with Antwan Thompson. Were Sheila Rawlingson to be deprived of the company of the man who had so effectively monopolized her time of late, Tanika would again have to compete for the attention of her other half against the exuberant body of (a now single) Sheila Rawlingson, because whore or no whore, she knew *every man in Anguilla dream at night of her freakin' pum-pum*. The threat posed merely by the thought of Sheila Rawlingson's delicate frame sauntering along the streets of Anguilla, endangering her perfect relationship, was enough to send a stream of tears flowing down Tanika's cheeks.

Gwendolyn Stewart listened attentively to the story, reassured her niece, sent her away with a smile. She grabbed the phone, made a few calls, asked a few questions. A matter as delicate as this could only be resolved with a bit of tact. Auntie Gwen spoke to Sheila herself. *I heah you boyfriend wan' get he visa extended.* Sheila's broken nerves found no reason to doubt Auntie Gwen's goodwill, to question her intentions. *I no wan' no trouble wit' Glen, you know, but if you promise to stay hush 'bout it, I can see wha' I can do.* Sheila never once revealed the name of the person who had enabled Nathaniel to stay on the island during those early days of primal love. And Gwendolyn never even had to ask for the favor. Just her presence in Akira Hart's office at Immigration bought Nathaniel Jones another six months on the island.

IX

Nathaniel spent three of the six months he managed to secure through the unspoken favor of an unnameable friend exploring the geography, topography, and history of the French Antilles with his wife. But the weather in Martinique was lousy and Sheila Rawlingson-Jones's mood deteriorated daily to the point where one day Nathaniel understood that the only solution was to go back to Anguilla to, one way or another, restore peace in the family he had wrecked with his presence. Three days later Nathaniel and Sheila's honeymoon came to an end as they found themselves back in East End, retrieving the dusty corners of his rented house from the grip of the sea blast, the geckos, and the insects. Once in Anguilla, Nathaniel Jones kept from his wife the details of a plan she despised and he had already put in motion, until the day when he returned home after an informal meeting with the Honorable Franklin Howell, Minister of Communication and Infrastructure, to find his wife barely recovering from a new fit of sadness. Nathaniel was perfectly aware of the source of her affliction, but he also knew that she remained reticent about the idea of the airline, so instead of comforting her, and with no prior consultation, he simply informed her that he would set up a partnership in which she would control the 66 percent of the company required by Anguillan law to operate a business on the island, *and if you're stubborn enough to insist on refusing, I'm sure I will be able to find a different business associate.*

The shock was enough to snap Sheila out of her sadness. She was enraged about Nathaniel's own obstinacy, about the secrecy with which he had been pursuing his interest, about the touch of fantasy—of naivety, even—that clouded his reasoning. *You ain' know de first t'ing 'bout aviation. You ain' even know de first t'ing 'bout Anguilla. How you wan' make any airline business like dat?* and Nathaniel's *That's why I need you to help me* detonated the full load of Sheila's frustration: *How kyan I help you understand anyt'ing when you ain' even listenin' to my first advice?*

Sheila used reason to expose the flaws in Nathaniel's plan, but he was blinded to the point where he saw in her arguments nothing other than stubborn opposition. *Don't be such a coward!* He knew as soon as he uttered the words that the young woman who had gambled her uncertain yet promising future just for the sake of sharing her life with him would find his offense intolerable. The disappointment that brewed inside her brought back to her eyes the tears she had recently managed to control. Nathaniel felt guilty, if also assured that he had broken her obstinacy. He felt responsible for her sadness, but embraced the opportunity to make his proposition all the more persuasive. *You can't live in this crisis forever, Sheila.* Nathaniel diverted the attention from his own blunder, made way for his final attack. *If we can't bring your family back to their senses, we'll have to buy them into it.* For the best part of an hour Nathaniel voiced—more to himself than to her—all kinds of ploys and stratagems, while she sobbed in the background.

Later that night Nathaniel sat at his desk, in front of his computer, writing an e-mail to his son, Dragon, summoning him to a godforsaken islet bustling with potential, spelling out further instructions regarding Jones Investments' other interests. That was the beginning of a few hectic weeks of activity for Nathaniel Jones. While Dragon ordered his broker to sell all their shares on Petrobras, Nathaniel walked in and out of a million offices, taking it upon himself to comply with the requirements and abide by the rules of commercial protocol in Anguilla. Guided by his instincts, Nathaniel knocked on the door of Deianira Walker, reputedly the best lawyer on the island. *I need an adviser.* The considerable cost of every hour of Mrs. Walker's time devoted to Nathaniel's project was settled with a check from his personal account in the Indigenous Bank of Anguilla.

Mrs. Walker's services could not just be bought—they had to be earned. But something in Nathaniel Jones's appearance struck Mrs. Walker as extraordinary and she found his approach agreeable and she saw a lucrative promise in their collaboration, so she decided to help Mr. Jones with his plans to build a local airline in Anguilla, got hold of the Civil Aviation Rules and Regulations, and *Don't worry, you don't have to go t'rough all of dis yourself. I'll examine de document and give you my opinion next week.* But Nathaniel would have none of Mrs. Walker's patronizing, if well-intentioned talk: he took home the five-hundred-page Bible of the air, spent days and restless nights detailing the commandments spelled in it. When Mrs. Walker called him the following week to set up an appointment to discuss the steps to take to continue the establishment of his company, he declined because *I haven't finished with the regulations yet.* When Nathaniel finally met Mrs. Walker a week later than expected, he showed up with a draft of his business plan and the charters of the future organization. Mrs. Walker read with interest: twenty to forty employees, mostly local; offices in several countries; linking routes to European destinations; further development and enhancement of the tourist industry; contribution to the integration of the member-nations of the Caribbean Community and Common Market (CARICOM) and the Organization of Eastern Caribbean States (OECS). Mrs. Walker's clean, tidy dreads fell over her face. She lifted her head with a slow, deliberate movement, removed her reading glasses with her left hand. The large black eyes that scrutinized Nathaniel Jones hid partially behind a wince of inquisition. *How serious are you about dis?* Dead serious.

So the rumor which had already made the rounds in Parliament House after Nathaniel's informal meeting with Franklin Howell found its echo in the private sector after he departed Deianira Walker's office that afternoon, leaving behind a draft of his business plan and the organization charters for his lawyer to amend. By the time Nathaniel entered his application for a work permit, everybody at the Labor Office knew exactly what this one was about, but because no one from the government or the private sector had issued a specific recommendation (be it positive or negative) for the case, fiddly hands went through it in detail with curiosity and apprehension, holding on to it longer than was needed, as long, in fact, as was necessary to get explicit instructions from the powers-that-be. After three conditional rejections due to insufficient information, invalid references, missed deadlines, Nathaniel's private account in the Indigenous Bank of Anguilla was finally reduced by the $3,000 fee that enabled him to be employed on the island for the following twelve months.

Sheila Rawlingson-Jones sat in silence and ignorance as Dragon pulled the plug on Jones Investments' real estate interests, as Nathaniel reviewed the details for setting up their company in Anguilla. She sat in ignorance and silence, watching Nathaniel get carried away by a project she disliked but no longer opposed, while the perfectly happy household of idleness where they lived got infected with the disease of purpose, with the stain of disagreement. Sheila Rawlingson-Jones sat, watching in silence, as Nathaniel worked away on the intricacies of his little dream until the day when the phone rang and she heard the familiar voice of Uncle Glen on the other end of the line. Sheila's first reaction was fear: she remembered Uncle Glen's furious opposition to Nathaniel, feared he might still be plotting against her husband. After weeks of anger and frustration, she discovered she still loved the man she had—perhaps so rashly—married. As it turned out, Uncle Glen had heard the rumor that started around

Parliament House before finding its echo in the private sector, so strictly speaking he was calling Nathaniel not his rogue niece, and he hardly acknowledged her on the phone, demanded almost immediately to speak to her husband.

Glenallen Rawlingson and Nathaniel Jones spoke for the first time as civilized human beings on the night when Sheila Rawlingson-Jones realized that the man she still loved was also an astute negotiator. Nathaniel fielded questions and depicted promising scenarios to Uncle Glen, while Sheila silently sensed her respect for the man she (yes, still loved but) had thought a hopeless dreamer grow by the minute. Nathaniel seemed comfortable finding the balance between the level of commitment he was prepared to show at this stage and Glenallen Rawlingson's mounting expectations. He steered away from trouble with ease, dropping matters when they became overly contentious, making ambiguous comments that could easily be adjusted to a different situation later on.

Suddenly, Nathaniel saw a glint of interest shine in Sheila's eyes. He adapted the nature of his performance immediately, complemented the measured tone of his voice, the composed nature of his speech, with a totally controlled attitude that replaced the frantic pacing of the room that had previously accompanied his conversation. His steps became shorter, the path he followed became regular, he moderated his gesticulation: his entire demeanor now glowed with the confidence of someone who knows exactly what he is doing. His intense eyes burned through Sheila's defenses as he spoke to her uncle.

There's just one more thing, Glen: you will never, ever hear from me again or have anything to do with this airline unless you speak to Sheila now. She had already surrendered when she heard him speak her name. *It's not about what I want you to tell her, it's about what she wants you to do.* Her heart jumped with fear, pride, expectation. *You know exactly what I'm talking about.* Sheila made her way to the phone with clumsy, hurried steps, and sat next to Nathaniel for the duration of her talk with Uncle Glen.

X

When Dragon Jones heard Nathaniel's instructions he had to double check to make sure his father was not playing a prank on him. *Pull out? I've been working on this for months!* Nathaniel was firm, radical, unequivocal about investing in the Caribbean. *I'll send you an e-mail with the details of the proposal.* A combination of anger and frustration delayed Dragon's response. By the time he was ready to string together a sensible answer there was only silence on the other end of the line. The screen of Dragon's phone was just the first victim of his fit of fury.

Nathaniel Jones had been away for a full year. During this time Dragon had taken the reins of Jones Investments. He believed in solid investments, long-term profitability, palpable projects; Nathaniel, on the other hand, relied on his (uncannily accurate) instinct and his volatile character to take advantage of the most unstable markets, profiting from speculation. Over the course of that year, Dragon had progressively turned the company's attention away from stock markets, concentrating instead on real estate. For months he had focused on a major deal that would become the largest in their portfolio, and he had engineered it from its conception, the first project of the kind he had worked on from scratch on his own. Just before the deal was sealed, though, Nathaniel made the call that cost Dragon his phone, sent the e-mail that derailed his plans.

To: Dragon@JonesInvestments.com
From: Nathaniel@JonesInvestments.com
Subject: Further Instructions

Dragon—
Here's what you have to do. Get your hands out of Borricone. Claim idiocy, it doesn't matter. Just say I got cold feet. Simply get out. I need you down here. I don't know too many of these people, don't know who to trust. My instincts tell me no one. Sell Brazil. I know you said we should sell months ago. Tough break, at least we still make a profit on that. Sell it all. Then open a new folder: Project Caribbean 1171. You will like this! This little island is bustling with potential. But unless you own a private jet, you can't get here. We'll redress that: a Caribbean airline to link the world with this godforsaken islet. We won't need much: three or four airplanes should do. I've been discussing with a few people the feasibility of the project. It looks like it'll take time but it can be done. Permits, routes, licensing, personnel, equipment, it's all too much for me to do on my own. Open a line of expenses for PC1171 and get yourself down here. Don't touch NASDAQ, there's enough there to keep us afloat if this whole business goes bust, and it'll be easy to run, even from here. Leave Charlie in charge of the office.

I look forward to seeing you. It's been too long. Receive my love.

Happy Easter,
Nathe

Move message to deleted items folder. *Message deleted.* Dragon did not reply. He spent a week sulking on his own, cursing Nathaniel for having chosen Anguilla above the Seychelles for his Easter holiday the previous year. Good Friday now came and went, as did Saturday and Easter Sunday, and then the day arrived when the final contracts for the Borricone deal were supposed to be signed. Dragon wore his best suit, an impeccable tie, his sharpest shoes. His presence in the boardroom was brief, his demeanor imposing. As he walked into the room the rest of the table sensed the difference in his attitude. Jones Investments was not the major player in the deal but in an agreement of this nature every piece of the puzzle was crucial. *Gentlemen, we have had a change of heart. We feel at the moment Croatia is not the right place to invest our money.* There was no apology, no explanation, no negotiation. Dragon left the room with the same air of superiority that had accompanied him when he had entered it, let no one get a glance of his wounded pride.

One phone call later, the money invested in BOVESPA was also as good as back in the company's account. As instructed, Dragon did not touch their NASDAQ stock. He felt an uncommon yet almost irresistible desire to trade technology for science but he repressed his instincts, and in the end canceled the operation. He called Charles into his office, gave him instructions, informed him of the purpose of his absence (to ascertain the potential of an activity suggested by Nathaniel). *You will be in charge of the operation until I return.* Without any further delay, Dragon bought a first-class ticket to Antigua and an inter-island connection to Anguilla in the only class available. CP1171's expense line had been opened. From his car, on the way to the airport, he called the only two people who made a difference in his life: his mother Dorothea, and his best friend Linda. *I'm late for my flight, I'm sorry. I promise to buy you a big gift and deliver it personally on my way back.* Dragon had no idea how long he would have to stay in Anguilla—it never even crossed his mind it could be forever.

Nathaniel knew the transactions he demanded would take some time. He also knew Dragon had been injured by his seemingly deliberate attempt to undermine his authority. But even through the four weeks of silence that followed his explicit e-mail, he could rest assured that his orders would be carried out, that at some point Dragon would show up with a tiny suitcase and a ton of beef. Nathaniel's token of trust was not to question Dragon's loyalty, not to force communication between them before Dragon had reestablished it himself. Dragon took no steps in that direction until the moment he got to Gatwick airport. *I'll be there at seven thirty in the evening, please have me picked up at the airport.*

XI

. . . The airline was a success from the start. We had to push hard to set it up on time, but once it was up and running our routes were so popular we even made a profit. I guess we just got lucky. It was a good season and people didn't care that we were brand new. I think we all thought it would stay like that forever. At least that was what we all hoped. Of course, it didn't. I don't know how it happened but some months later it all seemed to fall apart. We won the bid for that plane in Florida and suddenly the economic pressure was too strong. We overburdened ourselves, and our prospects for the future never looked like they could bail us out of our crisis. Real soon it was obvious that the airline was not economically viable.

How quick things can change, Grandpa. How sudden. When trouble hit us I think we didn't know how to hit back. I think we just soaked it in and hoped for the best. I don't know what else we could have done. We tried to apply simple strategies, we concentrated on marketing, we tried to survive. But the real problem, Grandpa, was not the business side. The real problem started from within. Once the crisis hit the company we began to blame each other for things that were not really our fault. Maybe we were already tired from the effort of setting up the airline. Maybe we just got cocky because in the beginning everything

was so easy. I don't know what it was, Grandpa, but I saw
our relationship, our friendship, disappear. I don't mean
only me and Nathaniel. I mean all of us: me, Dragon, Nathaniel, Sam. I saw all of us grow apart and do nothing to
help it, either. It was a terrible time, Grandpa. We weren't
friends no more. We were nothing but resentful partners.
We fought against what the other said just because of who
had said it. We were insulting and thoughtless. We just
couldn't hold it together. And throughout this whole nightmare, there was only one thing I could hold on to, only one
genuinely caring shoulder where I could lay my head . . .

    In the end, there were too many voices in Dragon
Wings, Grandpa, and every one of them had different
opinions. Everyone else on the island seems to have their
opinion about it too. I'm sure you have yours as well. But
I don't want to know. I ain't never want to know nothing
about Dragon Wings again. The details bore me and I just
don't want to have nothing to do with it no more. I don't
care where it ends up. I don't care how it works out. I ain't
going be here to see it and I ain't going make much of an
effort to find out, either. It can all crash and burn for all I
care, Grandpa, honest to God. I'm too tired. Dragon Wings
drained me out. It took more out of me than I was ready to
give. It involved a commitment I just couldn't keep.

    So, this is how it all ends. This is where I have to go.
I can see the trees outside. The sky is blue, the sun will
soon be out. I need to start again, Grandpa. I need to find
peace and happiness. How can I do that here? How can I
do that among my family? How can I look at you without
shame? I know you can't forgive me. None of you can.
I ain't even asking for forgiveness, all I'm asking for is
understanding. All I wish is that you read this and give
yourself a chance not to hate me. All along, the only thing

I have wanted has been a life of my own. I won't get that in Anguilla. I won't get that in the company of Nathaniel Jones. By the time you read this I'll be somewhere else, with someone else. And I'll be sending you all my love, all my good wishes. I hope you can do the same for me.

I love you, Grandpa. Please don't forget. I'll send you a postcard, I'll send you my details, and hopefully we can keep in touch. Please put in a good word for me with the rest of the family. If anyone asks, if anyone cares, tell them I'm alright, tell them I'll be fine.

I will take you with me wherever I go, Grandpa. Always.

Your SHE.

PART III

I

While Sheila Rawlingson-Jones compiled her magic list of potential local partners, only to spend the best part of a long month crossing them out one by one, Arturo Sarmiento experienced in full the frustration of his life. Entrapped in a failed career which offered no fulfillment and little promise, engaged in a relationship that was cemented by routine rather than passion, lodged among the memories of his childhood in a small apartment in the most dangerous city on the planet, Arturo knew that somewhere along the line something had gone terribly wrong. He had considered Dragon's offer in all seriousness, but had discarded it after coming to terms with the fact that the person Dragon thought he was addressing—the careless adventurer who had once been Dragon's best friend—had vanished in the maze of fear and violence and anger and frustration that was Caracas. Until the magnitude of the misery that surrounded him hit him in the face. The lightning went unseen. It was the sound, really, which made the greatest impression. And the blood—blood pouring like a river out of a nameless stranger's stomach, draining life from him by the minute, by the second, by the milliliter: just one of the hundred-odd lives claimed by the city every weekend; just another corpse to be piled up in the overflowing compartments of the morgue in Bello Monte; just another number reflected in the unreliable statistic published by the papers on Monday morning—maybe not even that much. Yet, a number that was tallied right beside Arturo Sarmiento; a number with a face, if not a name; a number that had instilled fear, sympathy, anger, even sadness in Arturo; a number that had sent him deep into his own thoughts; a number that had led to a resolution. *I'm leaving. I'm out of here, Eduardo. I'm out of this dump.*

Sheila had not yet reached the end of the first column of names on her list when Arturo Sarmiento showed up outside Dragon's house on the Tuesday morning when impetus was unwittingly injected into his efforts to build the fleet of a commercial airline. Just a few days after a conversation with Nathaniel in which his father had tried to get him fully committed in the construction of an actual, rather than a hypothetical, airline, Dragon found himself in a mental cul-de-sac, doubting his ability to live up to the task at hand, finding himself out of ideas, when the lucky strike of chance opened two unexpected avenues for him to explore simultaneously: within half an hour, Dragon had been offered a plane and he had found a pilot.

Meanwhile, Sheila had to wait until the morning of the day after the end of the extended celebration that is carnival in Anguilla to begin her pilgrimage around the island. Once that day arrived, she got out of bed long before Nathaniel Jones, made herself ready, and departed the house before he awoke. He did not notice her absence until he heard the front door slam shut. As soon as he rubbed his eyes, even before he looked at the time, he knew it was the tenth of August—the first anniversary of his wedding to Sheila. Nathaniel's immediate reaction was to assume she had gone to look for something: a cake, a gift, something. It never occurred to him that she had left the house to deliver the packages she thought, or maybe only hoped, would ensure the future of Dragon Wings. Half an hour later, once the clock had reached the time when he usually woke up, he tried for the first time that day to speak to his wife, but Sheila was out of reach until well into the afternoon, by which time Nathaniel no longer had any interest in reminding her that this was the anniversary of the day when she had officially added a hyphen and a Jones to her name.

Sheila Rawlingson-Jones did not have the remotest idea what was going on when she reached her home, long after dinnertime, to find her house full of flowers, dinner served in a romantic setting, and a sparkly silver dress hanging from her wardrobe. Since the disease of purpose had first infected the perfectly idle lodgings of the Jones-Rawlingsons, Nathaniel's den of love had progressively turned into the private workplace where the couple shared everything but each other's company. Consequently, in recent times Sheila's lurid demands had repeatedly been met with the various sources (time, energy, willingness) of Nathaniel's resistance, and conversely, on the less common occasions when Nathaniel took the initiative and tried to seduce his wife, he had also experienced the scorn of his neglected lover. Nevertheless, the fortress of abstinence that had been erected around Nathaniel's king-size bed during weeks of purposeful focus was hijacked for a night when forgetfulness was forgiven and enterprise rewarded, when lust was rekindled between a loving pair, when the not-so-distant memory of seven nights and one day of secluded pleasure was complemented with one more anecdote for their private diaries.

Yet, now there was no time for a week of debauchery. On the morning of the second day after the end of carnival in Anguilla, Sheila Rawlingson-Jones woke up at the same time as her husband, an hour later than usual. She shared her coffee with Nathaniel, pressed her lips against his, allowed a fragile string of saliva to linger between their slowly retreating mouths. Then she picked up the folder with the remaining twenty-four copies of the alluring proposition to invest in Dragon Wings and departed on a new excursion around the island to carry out the task she had appointed to herself.

II

This island is already getting on my nerves. Who in his right mind would come up with the idea to set up an airline here? Look at this: nothing but dry bush and rubble. The drive from one end of the island to the other takes you not only less time than you would need to count your problems, it also takes you through some of the ugliest scenery you have ever seen. Buildings in Anguilla look derelict long before they're finished. Even when they're inhabitable, everybody seems to have this delusion of grandeur that makes them think they will need a second floor to their house which they will be able to build almost immediately, so every house has a handful of girdles reaching out to the sky from all corners. All for nothing, anyway, because the salt water, the rain, and the sun take care of rusting the metal long before the drawings for the extension have been sketched. Assuming anyone uses drawings here, which is assuming a lot.

And these roads! Compared to these roads, Caracas is paved in gold. These are not potholes, they're craters! Except, of course, when you go to the west. The west is kept tidy, clean, and beautiful for the sake of the tourists. To think that this place is considered one of the most exclusive holiday destinations in the world. In the world! There's more luxury in the backyard of my house in Caracas than in this whole island. Luxury: an old school bus rotting on the side of the road; the remains of a discarded Caterpillar slowly fading into the bush on a construction site that has long been turned into a junkyard; an unrecognizable chassis, a dismantled engine, a set of wheels resting over split concrete blocks; a collection of truck tires littering someone's garden: the other side of luxury.

What do you do on your day off in Anguilla? Nothing. Every day is a day off. Every day. There was one week of "carnival" when I first arrived when everyone seemed desperate to party—if you can call the hullabaloo that took over town every night that week partying. But then again, everything is hard to describe in Anguilla: the stadium isn't a real stadium, town isn't really a town, and partying certainly isn't anywhere near close to what we call a party in Venezuela. Now, *that* is a proper party. And yet, even if carnival wasn't a real party, at least it was *something*. Since then, it feels like there is nothing to do in this place. On your day off, you drive around, you get depressed by the surroundings, you arrive in a beautiful beach and either scorch because there isn't a single place where you can take shelter from the sun, or you get extorted by a local mercenary for a chair and an umbrella on *his* beach. So you sit on your towel and you scorch, or you pay for your space and you don't (for fifty bolívares you can buy your own chair and umbrella in Venezuela, but after all, I *am* getting paid a pilot's salary for doing nothing at all). And then what? You read, you listen to some music, you walk. But with all this solitude at some point your thoughts *have* to catch up with you. Thoughts of home, thoughts of missed opportunities, thoughts of Alicia's fine ass. Thoughts of what the hell am I doing in this place? And what the hell *am* I doing in this place?

So you go, you look, you search for someone who might distract you for a little while. But tourists are so boring in Anguilla, so one-sided. They're all old and tired and ridiculously rich, or they've just married and have small children and are discovering that motherhood is the best way out of domestic disillusionment. And the locals are so fat and so loud, and they all hang out in gangs, and in the odd case that you find one who might be halfway attractive or appealing or something, you find soon enough you have been dragged into this entire community of people which is always surrounded by endless amounts of kids who seem to reproduce by themselves—and almost inevitably two of them, at least two of them, turn out to belong to the girl you were chatting up. And you don't want to know the name of her grandmother and you really don't want to know the name of the children, and by the time you know her first child's father is also on the beach, teaching his son by his second wife—the one he got after this one—how to swim, you're thinking, *He's so young, how did he get time to marry twice?* And how did you get time to give birth twice? And what the hell am I doing here? And before you find out that he *hadn't* had time to marry twice because her first child was a mistake that happened out of wedlock, and his second child is with a woman who was already married when he met her, such that in fact the guy isn't even married at all, by that time, you just walk away and return to the peace of your iPod and your solitude.

Even when it comes for doing nothing at all, a pilot's salary is hardly enough to allow you to eat out in most places in Anguilla. Not that you would want to throw away your money for an over-elaborate meal that has nothing to do with the sun and the sea and the Caribbean, anyway. The funny thing, though, is the food is generally not the problem when you go to a restaurant here. If you like your pretentious nouvelle cuisine and you don't mind eating three sticks of chopped carrots with one slice of beef from a huge plate which has been sprinkled with what looks like the chef's makeup, then you'd probably enjoy a few places on the island. What I'm sure no one can tolerate is the rehearsed stiffness of the environment where you eat your food. The view is generally picturesque but the service—the service! Most of the time islanders have an attitude that would make a madman happy to stay in his asylum. Even getting to your table can be dangerous, as someone might very delicately address you as *milord* or *milady*. Milord! Where the hell did they learn this sort of bullshit? You couldn't make it up, really! And then ordering your food is the next frontier, particularly if you've chosen one of those places where neither you nor the waiter actually know the meaning of the words written on the menu. However, the real torture doesn't start until the wine arrives. It would be so much simpler if they allowed their sommeliers to hold the wine like they grab their rum and pour it like humans do. Instead, you're faced with the farce of an amateur sticking his thumb under the bottle, holding it with his four fingers, pouring the wine with blank fear, and dribbling it all over the glass, the bottle, and the white tablecloth. Because this technique means half the bottle actually goes to waste, and because even the simplest plate on the menu is so extravagant it takes an hour to cook, you have to repeat the ritual until you get so bored—so, let's say, after the second glass—that you simply snatch the wine out of the waiter's hands and pour it yourself. The sneer of contempt you will get from the owner if he sees you disrespecting the strict etiquette observed in his restaurant will forever remain his way of greeting you in the future, but because you're the customer and the customer pays the bill, he won't say a thing.

Bottom line is I won't go out for dinner tonight. In fact, I will do absolutely nothing at all tonight. I will get home, cook myself some fish, and sit in front of the TV until I fall asleep. Exactly the same thing I did last week, and the week before last, and the one before that. Not because I'm sad or depressed or anything like that, but because there is simply nothing else to do in Anguilla on a Sunday. There's nothing else to do in Anguilla generally, but Sundays are even worse. At least if it were Friday I would know where to go. On Fridays the night comes alive at The Velvet. You can see the girls get horny to the rhythms of soca or calypso. They really can dance, these girls, really can shake those hips. But then they seem to disappear for the rest of the week. You never see them anymore. You certainly don't see them on a Sunday night. Sunday is the day of the Lord, and Sunday night must be the night of the Lord, or the husbands, or the goats, but they're sure not the night to be seen. Friday night is the night to be seen, to have some fun. Still, better one night of entertainment a week than no night at all. I'll just go home, cook, sit in front of the TV, and wait till next Friday. Let's see what I can catch then.

III

While Sheila Rawlingson-Jones spent the best part of the month that followed the extended celebrations of carnival in Anguilla crossing out the names included on her pointless list, Dragon suddenly found himself immersed in negotiations to buy a Trislander from the Dominican Republic. The addition of Arturo Sarmiento to the company was an immediate boost, not only morally, but also pragmatically—he had knowledge of the technical detail that mattered; he could communicate with the negotiators in Spanish; he could ask the right questions and provide Dragon with insightful information. But there was one thing not even Arturo could fix: the fact that, once again, even if the plane proved ideal and the price right, Dragon Wings could not afford to purchase it.

Although the plane was, in fact, far from ideal, its general condition anything but clear, and the story behind it positively shady, the times did not allow Dragon and Co. the luxury of selection. For very much the same reasons why beggars cannot be choosers, Dragon and Arturo found themselves piecing together a puzzle, with the main objective of finding out whether the aircraft in question would actually be legal. The Trislander had been privately owned by a Dominican businessman who had leased it to a small company which had used it as a cargo plane to run the route between Santo Domingo and San Juan de Puerto Rico. It had been stripped of its inside but all the interior had been kept in the hangar at the airport so the plane could be cleaned (industrially, the Dominicans worryingly insisted) and restored to its original configuration.

In technical terms, the Trislander would provide considerable improvement to the commercial potential of Dragon Wings. Averaging a speed of 140 knots/hour, it could take seventeen passengers anywhere from the Virgin Islands to Antigua within an hour: flights to St. Barths, Nevis, and Barbuda—destinations with the same scent of exclusivity as Anguilla—could become Dragon Wings's niche; direct flights to Statia could exploit the appeal of scuba-diving day trips in one of the most privileged locations in the Caribbean; meanwhile, daily flights to St. Kitts and Antigua would appease both the government's and the HTA's desire (condition, in fact) to use the airline as an air-bridge to destinations other than St. Martin, which linked the region with Europe.

The seventeen-seat Trislander was perhaps not the best option to deploy an intricate net of connections from Anguilla to the rest of the Windward Islands, or even the rest of the Leeward Islands, but it was the only option readily available to Dragon Wings, and seventeen seats were better than nine, and two planes were certainly better than one, and US $150,000 seemed like a reasonable price, and a Trislander, with its distinctive third engine above the rudder, could become a trademark around the islands for an emerging airline. So, Dragon pressed on with the investigation, found that Mr. Alexandre Martínez was a respected businessman from Santo Domingo involved in a number of enterprises in the city, from real estate management to waste disposal. Dominair, the cargo airline which had leased the Trislander for the past five years from Alexandre Martínez, claimed they could transfer *anything* from door to door between the Dominican Republic and Puerto Rico. The price list included a section for livestock—chickens, goats, pigs—and fresh food. It also encouraged customers to "challenge us": an attitude which did nothing to appease

Dragon's concerns regarding the legality of the aircraft and the company.

But the time was not ripe for Dragon's trust to play any role in the negotiations, because after his third conversation with Alexandre Martínez the next obvious step should have been to go to Santo Domingo to carry out a personal inspection of the airplane, to have a look at the logbooks, to make certain the condition of the interior of the plane was acceptable, to begin the actual transaction, to dispense with all this talking. Except, of course, Dragon could not do this, because he had no means to fund the trip, because even if the trip were to be financed by Jones Investments' PC1171 "expense line," the company still had no means of funding the purchase of the machine, because there was no way in hell he would allow Nathaniel to make use of Jones Investments to assemble Dragon Wings's fleet of aircrafts. So Dragon stalled the negotiation, sat on his hands, stopped contacting Alexandre Martínez, and simply watched as the month of September slowly turned the dream of a commercial airline in Anguilla into smoke.

IV

Sheila Rawlingson-Jones parked her 4x4 SUV on the muddy road at the top of the steep hill that led to Gwendolyn Stewart's house in Island Harbour. She looked in the backseat and pulled out of a thick folder one of the numerous files with the details of the proposition to join Dragon Wings. Sheila dipped her small sandals in the mud as she walked around the house, hips unusually close together, their swaggering consciously restrained, to find Auntie Gwen sitting on her reclining chair, gazing at the indigo sea from her backyard. Auntie Gwen hardly said a word once she caught sight of Sheila, simply let out a warm smile that served the purpose of a welcome. Sheila was ashamed to conduct business with the unnameable friend who not so long ago had made possible the prolongation of her happiness with Nathaniel Jones, but when she brought up the episode Auntie Gwen acted as if she had forgotten all about it. *Tell me, nuh. Wha' brings you here? I know is not for me you come.* Auntie Gwen sent a scrutinizing—sharp, avid, alert—look in the direction of the file Sheila held between her hands. Sheila understood that at her old age, Auntie Gwen felt she did not have much time left to waste on small talk. *Auntie Gwen, I wan' talk business wit' you for a little while.*

Business propositions and personal requests were all Auntie Gwen ever got these days. Hardly anyone bothered to visit her at all unless they had a problem that needed solving. She had reached that stage of life where there was no longer any point in asking how she was, where hardly anything at all could make her feel better—or worse. Auntie Gwen was fully aware of everything that happened around her, she was in complete control of her faculties, she still possessed her characteristic willpower, her overwhelming force, that commandeering look in her eyes that told you she had the power to steer the interests of the Stewart family in one direction or another. But her weathered body was not fit enough to allow her to be at the helm of things the way she might, the way she had been all her life. Auntie Gwen's old age made her feel tired from the time she opened her eyes so early in the morning it was still dark, to the time when she gave herself to the irregular, restless slumber that filled her nights. So Auntie Gwen hardly ever felt the urge, the drive, the need to interfere in the way the family's interests were looked after by her six younger siblings—Fabian, Evaristo, Darius, Connor, Bacchus, and Attila, her only sister, the youngest of the bunch, who had been given a tyrant's name after her father read it somewhere and took it as some sort of sign. When the midwife told old Connor Stewart that Attila was a boy's name he simply laughed it off. *No sir, you're wrong: Attila dis baby's name and is plain for everyone to see she ain' got no stick between she legs.*

Like every family, the Stewarts had their disputes, but every time Evaristo insisted on creating a recording studio in Anguilla to help propel the career of local musicians such as his latest sweetheart, K-Sandra, or Attila demanded funds were made available to purchase a mansion in Harbour View that was in keeping with the stature and the prominence of the family in Anguillan society, Gwendolyn would emerge, of her own accord and long before anyone mustered the courage to summon her, as the ultimate authority to settle the issue with her usual resolve. *Is for pimps and bad ras dem houses made, an' if is pimpin' pimp you come trouble me 'bout I already tastin' enough of dat wit' Evaristo an' all his music-business foolishness, you know.*

But in recent times the occasions when Auntie Gwen would venture out of her self-imposed exile in her house on the hill in Island Harbour, overlooking Silly Cay, Scrub Island, and the great expanse of the deep indigo sea were few and far between. The last time Auntie Gwen had left her lodgings in Island Harbour by herself had been the distant day when she had traveled the long way to Akira Hart's office in The Valley, to help the cause of a seemingly indistinct old tourist who, unwittingly, had become a defining factor in the suddenly idyllic relationship her favorite niece, Tanika Percy, held with Antwan Thompson.

This time, though, Sheila's corner was not being backed by the sobbing requests of Auntie Gwen's favorite niece; this time Sheila did not have on her side Gwendolyn's secret ambitions to link—ally, really—the Stewarts with the Thompsons; this time all Sheila had in her hands to secure Auntie Gwen's favor was the carefully crafted proposal she casually held under her arm. This time Sheila only had the facts and numbers printed on her sheet of paper to convince Auntie Gwen that it was in the best interest of the Stewart family to get involved in Dragon Wings, to come to the rescue of what was, ultimately, the latest enterprise by a member of the Rawlingson clan from South Hill, one of the island's most notorious rivals of the Stewarts from Island Harbour.

But Auntie Gwen was a kind woman, a woman who had always tried to balance the weight of feelings against the arguments of reason in order to come up with the most advantageous decisions for herself and her family. She had not always succeeded and at times she had seemed irrational or even ruthless, but Auntie Gwen had never concerned herself excessively with keeping a spotless reputation: she had learned too early in life that people like you most when they need you most, that the best way to make an enemy is to help people when they are in desperate need, that the status she had come to enjoy in Anguillan society made her vulnerable to envy but also allowed her to get away with a certain amount of unpopular behavior. Presently, Auntie Gwen felt an unfamiliar sympathy for Sheila's request—perhaps triggered by the distant memory of the last time she had actively (physically) sought to further her interests. At the same time, Auntie Gwen felt an irrepressible mistrust—a disposition bordering on scorn—for the Rawlingsons. Of course, Auntie Gwen knew that, of all the Rawlingsons, she was facing the one rogue element in the family, and she knew that any influence she could gain in Dragon Wings now would be influence she would be taking from the hands, the control, of the rest of the Rawlingsons in the future. Yet, rogue or no rogue, no Rawlingson was likely to deserve her trust.

As Auntie Gwen entertained these thoughts, the welcoming smile which she could not help but show whenever anyone—even a Rawlingson—came to visit, ran away from her withered face. Sheila saw in the full extent of her wrinkled expression that it was about time she retraced her steps around the house, left the enemy camp, allowed the terms of her truce to speak for them-selves. Somewhat reluctantly, Auntie Gwen agreed to take a look at Sheila's proposition, telling her (and herself) that, ultimately, it would be the numbers contained in the orange folder that would have to determine the outcome of this unusual conversation.

Three days later, Auntie Gwen summoned her little brother Bacchus to her home in Island Harbour. *I wan' you take a close look at dis before you go into de board meetin'.* Bacchus browsed attentively the bunch of papers Auntie Gwen handed him. A look of dis-dain surfaced on his face as soon as he realized this was about the airline the Rawlingsons were trying to set up. There was a sudden reproach in his voice, an unusual strain of disobedience. *Is de numbers I talkin' 'bout, not de names.* Bacchus knew far too well that Auntie Gwen's privileged status among the Stewarts and, in-deed, among the rest of Anguillans was not merely a matter of tradition. He knew there was absolutely no hope in any attempt on his side to dissuade Auntie Gwen from her latest inclination.

Nevertheless, he still, somehow, managed to gather the strength to voice his dissent before capitulating. *You proposin' a partnership wit' de Rawlingsons?* The weight of contempt shackled his voice, reduced his words to a croak. Auntie Gwen knew perfectly well the question was rhetorical, and she was far too old to have to repeat herself in the first place. The sparkle in her dimmed gray eyes told Bacchus all he needed to know. So he slid the orange folder under his armpit, and with a dose of curiosity to spite his resentment, he turned around, headed west to review the details of Sheila's alluring proposal.

V

While Sheila Rawlingson-Jones spent the best part of the month that followed the extended celebration of carnival in Anguilla crossing out the names included on her pointless list of potential investors and Dragon found himself immersed in similarly pointless negotiations with Alexandre Martínez concerning the purchase of a Britten Norman Trislander which, regardless of the price, they could not afford, the board of directors of the Indigenous Bank of Anguilla had their monthly meeting to discuss the direction the institution would take regarding several matters of immediate interest.

Not very high on the list of such matters was Dragon Wings's application for a credit of US $1,000,000, which failed to meet the minimum conditions and therefore should have been dealt with within seconds. But Glenallen Rawlingson wanted to turn the board of directors of Anguilla's only indigenous bank into the sounding board on which he could test the appeal, the popularity, the reach of this outlandish project, and Glenallen Rawlingson wanted to gauge the reaction that this specific proposal would provoke on the rest of the bank's board because, if nothing else, that would give him a reasonably accurate idea of how much interest or even support the Joneses had been able to garner on the island to that moment, so when Glenallen Rawlingson brought up the application for US $1,000,000 to set up a local commercial airline he did so almost inconspicuously, as if he did not know the exact details surrounding the project, and he left it there, lingering in space, awaiting his peers' reviews.

That's why no one was more surprised than Glenallen Raw-lingson when what should have been a straightforward rejection sparked the most heated argument to have taken place in the directors' conference room of the bank's building in The Valley not only since its recent rebranding as the Indigenous Bank of Anguilla but also during its previous incarnation as the Bank of the Leeward Islands. Bacchus Stewart, Glenallen's lifelong nemesis, showed not so much interest but total familiarity with the business plan. The youngest of Auntie Gwen's brothers, Bacchus was only five or six years older than Glenallen Rawlingson but over the years had bred the most genuine hatred for him, resulting in the sort of competition that is best described as vicious, deliberately seeking to overshadow his achievements, to smear his reputation, just because Glenallen had taken part in the single most important event in Anguillan history, the revolution against St. Kitts well over four decades earlier, and Bacchus hadn't. Consequently, and almost coincidentally, Glenallen, like Bacchus's nephew, Walter Stewart, his brother Fabian's son, had been involved in Anguilla's earliest experiences as a democratic nation.

Just a teenager at the time, though, Glenallen had not shared Walter's fascination with politics, instead putting to good use his connections with the highest echelons of the young country's revolutionary elite to profit from a wide array of commercial ventures on an island that boasted absolutely no infrastructure, no services, no commodities at all. For the following four decades Bacchus Stewart busied himself shadowing Glenallen's every move, making certain that whatever he did, Bacchus did better. Thus, when in 1973 Glenallen bought a taxi, Bacchus bought three and operated a taxi company from Island Harbour which he called Glennbeat, only for him to realize later that the business model was unviable and that he would have to sell the cars before they were eaten by the rust if he wanted to save some of his capital. Similarly, when Glenallen decided to open a restaurant in South Hill, Bacchus did everything in his hands to have the Stewart family build the largest hotel on the island; when Glenallen decided to buy a piece of land, Bachus would double Glenallen's offer, and when he was faced with a seller who did not want to sell to the Stewarts or who had already taken Glenallen's money, he would endeavor to secure a piece twice the size Glenallen had bought, regardless of the price, without even remotely thinking of its use. By the same token, when Glenallen Rawlingson had joined efforts with Alwyn Cooke in 1979 to create the Bank of the Leeward Islands, Bacchus Stewart had embarked on his very own crusade to have Auntie Gwen move ahead with the formation of the Anguilla Home and Trust Bank, which had opened its doors to the public in 1982. So it might well have been by the agency of some perverse divinity or principle of cosmic order that Glenallen Rawlingson and Bacchus Stewart were forced to sit in the same boardroom ostensibly working together toward the same goals, once the Caribbean Central Bank in St. Kitts intervened in the affairs of both the Bank of the Leeward Islands and the Anguilla Home and Trust Bank and ordered their merger shortly before Nathaniel Jones's first arrival on the island.

Glenallen Rawlingson had had to withstand Bacchus Stewart's presence long enough to understand that his enthusiasm for a venture that was being spearheaded by his niece Sheila should send alarm bells ringing all around, but his world really turned on its head when Godfrey Ryan, the owner of the Arawak Cave, one of the island's oldest and best hotels, expressed utter indignation at having to discuss any more of this white man's fantasy. *We talkin' talkin' talkin' 'bout dis nonsense for weeks already in the HTA, an' dey goan give dem plenty money just so. I ain' wastin' my time wit' dem people no more, you know.* This was the first thing Glenallen Rawlingson had heard about the HTA's agreement to commit approximately half of its budget for the year to guarantee the longevity of an initiative that, if successful, could potentially bring about the most dramatic transformation in the island's tourism industry since its emergence in the mid-1980s. This was also all Glenallen Rawlingson needed to know to understand that Sheila's efforts to find independent means to fund Dragon Wings had far exceeded his expectations, that the Joneses would be able to press ahead with their plans with or without him. The time had come to act, and to act quickly, if he wanted to prevent the Stewarts from getting any leverage in the enterprise.

Unbeknown to the Joneses, they had just landed the most important victory in their bid to turn a hypothetical airline into a fully operational business, because though Sheila's application for a US $1,000,000 credit would not be accepted by the Indigenous Bank of Anguilla, the heated discussion sparked by it was a sign that a number of prominent players in Anguillan society had strong feelings about the prospect of Dragon Wings becoming Anguilla's flag carrier in the immediate future, and that at least a portion of them were prepared to clear the way to make the process as simple for Nathaniel and Co. as possible.

VI

O h, Dragon! Can't it wait till Monday? I know it can't but I'm just making it clear that I'm taking one for the team right now—one that I'll make sure to redeem on a future occasion. After weeks of doing nothing, there are finally some signs that I might, after all, get to actually work on this island. I met this girl at The Velvet last Friday and agreed to go out with her tomorrow night. It's our first date, Dragon—I swear I'll make it to Antigua the day after tomorrow. There is, of course, nothing to do: the slot has been booked, sleeping arrangements have been made, I must go. My Venezuelan license is endorsed by the FAA, and we're ranked in Category 1, anyway, so They should just give me a stamp and allow me to fly! I know I haven't flown in over two years, I'm kidding. It's just that I met this girl at The Velvet and . . . Oh, never mind, okay, tomorrow, first thing in the morning, departure time six forty-five a.m. Fine. I'll be there at six o'clock. Don't worry, I won't miss my flight.

The day will be a drag. I need to validate my license and pass the theory test of the ECCAA to get local certification. I promised Dragon weeks ago I would look into the rules and regulations to verify that standard procedure around here matches procedures in Venezuela. I'll have to find the book, have a look at it on the way to Antigua tomorrow morning. Dragon's still upset. He looks distracted, almost lost. Is he worried I might miss my flight? It's not me you should be worrying about, Dragon. I have kept this to myself for weeks but maybe the time has come to get it off my chest. I don't really care if this airline works or not, all I care about is my salary, and I'm getting paid, but if something doesn't change soon I won't be getting paid for long. *Dragon, we need to talk. I'm not convinced about this airline, man. If I go back to my old job my boss might still take me back, you know. I don't know if this was the right decision.* He thinks this is a scheme. He thinks I'm doing this to get out of going to Antigua tomorrow. He doesn't think I'm talking sense. Reassure me, Dragon. Convince me. Nothing. Dragon's just lethargic, absent—in fact, disinterested. *Answer me this, Dragon: How do you plan to make this business work? Why do you suppose anyone would go into that dreary office in the Business Center and come out of it with a ticket in their hands? Explain to me why anybody in Antigua or St. Kitts would fly with us? Do you plan to open one of our swanky offices on every island in the Caribbean?* I didn't really mean to be this blunt but at least I'm getting a reaction. Dragon is irritated. I can see it in his eyes, in the angle of his shoulders. He hits back at me with what might have been an insult but is in fact only a question. *Of course I have a suggestion. I wouldn't be saying this if I didn't have a suggestion. I never wanted to be a businessman, Dragon, but I have become one. Our only hook in this market must be our prices. It seems clear to me that if we want to make this work we need to turn Dragon Wings into a budget airline. Forget about offices anywhere—run the business through the Internet. Contact travel agencies, speak to the major airlines we will be looking to feed off from, establish allegiances. Buy placards in the airports we want to service, get our name in the in-flight magazine of BA, or Air France. Forget about personnel and concentrate on advertising instead. This is your business, Dragon, and you run it however you want to, but it seems to me at the moment you have no prospects beyond fulfilling our most immediate needs, no plans for the future at all.* This has him thinking. His attitude is no longer aggressive, his gaze, though thoughtful, no longer lingers idly. Dragon's far away, entertaining thoughts that I planted in his head. Big point for me. You owe me, Dragon, but I won't tell you just yet. *I have some packing to do. I'll be at home.*

Packing for what? Every island is the same, I'm sure. Same temperature, same air, same sea, same girls. A couple of days in Antigua, validating a foreign license, taking a certification test: another drag. Antigua, Anguilla, even Margarita, all the same. *Charmaine, how are you doing, love? I'm so sorry, I won't be able to make it tomorrow evening. I have to travel to Antigua for business. Yes, a pilot thing, you know.* She tries to disguise her disappointment with a touch of boredom in her response but I can see through her pose. *You wouldn't have time for a quick drink tonight, would you?* A man who can't drink, can't afford to pay for dinner, and has just canceled a date for the following day can't expect to get much out of the evening but these are the kinds of things a pilot can get away with sometimes. *Great! I'll see you there at nine thirty.*

A relatively early night becomes a very late one when you have to be at the airport at six a.m. And now I have to study the local rules and regulations. Thank God I stopped myself from having another whiskey. I don't think I could handle a hangover today. Dragon Wings: a commercial airline in Anguilla. These people don't have a clue. I swear, if this thing works out, no project in life should ever fail. And now they send me away precisely the day when I have a date. She's hot, that little girl. And this is so boring: codes and distances and language and procedure. I'll have to assume that safety regulations are more stringent in Venezuela than in the Eastern Caribbean. I'll have to give that little girl a call once I'm back, try to get inside her pants. I should be okay for the medical—I hope my eyesight's still fine. Fire and water drills: piece of cake. My IFR might be a little bit rusty but I should be fine. To be a certified pilot again— I'd forgotten the joy. I'll have to go celebrate with that girl. But before that maybe I can catch up with some sleep on the way to Antigua . . .

VII

A rt's arrogance and his lack of tact initially put me off the idea, but I haven't been able to get it out of my mind since he mentioned it. It will undoubtedly be the cheapest, easiest, quickest way to set up this airline. It is absolutely crucial that we become operational by December 1. That is only two and a half months away. The HTA loan and government subsidy will only come to effect if we can provide services to Antigua and St. Kitts to link up to flights arriving from London. I don't see how we can open offices and develop teams in both those islands in the next two months. We need two aircrafts, at least, with their respective crews. The negotiation with the Dominicans who own that Trislander have been stuck by our lack of funds. I absolutely refuse to keep draining Jones Investments for the sake of Dragon Wings. But Sheila at least seems to be making some progress in her search for local funding. Where is Nathe? He is never late for a meeting—least of all a *business* meeting.

The sun is particularly hot today. There is a breeze but the air is still sultry, humid, heavy. Everyone complains about September in Anguilla, everybody leaves the island. I asked Nathe to meet me in my favorite bar down in Sandy Ground but it turns out it has shut for the rest of the summer. Everything is shut. Just over a month ago we were celebrating carnival, partying all day and all night for two full weeks, and now, look at this: The Valley, a ghost town. Thankfully, we haven't had a hurricane so far this year and none seems to be forming at the moment either. However, as you drive through the island at least half the buildings are hermetically sealed with hurricane shutters. The traffic has shrunk by half, and the people who have stayed are in no hurry to get wherever they are going. It's the middle of September and suddenly there are no tourists on Anguilla: the expats, all gone; the restaurants, all seventy of them, shut; the hotels, all thirty-five of them, closed; and the ones that aren't should be, because they are totally empty. Supplies in the supermarkets have been halved and a public service announcement floods the radio and the TV every half hour with warnings and suggestions of preventive measures in case of a storm. Somehow, it feels like everyone who has stayed here is patiently waiting for something, anything, to happen: for time to go by, for October to bring respite, or simply for disaster to strike.

In the meantime, I sit alone in the Business Center, waiting for Nathaniel to arrive (late) to a business meeting in which I will put forward as an organizing alternative a proposition which, I know, doesn't correspond with the original plan he envisioned for the airline. I have read the company charter, I have seen the business proposition Nathaniel showed Deianira Walker. What he had in mind was more of a little empire than a little airline. But Nathaniel is a dreamer, and this time his dream will have to be amended if it is to come to exist at all. Is there any other way of getting Dragon Wings started? Is there another solution? I got in contact with some specialists and apparently the process is quite simple: all we need is a specific application with its program and a server to support it. They seemed confident they would be able to set up the page and have it running within six to eight weeks. Art will be licensed to fly in nine weeks. We must make our first flight in eleven. There won't be much time to test things but making the deadline would already be a major success.

I can hear Nathaniel's car pulling into the parking lot. Nothing else seems to be going on today, so I have no doubt it's him.

Two minutes later I can hear the echo of feet tramping up the stairs: Tuesday morning, and it is that quiet.

What the echo didn't tell me is that there were more feet walking up those stairs than belong to one person. Sheila walks through the open door first and suddenly the thick, soggy air inside the office is lifted by a gust of freshness. She wears a tiny turquoise strap top and a very short pair of shorts. She looks taller than she is on those high platform sandals she's wearing. Nathaniel follows. The heat looks less flattering on him, his hair drenched and a visible trail of sweat soaking his white shirt from the bottom of his neck down the middle of both his chest and back. He has a wide smile, though, and a large dose of enthusiasm. *Good news!* He doesn't even stop to apologize for his tardiness. His hands rub; Sheila looks at him victoriously. *We've found a local partner.*

This, of course, is not only extraordinary but also unexpected news. *What? When? Who?* Sheila's efforts to draw one of the wealthy families into the venture has finally paid off. *I tell you all along dat somebody goan bite. In de end is Uncle Glen step up wit' de money.* Glenallen Rawlingson, the tower of a man with the boisterous guffaw and the disdain filtering through his smile, has suddenly, after weeks of skepticism toward the project, after months of antagonism against Nathaniel, come to the rescue of Dragon Wings. *How come? What's made him change his mind?* The two lovebirds look to have renewed their vows. They speak over each other, they hold each other tight, they laugh at what the other is saying and fail to answer my questions, or to even finish a sentence.

He musta seen de light, and just her sweet wide smile tells me everything I need to know. *He wants more than anything to keep the Stewarts from entering the business. So much so that he's prepared to put a quarter of a million dollars in cash for shares.* We should listen to what the Stewarts have to say, that much is obvious to me. *No, man, now Uncle Glen seen de light we no need no Stewarts,* and the cackle that sends Sheila's body into sexy little spasms again transports me to a land far away from the corporate world. *We've already signed an LOI. He's ready to move ahead, and so are we. We're in business, Dragon.* I cannot believe my ears. All of a sudden, and implausibly as it seems, Nathe tells me we're in business. *Dat ain' even de best news: Uncle Glen tell me unofficially an' all hush-hush de bank kyan't give we cash but dey wan s'port de airline so dey goan make it easy for we to borrow for planes. Yessir, we is in business!* One meeting, and Nathaniel and Sheila rediscover the enthusiasm that September has been draining out of all of us. *Was there something you wanted to discuss, or should we just go celebrate somewhere?* There is nowhere to go but Nathe will listen to no reason. *Who cares! Let's buy a case of champagne and celebrate at home.* A case of champagne. In September. Wishful thinking. But Nathaniel is right: there is no point in working today. How could I possibly spoil this moment with what I have to say? How could we concentrate on the advantages and disadvantages of my new (adopted) idea? How could we consider anything objectively with the exhilaration of such a breakthrough hanging over our heads? *What I wanted to talk about can wait till tomorrow. Let's celebrate!*

Old pâté, bad cheese, and a lot of champagne is all we can muster for an improvised celebration at Nathe's home in East End. But despite the poor provisions, the hot afternoon has turned into a beautiful evening and we enjoy it outdoors,

in Nathe's garden, on a hill, overlooking a small eastern lip
of the island that winds into the endless sea. The effect of the
champagne, the burning glow of the sun slowly nearing the
horizon, trigger an urge in me to prepare a bonfire. I gather
bits and pieces from all around the garden and before long
we have a sizable pile of dry wood and branches ready to
burn. We wait until the evening turns dark to light the fire
and send the cork of another bottle of Moët soaring through
the skies. Nathe and Sheila playfully dance to the tune of
some old-fashioned melody and, for once, they look genuinely happy. I should be glad, but I'm not. I know this sounds
selfish but she is so beautiful it simply cannot be helped. She
looks even more beautiful in the red warm glow of the fire.
I need to move away from them so I approach the flames,
watch them soar higher than I predicted, sit as close to them
as the heat will allow me, sip my champagne awed by the
shape of the orange tongues, tracing the trail of the plume of
smoke, trying not to listen to those two laugh with each other.

I have lost sense of time. The only chronological reference
I can find is an empty bottle by my side. The night is still
young and beautiful—the stars lay their claim to every inch
of the clear sky—but too much to drink and too little to eat
combine to make me sluggish. Sheila still dances like a dervish but Nathe has retired to his hammock and appears to
be half asleep. A new song plays on the iPod and Sheila
approaches—freshly poured glass of champagne in hand—
with irresistible resolve. We dance two, three, four consecutive songs. I'm no longer sluggish but I'm tired and sweaty
and thirsty. I go inside, pour us another round, and return. I
can see Nathe has lost his battle against sleep. A slow song,
a romantic song, slots into the machine. Sheila can't stop
moving anymore. She starts dancing to this tune as well and

suddenly, here's the nightmare I had not yet dared fantasize about. She stands so close to me I can feel her bosom against my chest. She is so beautiful. She is so graceful. She smells so . . . My hand around her waist, my nose, her breath. I can hear her breathing. I can feel her heart beating. Can I resist? Could anyone?

Did our lips meet? Did our tongues? What else? Did anything? And what if they didn't? Does it matter?

I wake up, dressed, contorted and still slightly drunk, on Nathaniel's white couch in his living room. He no longer sleeps on the hammock. In fact, he and Sheila are nowhere to be seen. The bedroom door is shut. I look for my shoes, a glass of water, my car keys. A clumsy note on the kitchen counter: *We need to talk. But please don't call until the afternoon.* I should have mentioned it was business. I should have addressed it to him.

VIII

Nathaniel Jones saw very little of his wife during the rest of the week that followed the extended celebration that was carnival in Anguilla. In fact, Nathaniel Jones would not see very much at all of his wife during the better part of the month she spent crossing out one by one the names of potential local investors for Dragon Wings. Until the Monday afternoon when Glenallen Rawlingson himself, the man at the very top of Sheila's pointless list and the only name that could really make a dramatic difference in the fortunes of the airline, called Sheila Rawlingson-Jones. *I been t'inking 'bout dis strange business proposition you make me de other day, you know. I mean, every old way you look at dis is madness, nuh, but for some reason I don' even reach to unnerstan', I jus' kyan't stop t'inkin' 'bout it. An' you know is sometin' good an' interestin' you have cookin' in you hands if Glenallen kyan't stop t'inkin' 'bout it. Why you don't set up a meetin' wit' Nathaniel later today, Sheila, I wan' have a little conversation wit' de man.*

The second time in their lives Glenallen Rawlingson and Nathaniel Jones had a civilized conversation was the Monday morning when the former came to the latter's house in East End with a draft of an LOI in his pocket and a single condition. *I kyan make dis fancy dream of yours come true, you know. I dunno why I would want to, but I do. You make so many mistakes already, but is still not too late. I kyan help you rectify dem, under one condition: by no means are de Stewarts to get involved in dis airline, you understan'? Dat ain' negotiable. Is me or dem you*

wan, you kyan't get bot', an' if is me, you have to decide roight now, and
with this, Glenallen pulled the folded LOI out of his back pocket.

The agreement was not binding, the final figures were not
even discussed—although a quarter of a million dollars was mentioned as a plausible sum—and nothing was officially finalized,
but Nathaniel saw this as the greatest coup of his Caribbean life.
He had agreed to meet Dragon in the Business Center that day
to discuss the future of the operation, but suddenly it seemed im-
proper to work during such a wonderful occasion. He showed up
late and merry at the office, improvised a drunken celebration at
his home, spent most of the night watching Sheila dance like a
dervish, before she resolved to combat his weariness, his inebria-
tion, to ravish him repeatedly with an ardor, an intensity, which
differed from any other night—as if her delirious mind had mis-
taken him for someone else, as if they had never made love before,
as if they were in a different place.

This was only two weeks after the Thursday morning when Arturo Sarmiento departed for Antigua on what had been intended as
a two-day journey to validate his commercial pilot license. Arturo
was concerned about his future; Arturo had absolutely no faith
in the project; Arturo had no doubt whatsoever that, even if the
airline were to come to fruition, the venture would eventually fail.
Further negotiations for the purchase of the Trislander were being stalled by a lack of funds; the uncertainty regarding the actual
machinery the airline would fly meant the search for pilots could
not be carried out in full; no planes and no pilots meant the routes
to be flown remained undecided; which in turn meant no team of
employees could be assembled anywhere. The hope was that once
the first domino fell, the rest of the pieces would follow automatically. Now that an injection of hope and an unofficial promise of
further credit had been extended to the company, the soundness
of such plan would come to be tested.

Arturo Sarmiento departed for Antigua on what was intended

to be a two-day journey to validate his commercial pilot license, but Arturo Sarmiento's flying instincts were less forthcoming on a Thursday morning of little sleep and much travail. His eyesight was fine, his physical went smoothly, and the emergency drills were, as expected, a piece of cake. But his Instrument Flight Rating (IFR) was appalling, his navigation exam a failure, and he did not actually have an Air Transport Procedure (ATP) license in the first place, which meant he could only fly aircrafts that weighed less than 12,500 pounds—nothing bigger than a Twin Otter.

Arturo Sarmiento's flying instincts didn't resurface as swiftly as he had expected, but the knowledge instilled in his brain had not vanished completely, not even after long years of absolute neglect. During a challenging morning of little sleep and much travail, Arturo was able to prove his erudition in aviation law and to show his mastery of aviation procedure; he was flawless in his manipulation of the machine's systems and electronics, cruised through the sections on planning, monitoring, and performance, and he managed to get a decent Visual Flight Rating (VFR). However, his dismal performance on IFR Communication, his lack of accreditation on ATP, his less-than-subtle touch on the simulator prompted the inevitable: he would need to take a ten-week course and pass the relevant exams at the end it, before his commercial pilot license could be validated.

So, what had been intended as a two-day journey to validate his license had to be extended indefinitely for Arturo Sarmiento to find the only ECCAA-approved instructor on the island and begin his course as soon as possible. Arturo Sarmiento spent two days looking for Michael Haywood, an American pilot with thinning hair and high blood pressure who gave the impression of being constantly drunk. After Art turned every stone and called every number in the phone book, Michael finally surfaced on Sunday afternoon, having just returned from a fishing trip. His dismissive attitude and patronizing tone of voice instantly struck a dissonant chord in Arturo Sarmiento. The two disliked each other immediately, but Michael desperately needed the money and Arturo desperately needed an ECCAA-approved instructor, so, from the very outset, it was perfectly clear that this was going to be, strictly and exclusively, a business-oriented relationship in which the priorities were money on the one hand and expediency on the other.

If we start the course next week we might just make it for the examinations at the end of November—you've missed the enrolment deadline but I have my connections. Favors, like everything else, had a price with Michael Haywood, but that neither surprised nor upset Art's South American disposition. *Cash only, my friend.*

Michael met Arturo Sarmiento on Monday morning with a washed-out copy of a token contract. *Here's 50 percent of your fees in cash. I'll bring the rest once you get me onto the examination list.* Michael gravely asked his pupil to print his name and sign at the bottom. Arturo Sarmiento returned the following Monday—and every Monday thereafter for the following ten weeks—for an intensive course that would allow him to rejoin the ranks of legal commercial pilots before the end of the year.

IX

This is the only way we are going to be able to set up this business in time. We have no alternative, Nathe. He paces the room patiently and tries not to show his anger, not to let it affect his demeanor. He is being civil and hearing me out but I know inside his mind he's already half-way through his answer. *We have to be realistic about this, Nathe, we have to be flexible.* His fingers entwine, his pace slows down, he wrings his hands.

Before allowing me to reach my conclusion he butts in: *We cannot turn this into a budget airline.* His eyes pierce me right back to my seat. His eyebrows are raised, his forehead wrinkled, his entire face disfigured with aggression. *This is not the place to make anything budget, these are not budget customers.* And then something or other about thousands of dollars per night, exclusivity, golfing paradise, elite . . .

Nathe, we can't afford to rely exclusively on tourists for this. His eyes bulge with anger—too much anger for the nature of our conversation. There's something wrong with Nathaniel, something's eating away at him. *We have to appeal to the local population, Nathe. Everyone is related in these islands, everyone has a cousin somewhere.*

I walk away from him, head toward my desk, pull a bottle of whiskey from one of the drawers, pour ourselves a drink. Nathaniel swishes the booze in his mouth, savors the heat on his tongue, before carefully placing the glass on the desk. *This has got to be a cleanly operated, fancy, efficient airline, Dragon.* He insists on the importance of image, on the advantages of ubiquity, on market strategies to make our launch a noteworthy event, but I can tell there is something else, perhaps something unrelated, troubling him. *Even if you want to target the local population, you cannot rely solely on the web: half these people don't even own a computer.* The steam train of Nathaniel's thought is rolling and I know it won't stop until it arrives at his final conclusions, as soon as he feels he has sufficiently demolished my argument. *Relying solely on the web would estrange us from most of the local community and harm our image in the eyes of rich tourists.* I sense in his use of the word *solely* his unique way of building a bridge between his position and mine. He knows that I'm right, that we cannot get offices in several islands at the same time in the next two months, and this is the extent of the compromise he is willing to make. But at least I know Nathe has come to his senses.

It is time we submit a full draft of our intended itinerary to the ECCAA, Dragon. This is what I have envisioned—and the final word is enough for me to understand that Nathe is now in control. *St. Kitts, Nevis, Antigua, Barbuda, and St. Martin are the destinations we can bank on at the moment.* With a sleight of hand Nathe acknowledges the time constraints that make the prospect of opening an office in each of these five islands impossible: suddenly, he shows interest in the digital option. *Can they program separate access for customers and travel agencies?* Nathe's anger is concealed beneath his pragmatism, but I can still sense it lying in wait, latent, tacit, simmering just under the surface. *As of Monday we'll have full-page adds in the* Anguillan, *St. Martin's* Daily Herald, *Antigua's* Observer, *and St. Kitts's* Sun. *I will include details of our homepage, so warn the programmers to set up a provisional front page with all our contact information while they put together the real thing.* Nathaniel's particular way of capitulating is so obtuse I don't know whether I should consider this a victory at all.

Nathe has adapted his ideas gallantly, reshaping mine in the process to the point where they no longer seem incompatible. But the day's work is far from over: he reaches inside a drawer in the filing cabinet, retrieves a thin folder, and throws it at me. It is the provisional schedule with departure times and estimated flight durations. Direct flights to Nevis and Barbuda are listed during the week with intricate island-hopping patterns; an early-morning flight to St. Kitts looks desolate next to the three daily commutes to St. Martin. *We're finding difficulties with Grand Case, in French St. Martin, and St. Barths, because they insist on pilots speaking French. The same goes for Dutch in St. Eustatius. But we already have licensing for Juliana, in Dutch St. Martin.* I can see that Nathe has put a lot of time into the elucidation of this plan. *We have a problem: we need a twenty-five-seater to have any chance of making a profit with the longer routes.* Nathe knows that the Trislander we are trying to get has a capacity of seventeen. *Where are we going to get that?* He acts surprised, looks straight into my eyes. *That's your job, Dragon, don't ask me how to go about it.*

He turns to me and approaches threateningly. I knew he would be disappointed with my proposal, but Nathe's rage is not being sparked by our chat. *I spoke to Alexandre Martínez last night: the Trislander is still on the market. I've already arranged a meeting with him this weekend in the Dominican Republic. Should I cancel?* I can see Nathaniel reviewing our options in his mind. *Get that Trislander, Dragon,* and he moves on: *Now, about those pilots—we cannot afford to disregard the two licensed pilots on the island.* The two, of course, are SamB and Ralph. I know Nathaniel intends to send out a message to the local community, a message of commitment as well as solidarity. *A partnership with Ralph, a native Anguillan, would be invaluable for us, Dragon.*

I stand my ground firmly: *Is that what you're going to tell the families of our passengers when our local stud crashes our Queen Air into the sea?* This time it's Nathe's turn to allow my snarky comment to drift past unanswered but recorded.

He looks like a man on the verge of a crisis. Does he know? He must know. But what can he know? He must know I'm in love with Sheila—that much is obvious. But can he blame me? Could anyone be blamed? I wonder where she is. I wonder what she's doing. I wish I could be doing it with her. I come back to myself and find Nathaniel leaning on the desk by the large window, scrutinizing me with wild, irate eyes. *I asked you a question.* I have absolutely no idea what it was. *Are you here now? Are you here at all?* He is furious.

I was listening, Nathe. He doesn't believe a word. *I knew this would be a major blow for you.* He is totally disinterested. *That's why I broke it down to the bare facts, Nathe.* I still haven't caught his attention. *It's not just the logistics of it, it's the economic factor and the practical side of things.* Nathaniel simply shakes his head. *Calm down, let me explain.*

Don't tell me to calm down when you and I both know perfectly well my wife is fucking another man.

What the hell? Is he talking about me? *You want to tell me what the hell is going on here?* I can see the fever inside Nathe's eyes recede under the effect of the booze.

I just told you. Don't act like you don't know—I mean, everyone must know by now, right? If even I know. And let's be honest, you've seen her: what's a woman like that doing with an old man like me, right? What could I expect? Is he genuinely feeling sorry for himself, or is Nathaniel drawing me into a trap here?

You're being unfair, Nathe, and you know it. You're being unfair to yourself, you're being unfair to her, and most importantly you're being unfair to me. I asked you to come here to talk business, Nathe.

His eyes grow wider and the expression in his face loosens as soon as he becomes aware. *You've fallen for her too.*

This had to happen. *Of course I have, Nathe: I see her all the time, I work with her every day. She's the most extraordinary woman—we all know that. We also know she's your wife.* This conversation is taking the strangest of twists but it's too late to change the course of it. Somehow, I thought my father was accusing me of cheating with his wife and I've ended up defending her. *Look, Nathe, I'm sorry, but I'm your business partner, not your marriage counselor.*

And that is how the end got started.

X

rturo Sarmiento returned to Anguilla with a suitcase full of failure, a dose of humility, and the tricky task ahead of him of catching up with time, but no one in Dragon Wings could take notice because before too long an injection of hope and an unofficial promise of further credit restored the element of urgency that the enterprise had lacked through the month of September. Shortly after the second time in their lives Glenallen Rawlingson and Nathaniel Jones had had a civilized conversation, the two were joined by Dragon and Sheila in Deianira Walker's office to sign a deal whereby Sheila's uncle would enter into partnership with the Joneses, purchasing 21 percent of the company in exchange of a quarter of a million dollars.

What followed after that was a period of hectic activity that started on a Friday morning when Arturo Sarmiento and Dragon Jones traveled to Santo Domingo to meet Alexandre Martínez and carry out the inspection of the Britten Norman Trislander that would make a large number of the initial plans for the airline seem achievable. The trip was long and complicated and all flights involved were predictably delayed, so before Arturo and Dragon met anyone that evening they had already spent several hours in various airports and departure lounges. That might have been why Dragon showed less tact than would have been advisable when a short, square, middle-aged man with strong arms, bowed legs, and a big round stomach introduced himself as Alexandre Martínez.

There was something utterly enigmatic about this man's presence, about the way he carried himself. He sported a bushy mustache that for some reason gave him an unusual air of elegance but that at the same time was incongruous with the old-fashioned glasses hanging clumsily—almost mockingly—from his nose. Dragon—exhausted by the journey, exasperated by the delay—totally disregarded the casual pleasantries prescribed by Latin decorum, intemperately asked whether they could take a look at the plane. But Alexandre Martínez proved to be tolerant as well as sensible, and *it's too late for that, tonight, Mr. Jones. There is no light, night will soon fall, and you are tired from your traveling. I hope you two will join us for dinner. We can go ahead with the inspection of the airplane tomorrow morning.*

Dinner was charming and a good night's rest was exactly what both Arturo and Dragon most needed, other than a suitable aircraft to start turning the dream of a commercial airline into some version of a reality. But the inspection of the Trislander the following day presented Dragon with a problem: to be sure, the plane's condition was acceptable and the interior had been safely stored in a dry place, to the point where it seemed never to have been used, and the three Lycoming engines sparked up in a hurry, and all systems appeared to work without fault—but when Arturo dove into the logbooks he spent an inordinate amount of time reading through them. His eyes sharpened, his body crouched forward as he read page after page. Arturo made no comment when Alexandre Martínez said something to him in Spanish but Dragon sensed he had found something he disliked. The self-consciousness of being observed deterred Arturo from continuing his investigation. He flicked through the rest of the logbooks, jumped off the plane, handed over the material to its owner. But the discovery of something unusual had already been made.

Hands were shaken, pledges exchanged—*Either way, I will be in touch with you very soon*—and behind remained the old-fashioned specs which sheltered the dark eyes of a shrewd businessman.

On the way back to Anguilla Dragon asked Arturo's opinion. *The engines' books have been tampered with. The left engine is slightly older than the right one—allegedly fifteen and twenty thousand hours each.* Arturo was unequivocal, yet inconclusive: *You can be certain they're older than that, but this doesn't mean anything is wrong with them.* Dragon sought in Arturo the sort of authoritative advice he was absolutely not prone to give. *It might be they're just trying to get as much money for their plane as they possibly can.* Arturo simply would not commit. *I couldn't hear any misfiring, I couldn't trace any malfunction in the system.*

Dragon had his back against the wall. He could sense that all the spiel Alexandre Martínez had given him about negotiations with a Costa Rican airline had been intended to build up the price of the Trislander, but at the same time he could not be fully sure about it. He did not trust Dominair but there was nothing in the records (not in the IATA's, not in the FAA's, not in the ECCAA's) that pointed toward anything illegal. He acknowledged an exotic appeal in the person of Alexandre Martínez but he did not feel he could trust him. On the other hand, he found himself out of options. *Given our current situation, Art, would you advise against us purchasing this plane?* Arturo Sarmiento gave the question two minutes' consideration before shaking his head from side to side. That was two minutes more than Dragon was expecting.

On Monday morning, with Art on his way to Antigua and the rest of the airline's high command in the Business Center, Dragon reached the office intending to put the domino-effect theory to the test. *We've got ourselves a nice little plane there.* He looked enthusiastic, optimistic, unconcerned. Indeed, he allowed his mind to drift so far away from their problems that he even neglected informing Nathe and Sheila about the conflicting data Art had found in the engines' logbooks. *There's no point in raising issues and potential objections if in the end I want us to go ahead and buy this plane: I'm just going to have to make an executive decision. It's not as if you could say Nathe is*

thinking straight right now, anyway. And it wasn't, because more than
ever Nathaniel Jones was reeling with pain at the thought of his
relationship—perhaps his last-ever chance at true love—ebbing
away, slipping through his fingers, dying the death of the brown
pelican, impaired by its own need to feed itself, unflinchingly
crashing headfirst into the sea time after time after time to catch
the fish that would keep it going, jeopardizing its future with every
fresh attempt to fulfill its present desires, every blow damaging its
vision minimally, almost imperceptibly, but cumulatively, sentenc-
ing it to an old age of blindness and hunger and trial and error
and its large beak scooping nothing but salt water and solitude
and despair.

But at the same time, Dragon's frame of mind was far distanced from right, and even on that Monday morning when he
got together with Sheila to discuss the details of the US $150,000
loan application to the Indigenous Bank of Anguilla for Alexandre
Martínez's Britten Norman Trislander, he allowed his attention
to waver, and he indulged in the pleasure of Sheila's beauty, so
effortless, so pleasing. Could Nathe be right in his suspicions? Was
there anything to tell him that Sheila could, indeed, be leading
a double life? Or was his father testing him, testing his loyalty,
staging a crisis just to see on which side of the divide he would
land? There was intent behind Sheila's nonchalance, there was a
thought process—no question about it. But could she be so cool?
Could she carry on living this fantasy in full while she polluted it
with the presence of someone else, of an outsider, of an alternative? *He-llo-o! Planet Eart' to Dragon Jones, is anyone dere?* and Dragon
was brought back from his daydreaming to face the reality of a
loan, of instructing Deianira Walker to draft the contract they
would fax Alexandre Martínez later that week, of the company
logo and the first full-page ad that would flood the media of the
Leeward Islands during the first days of October.

XI

October was the crucial month—the month that would
determine whether some version or other of the original
plan to set up an operational airline based in Anguilla by
December 1 would be realized. October was the crucial month
and a meeting between SamB and Dragon Jones on Friday, October 1, at SamB's West End quarters turned out to be the crucial meeting. SamB had known ever since the moment he had
rejected Dragon's first offer that he would be hearing more about
the project in the future, had been awaiting Dragon's second visit
with anticipation. But SamB had followed closely the developments surrounding Dragon Wings and the longer he did so the
more convinced he became that this project would, in the end,
never come to be. This, however, had been before an injection
of hope and an unofficial promise of further credit had restored
the element of urgency that the enterprise had decidedly lacked
through the month of September.

SamB was not aware of Glenallen Rawlingson's incorporation into the company, nor did he know about the quarter of a
million dollars he had brought into the venture; SamB had not
heard that Dragon Wings had applied for a US $150,000 secure
loan to purchase a Britten Norman Trislander with dubious pedi-
gree and tampered logbooks, nor was he at all acquainted with the
high levels of support the Stewarts had shown toward the project;
SamB had not bought the *Anguillan* that afternoon, so he had not

seen the full-page ad for Dragon Wings spread on the center page. So SamB listened attentively as Dragon put forward his proposal in self-assured fashion, equipped with the confidence of someone who knows he soon will get what he came looking for.

This is no longer a project, Sam—this is a reality. SamB's expression remained unchanged as he weighed his suspicions against the soundness of Dragon's arguments, as he entertained the possibility of all this being more than pure charlatanry. *There is absolutely no reason why you shouldn't join us at Dragon Wings, Sam.* Dragon produced a thin folder and slid it over the glass table in the direction of his friend. The front cover showed the company logo over a bright turquoise background: a pair of orange dragon wings seen from the side, spread upward in full flight, sitting above the name of the airline (also in orange) on the bottom of the page.

Seemingly unimpressed, SamB turned the page, faced the intricate details of the schedule Nathe had proposed to the ECCAA. *Initially we have envisioned eighteen return flights, tallying up to over one hundred legs per week.* Dragon knew his words were of little use at this late stage in his attempt to sell the idea to SamB, but his anxiety was too pressing, his expectancy too large to bear in silence. *We are trying to get a third, larger aircraft before the December 1 deadline, but even without it, we will go ahead with what we have.*

SamB had stopped listening. It was not Dragon who was going to persuade him to change his mind but the actual progress the organization might have made in the previous months, and the commercial potential the airline might carry into its opening flight on December 1.

DRAGON WINGS
WINTER FLIGHT SCHEDULE

Time	Queen Air	Frequency	Flight #
07.00 - 07.10	AXA - SXM	Daily	100
07.40 - 07.50	SXM - AXA		101
08.30 - 09.10	AXA - NEV	Tue	300
09.40 - 09.50	NEV - SKB		311
10.20 - 10.55	SKB - AXA		311
08.30 - 09.10	AXA - NEV	Wed	410
09.40 - 10.10	NEV - BBQ		410
10.45 - 11.30	BBQ - AXA		401
08.30 - 09.10	AXA - NEV	Mon & Sun	430
09.40 - 09.50	NEV - SKB		430
10.25 - 11.00	SKB - BBQ		430
11.30 - 12.15	BBQ - AXA		401
08.30 - 09.10	AXA - NEV	Thu & Sat	520
09.40 - 09.50	NEV - SKB		520
10.20 - 10.55	SKB - ANU		520
11.25 - 12.15	ANU - AXA		511
08.30 - 09.05	AXA - SKB	Friday	440
09.35 - 09.45	SKB - NEV		440
10.20 - 11.05	NEV - BBQ		440
11.35 - 12.20	BBQ - AXA		401
12.00 - 12.10	AXA - SXM	Tue & Wed	110
12.40 - 12.50	SXM - AXA		111
13.10 - 13.20	AXA - SXM	Mon	110
13.50 - 14.00	SXM - AXA		111
13.10 - 13.55	AXA - BBQ	Thu & Sat	400
14.25 - 14.55	BBQ - NEV		411
15.25 - 16.05	NEV - AXA		411
13.10 - 13.55	AXA - BBQ	Fri	400
14.25 - 15.00	BBQ - SKB		421
15.30 - 16.05	SKB - AXA		421
13.10 - 13.55	AXA - BBQ	Tue	400
14.25 - 15.00	BBQ - SKB		431
15.30 - 15.40	SKB - NEV		431
16.10 - 16.50	NEV - AXA		431
13.10 - 13.55	AXA - BBQ	Sun	400
14.25 - 14.55	BBQ - NEV		441
15.25 - 15.35	NEV - SKB		441
16.05 - 16.50	SKB - AXA		441
17.15 - 17.25	AXA - SXM	Daily	120
17.50 - 18.00	SXM - AXA		121

Time	Tri-islander	Frequency	Flight #
08.45 - 09.30	AXA - SKB	Mon	310
10.00 - 10.15	SKB - NEV		310
10.45 - 11.35	NEV - AXA		301
11.45 - 12.55	AXA - ANU	Tue, Thu & Sat	500
13.30 - 14.00	ANU - BBQ		610
15.50 - 16.20	BBQ - ANU		611
16.50 - 18.00	ANU - AXA		501
12.40 - 13.50	AXA - ANU	Wed and Sun	500
14.20 - 15.05	ANU - SKB		620
15.35 - 16.20	SKB - ANU		621
16.50 - 18.00	ANU - AXA		501
14.20 - 15.10	AXA - NEV	Fri	530
15.40 - 16.20	NEV - ANU		530
16.50 - 18.00	ANU - AXA		501
14.30 - 15.20	AXA - BBQ	Mon	540
15.50 - 16.20	BBQ - ANU		540
16.50 - 18.00	ANU - AXA		501

DRAGON WINGS
WINTER ITINERARY

	07.00	08.00	09.00	10.00	11.00	12.00
MON	AXA - SXM: 07.00 - 07.10 SXM - AXA: 07.40 - 07.50	AXA - NEV: 08.30 - 09.10	NEV - SKB: 09.40 - 09.50	SKB - BBQ: 10.25 - 11.00	BBQ - AXA: 11.30 - 12.15	12.15
TUE	AXA - SXM: 07.00 - 07.10 SXM - AXA: 07.40 - 07.50	AXA - SKB: 08.45 - 09.30 AXA - NEV: 08.30 - 09.10	NEV - SKB: 09.40 - 09.50	SKB - NEV: 10.00 - 10.15 NEV - AXA: 10.45 - 11.35 SKB - AXA: 10.20 - 10.55	AXA - ANU: 11.45 -	AXA - SXM: 12.00 - 12.10 SXM - AXA: 12.30 - 12.40 12.55
WED	AXA - SXM: 07.00 - 07.10 SXM - AXA: 07.40 - 07.50	AXA - NEV: 08.30 - 09.10	NEV - BBQ: 09.40 - 10.15	BBQ - AXA: 10.45 - 11.30	11.30	AXA - SXM: 12.00 - 12.10 SXM - AXA: 12.30 - 12.40 AXA - ANU: 12.40 -
THU	AXA - SXM: 07.00 - 07.10 SXM - AXA: 07.40 - 07.50	AXA - NEV: 08.30 - 09.10	NEV - SKB: 09.40 - 09.50	SKB - ANU: 10.20 - 10.55	ANU - AXA: 11.25 - 12.15 AXA - ANU: 11.45 -	12.15 12.55
FRI	AXA - SXM: 07.00 - 07.10 SXM - AXA: 07.40 - 07.50	AXA - SKB: 08.30 - 09.05	SKB - NEV: 09.35 - 09.45	NEV - BBQ: 10.20 - 11.05	BBQ - AXA: 11.35 - 12.20	12.20
SAT	AXA - SXM: 07.00 - 07.10 SXM - AXA: 07.40 - 07.50	AXA - NEV: 08.30 - 09.10	NEV - SKB: 09.40 - 09.50	SKB - ANU: 10.20 - 10.55	ANU - AXA: 11.25 - 12.15 AXA - ANU: 11.45 -	12.15 12.55
SUN	AXA - SXM: 07.00 - 07.10 SXM - AXA: 07.40 - 07.50	AXA - NEV: 08.30 - 09.10	NEV - SKB: 09.40 - 09.50	SKB - BBQ: 10.25 - 11.00	BBQ - AXA: 11.30 - 12.15	12.15 AXA - ANU: 12.40 -

	13.00	14.00	15.00	16.00	17.00
MON	AXA - SXM: 13.10 - 13.20 SXM - AXA: 13.50 - 14.00	AXA - BBQ: 14.30 -	15.20 BBQ - ANU: 15.50 -	ANU - AXA: 16.50 - 16.20	AXA - SXM: 17.15 - 17.25 SXM - AXA: 17.50 - 18.00 18.00
TUE	AXA - BBQ: 13.10 - 13.55 ANU - BBQ: 13.30 - 14.00	BBQ - SKB: 14.25 - 15.00	SKB – NEV: 15.30 - 15.40 BBQ - ANU: 15.50 -	NEV - AXA: 16.10 - 16.50 16.20 ANU - AXA: 16.50 -	AXA - SXM: 17.15 - 17.25 SXM - AXA: 17.50 - 18.00 18.00
WED	13.50	ANU - SKB: 14.20 -	13.05 SKB - ANU: 15.35 -	ANU - AXA: 16.50 - 16.20	AXA - SXM: 17.15 - 17.25 SXM - AXA: 17.50 - 18.00 18.00
THU	AXA - BBQ: 13.10 - 13.55 ANU - BBQ: 13.30 - 14.00	BBQ - NEV: 14.25 - 14.55	NEV - AXA: 15.25 - BBQ - ANU: 15.50 -	16.05 16.20 ANU - AXA: 16.50 -	AXA - SXM: 17.15 - 17.25 SXM - AXA: 17.50 - 18.00 18.00
FRI	AXA - BBQ: 13.10 - 13.55	BBQ - SKB: 14.25 - 15.00 AXA - NEV: 14.20 -	SKB - AXA: 15.30 - 15.10 NEV - ANU: 15.40 -	16.05 ANU - AXA: 16.50 - 16.20	AXA - SXM: 17.15 - 17.25 SXM - AXA: 17.50 - 18.00 18.00
SAT	AXA - BBQ: 13.10 - 13.55 ANU - BBQ: 13.30 - 14.00	BBQ - NEV: 14.25 - 14.55	NEV - AXA: 15.25 - BBQ - ANU: 15.50 -	16.05 ANU - AXA: 16.50 - 16.20	AXA - SXM: 17.15 - 17.25 SXM - AXA: 17.50 - 18.00 18.00
SUN	AXA - BBQ: 13.10 - 13.55 13.50	BBQ - NEV: 14.25 - 14.55 ANU - SKB: 14.20 -	NEV - SKB: 15.25 - 15.35 13.05 SKB - ANU: 15.35 -	SKB - AXA: 16.05 - 16.40 ANU - AXA: 16.50 - 16.20	AXA - SXM: 17.15 - 17.25 SXM - AXA: 17.50 - 18.00 18.00

AXA=ANGUILLA | SKB=ST. KITTS | NEV=NEVIS | BBQ=BARBUDA | ANU=ANTIGUA | BOLD=TRISLANDER | UNDERSCORE=QUEEN AIR

Two or three minutes passed, and they were the longest in Dragon's existence. *There aren't enough flights to Juliana.* Dragon's face lit up as soon as he was able to process SamB's words. *We have only been awarded three daily flights by the authorities at St. Martin—that's half as many as Winair—but so far we haven't been able to squeeze them all into the itinerary.* SamB nodded absentmindedly. *Your stops are too long: you will need fifteen minutes max per stopover. Like that you can make room for a flight at noon to St. Martin to feed the Miami flight.* SamB's detailed knowledge of the airline business made Dragon and his contingent seem every bit as amateur as they were. *You have full liberty to make any changes you deem necessary, Sam.* But Dragon was moving too fast, because in his desperation to have SamB join Dragon Wings he had failed to notice the latter's use of the second-person *you* in his speech, or if he had heard it he had chosen to interpret it as an editorial, general *you*, because no reasonable argument could be brought forward against SamB jumping onboard Dragon Wings, or so Dragon thought, or so Dragon wanted to think.

But SamB made it clear he was making no changes at all. *I'm just giving you a piece of advice because I like you, that's all.* And Dragon understood that this was the cue for the real negotiation to start. Because Dragon still harbored no doubt in his mind that SamB was prepared to join Dragon Wings—but the question that had suddenly, unexpectedly, but also quite reasonably arisen was at what price would he have to be bought. SamB leaned back in his chair, looked straight into Dragon's blue eyes. *The truth, Dragon, is you need me. Desperately.* Dragon had no nerve to deny such statement. *Here are my conditions: I want my job title to be Chief Pilot. I want a 10 percent increase in my current salary. And I want a 10 percent share in the company.*

The time for friendly favors had clearly passed, but Dragon was neither surprised nor disturbed by the shift in SamB's attitude. Dragon Jones was not surprised or angered, but he was also not ready to give away 10 percent of an enterprise that had finally found the cash to move forward and the credit to build a small fleet. The prospects for the future had never looked more promising and *you know I cannot possibly afford to give you 10 percent, Sam. That amounts to a signing bonus of 100K.* But SamB's stare never dropped, and his attitude was unrelenting, and, *Don't be so hasty, Dragon, consult your partners and let me know.*

The following day, Dragon Jones called for an extraordinary meeting of the board of directors of Dragon Wings, including its new partner, Glenallen Rawlingson, who fiercely opposed the idea of Samuel Bedingford joining the airline as a shareholder. *This is our only chance of getting an expert pilot with experience in the region to lead our operation, Glen,* and Nathaniel Jones agreed with his son *but there is absolutely no way we can afford to part with 10 percent of the company.* Officially, Sheila remained the largest shareholder in Dragon Wings with 45 percent, although up until that point percentages had made a very small difference, since every decision had been reached collectively and unanimously. *If de man ask for 10 percent, go offer him foive.* Glenallen Rawlingson was still against offering Samuel Bedingford anything at all, but he saw in the way the negotiation took shape an opportunity to profit from the situation and, *I only agreeing to givin' away dem shares if I kyan purchase de same amount at de same time as he for a preferential price.*

The first call of the day on that hot, stale, muggy Monday morning right at the start of October was to SamB. Five percent was not what he had requested, and even 7 percent seemed a far cry from what he had in mind, but *successful relationships are built on compromise, Dragon, and if this airline is going to survive the first year or two, we're going to have to be ready to meet each other halfway,* and before SamB could describe this as his first gesture of good faith, Dragon had already noticed the friendliness restored in his tone of voice—a change that in his mind was well worth the final half percent of the word *compromise.*

The second call of the day on that hot, stale, muggy Monday

afternoon was to Deianira Walker's office to arrange an appointment to make the suitable amendments to the legal scaffolding
that held Dragon Wings together, to bring Samuel Bedingford into
the equation, to increase the company's capital by US $70,000, to
raise Glenallen Rawlingson's stake and reform the corporation's
statutes. Thus it was that right at the start of October, the crucial
month in the realization of an extravagant fantasy, what once had
been no more than a mature man's dream, a young professional's
adventure, and a local woman's brave token of love was trans-
formed into a complex joint venture directed by a board that no
longer required unanimity (but a two-thirds majority) to reach a
decision and which now comprised Sheila Rawlingson-Jones (38
percent), Glenallen Rawlingson (28.5 percent), Nathaniel Jones
(13 percent), Dragon Jones (13 percent), and Samuel Bedingford
(7.5 percent).

October was the crucial month in the realization of some version or other of the original plan to set up an operational airline
based in Anguilla by December 1, and if the crucial meeting was
that between Dragon and SamB, the crucial element was the fulfillment of an unofficial promise to equip Dragon Wings with a
preapproved credit line to finance the purchase of a Britten Norman Trislander through a secured loan from the Indigenous Bank
of Anguilla. Sheila Rawlingson-Jones monitored the transaction—
slow, time-consuming, fastidious—but with completion all but a
certainty, the next urgent step was to devise a plan to form a small
team of two or three workers in each of the airline's destinations.

Dragon Jones spent the best part of the forty days that followed flying from one island to the next, getting to know in detail
the staff at Juliana Airport in St. Martin, the premises at Robert
L. Bradshaw Airport in St. Kitts, evaluating candidates at Amory
Airport in Nevis and Codrington Airport in Barbuda, haggling
for a better rate for a counter at V.C. Bird Airport in Antigua, vig-
orously driving forward a spontaneous plan that to a large extent

was still in the making. Six weeks later—just three weeks before D(ecember 1) day—he embarked on the five-day tour of the Leeward Islands—starting in St. Martin and finishing in Antigua— that would bring an end to the flurry of recruitment that had possessed Dragon Wings. By then, SamB had already contracted the services of Ngowe Adabor, the Nigerian pilot with the round face and startled white eyes, Joost van der Minden, a Dutch skipper with little experience but linguistic versatility, and Lauretta Williams, a Jamaican stewardess with long legs and thin ankles arrived from BWIA after their latest staff reduction.

Meanwhile, Nathaniel Jones—enthused as ever with the importance of corporate image—looked into the possibility of having the two-aircraft fleet coated in the customary colors of Dragon Wings. The original quote sent to him by Pinturas Borinquen, the Puerto Rican propeller plane painting company, suggested a white background with two stripes on either side of the hull—one turquoise, one orange—and the logo of the airline on the rudder. But Nathaniel was not ready to hold back on anything, so he requested a second quote for the hulls and wings in turquoise and *Dragon Wings* to be etched in orange across the body of the planes. The second option was more than double the original price and well exceeded their budget for aircraft refurbishment, but Dragon was too busy assembling a half-acceptable team of employees, and Sheila could waste no time on anything other than procuring the V2 registration for the Trislander, and SamB only thought of pilots and route guides, distances and procedures, and Arturo Sarmiento spent half his weeks in Antigua and the other half complaining about his instructor, and Glenallen Rawlingson took no part in the day-to-day running of the business, so Nathaniel Jones disregarded the airline's budget and *how soon can you have them ready?* David González at Pinturas Borinquen sensed the importance of his answer, felt obliged to promise the world, or what amounts to the same thing: *Two weeks from the time you land in San Juan.*

But once the deal was closed and the down payment made and the planes flown to San Juan, complications began to arise. The paint was, of course, hard to get; the exact shade of turquoise, elusive; the logo, difficult to reproduce. In the face of these mundane if predictable problems Nathaniel's patience revealed itself as thin as David González proved resourceful in his fabrications. Two weeks soon turned to three, to four, to five, and they might well have carried on tallying way past the boiling point of Nathaniel's rage, but luckily for him and the rest of his partners David González called one Wednesday morning to let everyone at Dragon Wings know that everything was okay and that the planes would be ready for pickup on Friday—twenty-three days late, yet still on time.

SamB, Ngowe Adabor, and Joost van der Minden, the young Dutchman with the face of a toddler and the build of a rake, flew to San Juan on Friday morning to find that the Queen Air and the Trislander that sat so beautifully on the runway had been covered in a shade of turquoise that was slightly too blue, not green enough, too deep, and, crucially, not ready. The excuse escaped SamB's ears, who was only interested in knowing when the airplanes would be fit for flying without damaging the paint job— *Tomorrow, Mr. Bedingford, without doubt*—and in forcing Pinturas Borinquen to take care of the three pilots' accommodation in San Juan for the night. It was then, during a fortuitous and unplanned stay in Puerto Rico, that SamB heard the news that would feed his greed and trigger his imagination into devising an ambitious plan of expansion for the nascent airline: Air Tampa—a small regional carrier—would have its assets—including four nineteen-seat Do 228s and four thirty-seat Short 330s—liquidated.

Long before Dragon Wings's inaugural flight, SamB already considered replacing and upgrading its current fleet the key for the long-term success of the company.

XII

It was quite easy, really. The toughest part was to put up with that prick, Michael Haywood. Back to little, gullible Anguilla. I quite liked spending time in Antigua—it's still a hole, but at least it's larger, livelier, better than this. *Drunken idiot, I don't know who he thinks he is. Anyway, that's enough about me, let's talk about you.* Her tits must be fake, but to be honest, who cares? Damn, I might have made a mistake there—she has absolutely nothing to say. Don't talk, honey, just shake those hips and look away. She is cross-eyed and that really drives me insane. It's like she's talking to two different versions of me at the same time. One eye talks to my eyes or my mouth—I have noticed her watching my mouth with hunger—and the other eye talks to my elbow, or my shoulder, or the Guinness poster by the bar: suddenly you're not there anymore, suddenly I'm not me.

Oh, it was nothing much. Most of it was boring stuff: hours and hours with an instructor, that Michael Haywood. I swear, I don't know who he thinks he is. I guess he was alright for what I needed him. I guess I wouldn't have been able to fly tomorrow if it hadn't been for him. So, tell me, where do you live? Please do tell me where we're going to finish the night—at your place or mine. I can't stay here forever, I need to fly tomorrow. And I definitely can't look at those crossed eyes for much longer. The way her left eye looks out into space really freaks me out.

But her fake tits look great—they *must* be fake—and her tiny, little waist seems so fragile, and her ass looks so fine, and I'm going to do her from behind anyway so I won't have to watch her squinting left eye staring into nothing while she looks at me.

It's been really hectic, yes. Everyone in the office has been very busy, very stressed the last couple of weeks. Last week we had trial runs to the different destinations. That's why you've seen so many flights come in and out. No, I couldn't fly until this week but I still went as navigator a few times, just to get used to the aircrafts and the routes. I can't keep on talking about this. It's what I do all day, I don't want to waste my nights going through it as well. And I can't look at her eyes anymore. *Let's go dancing.* That millenary island dance, so erotic, so submissive: face away and arouse me. It's a bit like a mellow version of pole dancing in which you are, quite literally, the pole. I like being the pole. I'm certainly relieved not to see her look at me somewhere I am not. There's no way I'll be able to handle those eyes in the morning. I'll have to take her home tonight. The way she shifts the weight of her body from one leg to the other, swaying her butt gently, tells me this will be a good night.

I hold her tight, I bend with her, and suddenly, in the distance, a pair of eyes shine in the middle of the dark room. That loose silver dress is something else. Her thin legs make her look svelte, her delicate movement carries something more than elegance with it, something lustful. I know that girl. I've seen her before, but between the distance and the darkness I can't make out who she is. My dancing partner has noticed my distraction. She's bent forward, holding her knees with her hands and thrusting herself backward. And yet I can't take my eyes from that other face. I *do* know you. Of course I know you. I bet a wild instinct lies beneath that exuberant body. *Why don't we go somewhere else, somewhere quieter.* Meanwhile, I *will* see *you* again.

The night was long and I had nightmares after I got back from dropping her off at Stoney Ground. I feared her eyes in the morning and it turns out I dreamed of them all night. I was in a forest being watched by thousands of birds, all of which looked away, and I tried to catch them watching me but they never faced me, and I tried to chase them but they weren't scared, and that made *me* scared. But all that is gone now, because now I have four gold stripes on the epaulets on my shoulders and four gold rings on the sleeves of my jacket, and they make me untouchable.

Eight passengers at the back get an especially cordial treatment because this is Dragon Wings's inaugural flight. I was chosen to do the honors out of the pool of four pilots as a reward for my "effort and commitment." Not that I give a shit, but it *is* nice to be in control of a commercial flight once again. To be the skipper, the captain, the law. *Clayton J. Lloyd control, this is Dragon Wings flight 100 to Juliana Airport, requesting permission for takeoff.* The traffic of private jets hasn't really started yet and we are the first scheduled departure of the day. Anguilla has a long runway, Juliana's is even longer, and the flight time is around seven minutes. Literally up and down. This couldn't be easier. Gentle push forward of the left throttle, turn right, and the empty runway opens up in front. Full throttle, forty knots, sixty, eighty, liftoff, and the most outrageous fantasy in the history of this never-never land comes true.

PART IV

I

The end of Dragon Wings was ordained long before a Beechcraft Queen Air painted in the wrong shade of turquoise—slightly too blue, not green enough, too deep— took off from Clayton J. Lloyd International Airport on the morning of December 1 to take eight passengers to Princess Juliana International Airport, seven minutes away, across the channel, on the Dutch side of the neighboring island of St. Martin. Dragon Wings would only exist as long as Dragon Jones remained in the company, but it had been an integral part of Glenallen Rawlingson's scheme from the very moment he agreed to buy a 21 percent stake in the business eventually to rid it, and possibly even the island, of the Joneses—senior, junior, and, if necessary, also in-law—in order to gain complete control of the airline.

The conditions SamB had imposed to join Dragon Wings initially seemed to hinder Glenallen Rawlingson's prospects, but after closer consideration he understood that the occasion presented him instead with the perfect opportunity to secure control of the board of directors without raising much suspicion: Glenallen knew that the Joneses would agree to anything within reason to get the candidate they wanted as their chief pilot, including parting not only with the 7.5 percent share demanded by SamB but also an additional 7.5 percent which would simply be transferred from Sheila's stock to his. Just like that, the Joneses were relinquishing 15 percent of a company in which Glenallen already

owned 21 percent. All he had to do now was get SamB on his side
and together the two of them would have the power to block any
initiative proposed by the Joneses: the path to seizing the Anguillan flag carrier from the hands of these foreigners had already
been outlined. It was a path in which SamB played a prominent
role, and the time had come to start traveling it.

But Glenallen Rawlingson was not the only person in Anguilla plotting against the Joneses and their airline; secretly and
manifestly against the wishes of his sister, Bacchus Stewart had
begun devising a plan to ensure the downfall of the future airline
from the very moment he realized he would be forced in his capacity as director of the Indigenous Bank of Anguilla to support
the venture. Bacchus had plainly refused to enter into a partnership with the Rawlingsons and he had made so much clear to
Gwendolyn on a visit just a day or two after he had read back
to front the proposal Sheila Rawlingson had left at Auntie Gwen's
house in Island Harbour. *Is for dat you de strong man in de bank, you
know. You ain' got to do nuttin' for youself if you kyan do it t'rough de
bank. Dem white folks love playin' 'roun' wit' odder people money, you know.
Go ahead. Give 'em plenty money from de bank: dem goan go spen' it all
an' come back for some more. Tzaz, dat when you get dem good, boy,* and
Auntie Gwen's words got lost in a cackle that was part laughter,
part cough. Gwendolyn's plan was consistent with the way things
had worked at the Stewarts' bank before the Caribbean Central
Bank had intervened and merged it with the Bank of the Leeward
Islands, but Bacchus knew that given the present circumstances
he would not have the same liberty of action he had enjoyed at
the Anguilla Home and Trust Bank. Uncannily, Bacchus Stewart
had not even had to raise the issue at the meeting of the board of
directors of the Indigenous Bank of Anguilla, because Glenallen
Rawlingson had done so instead, and not only that but he had
also proposed to back the financing of their aircrafts with secure
loans. For once, Bacchus seconded Glenallen's motion, and for

all practical purposes in Anguilla, a motion that enjoyed the support of the Stewarts and the Rawlingsons was a motion that was approved pretty much automatically. The Rawlingsons and their pitiful little airline had walked right into Bacchus's trap, and he hadn't even had to deploy it.

Yet, all through the month of December neither Glenallen Rawlingson's nor Bacchus Stewart's mischievous plots gained much relevance, because, all predictions to the contrary, it was the Joneses who laughed first. Dragon Wings's aggressive strategy to break into the regional market saw the company slogan (*With Dragon Wings paradise is just one hop away*) printed everywhere, from newspapers, to placards, to magazines all over the Leeward Islands, but it was the price war triggered by their schedule of daily flights to/from each of their five destinations which earned the airline the favor of most passengers. The slow start at the beginning of December turned out to be the ideal introduction for Nathaniel and his crew into the practical issues surrounding the business. Occasional miscommunication, double bookings, and technical glitches proved inconsequential because the relevant flights were half-empty anyway, and solutions were available. Pretty, distinctive, small, and cheap, Dragon Wings was the sort of operation that everyone was willing to forgive, and soon enough even some of the regional newspapers engaged the airline to distribute their product abroad. If Dragon Wings's attempt to take the region by storm had posed a palpable danger of overexposure, heading into the most important week of the year in Anguilla it seemed as if the gamble was paying off.

The peak of the high season in the Caribbean spans the fortnight between Christmas Eve and Epiphany. That's the period during which the core of the yearly income is generated, certainly in the tourist industry—and tourism is just about the only major industry there is in Anguilla. Dragon Wings faced the same challenges as the rest of such industry during this period: for twelve

consecutive days Dragon Wings faced the organizational challenge of catering to the most demanding clientele imaginable, of
providing efficient service, of adapting to the constraints of a tight
schedule, of turning a makeshift airline into a smooth operation.
The team at Dragon Wings was not experienced enough to fore-
see or prevent the problems that would arise, nor had they worked
together long enough to achieve the coordination necessary to run
a business from a handful of different locations. In fact, Dragon
Wings was in no way prepared to face the peak of the high season
in the Caribbean, so when the Jones family nucleus and their associates encountered the same challenges as the rest of the tourist
industry in Anguilla, the shortcomings of their organization
inevitably became exposed.

But the Joneses had resilience and commitment and luck, and
the problems that arose were not all that serious, and delays were
to be expected from a brand-new operation. So December came
and went, and by the end of the first month in business, Dragon
Wings averaged a seat occupancy of close to 70 percent, and though
punctuality was rather low (on the 80 percent range), most flights
had only been slightly delayed, and passenger satisfaction seemed
acceptable, and passenger yield remained high. Thus, regardless
of separate plans to ensure the failure of Dragon Wings, the Joneses
managed to turn the challenges brought by the peak of the high
season in Anguilla into their first taste of success. Little did anyone know how sparing success would be in providing them with a
second tasting, but later on, when it was all over, it would be clear
to Dragon and Nathaniel that no matter how lofty, when weighed
against the resources and experience at their disposal, their
ambition had been disproportionate—indeed, foolishly so.

II

D espite the improvisations that had characterized the setting up of the airline during the weeks previous to December 1, things had gotten off to a good start in all areas:
SamB's expert eye had proven spotless in his choice of pilots, both
of whom were able and responsible. His awareness of human
limitations, on the other hand, seemed more amiss when Lauretta
Williams, the Jamaican stewardess with the long legs and thin ankles, showed up at the offices of Dragon Wings in the Business
Center one morning—dark rings crawling around her eyes, hair
wildly unkempt—asking when she would finally get a day off. She
had been assisting the passengers on the afternoon flight to/from
Antigua for the past ten days in a row, and was yet to meet the
person who would share such responsibility with her. The reason
she had not yet met the person who would share her job on the
flights to Antigua and any other journeys that required a hostess
was because such person was yet to be employed. It would still be
many days until Lauretta Williams could finally take a day off.
When she did, she took five all at once, and spent two of them
sleeping. Yet her complaint did not go unheard. Instead, it opened
the second phase of recruitment at Dragon Wings, this time not
so much an overwhelming flood as a steady flow.

SamB's expert eye had proven spotless in his choice of pilots,
and Dragon Jones's natural instinct for human behavior had once
again revealed itself because only two of the twenty-two people

Dragon had hired during the flurry that had been the recruitment process at Dragon Wings during the month of October had had to be dismissed. Added to these two replacements, the airline was looking to expand by two members the team at Juliana and to engage the engineers who had once served under Leyland Airways to complement the team of ECCAA-authorized engineers at Clayton J. Lloyd International Airport in Anguilla. This was the natural rate of growth for an airline which had been put together quickly and inexpertly by a group of people who had become associates more by the doings of chance than by thoughtful calculation. This was the natural rate of growth for a small airline which had shown more promise during its first few weeks of life than anyone could rightfully have expected.

As it turned out, this was all the growth Dragon Wings could have withstood, but the board of directors could/would/did not understand this, because Nathaniel Jones was more interested in building the small empire he had originally envisioned than he was in making a profitable business, and Sheila Rawlingson-Jones rediscovered her desire to distance herself from the enterprise she had once opposed so fiercely and which in time had become the only connection between her and the (white, old) man she began to suspect she no longer loved, and Glenallen Rawlingson was desperate to promote any sort of activity that would jeopardize the stability of the corporation to deploy his plan of conspiracy. So on January 17, when Samuel Bedingford put forward his ambitious plan of expansion for the airline, and he explained how *this whole venture has been focusing on the wrong targets from the start*, and he highlighted the impracticalities of building a heterogeneous fleet of planes, and *the Trislander was a good option when there was nothing else available but this is an opportunity to upgrade and correct the mistakes that were made in the early stages of the assembling of this airline*; in short, when SamB proposed to take the aggressive strategy that Dragon Wings had adopted to break into the regional market one bullyish step further by putting the Trislander back on the market and joining the bid for two of Air Tampa's Short 330s, Nathaniel's first reaction was not outrage but rather curiosity: *How exactly do you propose we finance two aircrafts that together will cost us over three-quarters of a million dollars?*

The answer to that question rolled off Glenallen Rawlingson's tongue without him so much as having to formulate the words in his mind before speaking them: *Considerin' our current liquid assets, de initial success of de operation, and de cost of de aircraft, it would not be unreasonable to request further support from the Indigenous Bank of Anguilla.*

The only one squarely against the idea was Dragon, who advocated for a more conservative strategy: *Six weeks into our operation is not the time to upgrade, Sam. Right now, what we need to do is consolidate.*

But consolidation was not as popular as expansion, and *we might never again get the opportunity to purchase a plane so fit for our operation,* and, *This will effectively launch us into the prolific French Antilles market,* and, *How can our profitability be hampered by flights to St. Barths, French St. Martin, Guadeloupe, and Martinique?*

Two months into the life of Dragon Wings and a few days into the lull that in January follows the peak of the high season, the airline's board of directors resolved that instead of concentrating on the successful management of its already considerably large area of operation, instead of gathering data from its performance in December and analyzing it to source the origin of the various difficulties encountered, instead of focusing on the development of a flawless, professional service, the company would explore the possibility of purchasing at least one if not two Short 330s—*There's no point in doing this by halves, if we're going ahead with it we have to do it all the way*—from Air Tampa, stretching its resources to the limit in order to adopt a policy of expansion that entailed forming additional teams of employees, mediating with individual governments simultaneously, and negotiating route concessions.

III

walk into the friendly, familiar environment of The Old Mill and am greeted by its ever-smiling owner. You would think we're family by the welcome I get in this place every time I come here. The dining room is small and generally cozy but there is hardly anyone here tonight, and tonight I need company. *I'll just eat at the bar, if that's alright.* Tex-Mex, pizza, barbecue grill (Anguilla's national dish): the usual reliable, simple stuff.

Boy, you lookin' rough, man. You workin' too hard! Angie, the bartender at The Old Mill, is all smiles, always joking, constantly on everyone's case. I enjoy exchanging a few pleasantries with her, even if they are always the same jokes, always the same tongue-in-cheek abuse. But my nerves are soothed by this simple chitchat and a cheap laugh works wonders while she fixes my rum-and-Coke, and the first sip tingles the taste buds on my tongue and all of a sudden the world of problems just recedes a little and I can breathe again.

This is the first night I have been able to take "off" since December 1. Work has been relentless since our opening flight and there is no sign of things slowing down. Suddenly, leaving the office at eight p.m. to go straight to the Mill for dinner has become an early night. I haven't been to the beach in three months, I haven't played golf in four. I think I was probably slightly more tan when I arrived from London last May than I am at the moment. This is not what I expected from work in paradise.

Two couples—white, sunburned tourists—walk in and sit in the dining area. They are just about the only people here, and the room becomes a bit sinister. At the bar, two of the usual suspects sit in their corners, like every night, staring into nothing, saying nothing, simply stirring their drinks with religious devotion. I have eaten my meal and prepare to join them in their ritual when, out of nowhere, Sheila Rawlingson walks through the door. Our eyes lock, we've made contact, and though she looks uncomfortable she has no alternative—she is almost forced by circumstance to approach me at the bar.

I wish Sheila wasn't here tonight. This is my first night off in weeks and now there is a sense of inevitability about our conversation drifting into Dragon Wings. We both pretend to be surprised to find the other here, we both pretend to be glad, but soon enough there is nothing else to talk about. *You here wit' SamB?* SamB is not in the rotation to fly tomorrow, but I've hardly been out with him since he joined us at the airline.

Nah, SamB and I aren't on the best of terms right now. He didn't take kindly to me not backing his plan of expansion for Dragon Wings last week. Even at that stage it was plain to see that SamB and I no longer enjoyed the same relationship as before, but something snapped with that vote that cannot be undone, something I hadn't seen coming up to that point. It's true that the Business Center and the airport lounge were the only places I had seen him in weeks, but the main reason for this was that work was hectic. Or so I thought.

Don' take it personally, nuh, we all been too stressy-stressy dem last few weeks. I get the feeling Sheila is no longer talking about SamB. Is she talking about herself? Is she talking about her relationship with Nathe? I don't want to think about Nathe tonight. I just don't want to think.

What have you been stressed about, Sheila? I didn't want to meet Sheila here tonight, but now that she's here we might as well make the most of the situation. She talks about routes, about prospects, about pieces of luggage left behind in some island or another.

You really don' t'ink we should buy dem big planes? Oh God, let me forget, please let me forget, just leave me alone and stop talking about this stupid airline.

"*Dem big planes,*" Sheila, *will be the end of us. You can mark my words.* I shake my head, eyes fixed on the empty glass in front of me, and ask for another rum-and-Coke.

Sheila grabs Angie by the wrist amicably, gives her an affectionate look, asks for a daiquiri. Christ, this woman is beautiful! She knows it as well, she just cannot help it. But Sheila is not teasing me tonight. As a matter of fact, I don't think Sheila is any happier to see me here than I was when I first saw her walk through the door. Why is she uneasy? Was she hoping to meet someone else here tonight? Maybe that someone else will still show up. Maybe she doesn't want me to see her with that other person.

Let's not talk about business, Sheila, okay? Let's just talk about something else.

She's startled by my comment. I've interrupted her mid-sentence and the silence that follows gives away the fact that we only have two things in common, and I don't want to think about one of them or talk about the other.

I'm drinking these too quickly. *Are you alright, Dragon?*

Am I alright? I just want *another rum-and-Coke, Angie, please.* Am I alright? No, Sheila, I'm not alright and you are not either. *Why do you ask? Can you help, Sheila, if I'm not?*

I feel the anger brewing inside my chest, I see the situation developing long before it gets that far, but something tells me to keep going, something doesn't let me stop. *Are you still having fun, Sheila?* Now that she has a reason to be serious, she looks less uncomfortable. She doesn't seem upset— there's certainly none of the anger brewing inside my chest in her expression—but she no longer needs to pretend. She sips her daiquiri solemnly, not restlessly, like it's a duty to be taken seriously, even though she knows there is no respite to be found in it. *I mean, that's what this is all about, isn't it? Just a bit of fun,* and she asks if I mean, life. Do I mean life? What do I mean? And what does she? No, I didn't mean life, *I was talking about something simpler,* but never mind. The rum is getting to my head. I should have gone easier on the booze. Oh well, too late now. *I was talking about you and me, Sheila, you and me, here, tonight.* Tonight and some other night. Some other night, like the other night. *You remember the other night, Sheila?*

What other night? How do you mean? She's good, this woman. What other night? Good, good. Very good.

The other night, by the bonfire, under the starlit sky, dancing to the music, that was fun, right? That was fun. That was lovely. *You are lovely, Sheila.* But you know that. Of course you know that. Why wouldn't you know that?

You need to go home, Dragon.

I need to go home. Do I? I'll go home if you take me, hun, that's for sure. *You want to go home with me?* C'mon, just come with me. I'll treat you right, I'll make you feel like a lady, not like the whore that you are. *I'll take you home, let's go,* and she looks at me with emotion—there is something in the glint of her eyes, something deep, something powerful, there is a passion to be found there, and I don't mean lust. I don't mean anger either. The anger is all stored up inside my chest, brewing, simmering, waiting to erupt. What is it, Sheila, that hides behind your eyes? *What?* C'mon, Sheila, tell me *What?* Why are you looking at me with those eyes? Maybe it's just compassion. Yeah, that's what it is, she's just feeling sorry for me, isn't she? But there's no need to be feeling sorry for Dragon, let me tell you. Dragon does what Dragon wants to do. *Come, let's finish all this business at my place.* Stop it? Why should I stop it? *What? What's the problem? You don't feel like whoring around with me? At least like that you'd be keeping it in the family.*

The sting of her palm on my cheek still pricks me. I'm sitting at the bar, finishing my rum. I must have had four or five. I had too many. My face is still cool from the water but my cheek burns with the shape of her slap. Sheila's gone. She walked out the door the same way she walked in, out of nowhere. At least she won't be meeting anyone tonight, she won't be whoring around. I guess I shouldn't have said that. I guess it's none of my business. To think that this was my first night off since December 1. Well, that's gone down well, hasn't it? Not quite as planned. Now I'm on my own in my private corner of the bar. I didn't want to be on my own tonight. I didn't want to be with Sheila either. To think that just a few months ago, back in the summer, everything—Sheila, SamB, Dragon Wings—seemed so exciting, so alluring, so much fun. What difference six months can make. All the fun has been sapped from this venture, and all we're left to think about is what might have been. What might have been, had things been altogether different. Meanwhile, the times are as trying as ever, and the only motivation to continue this ordeal is not to come out of it looking like a total fool. To save some face regardless of the cost—is that too dear a price to pay for dignity?

Enough self-punishing. Tomorrow will be a brand-new toiling day and I need my rest. *Let me settle my bill, Angie, please,* and, *This one's on the house.*

IV

The weeks that followed the peak of the tourist season in Anguilla saw the return to the island of its natural pace of life, as the periodic invasion of foreign visitors receded with predictable regularity on or around January 6. The calm weeks that followed Epiphany brought back to Anguilla a dose of the quietness that during the rest of the year is nothing less than customary—except that then it came impregnated with the mixed emotions evoked by the relative opulence left behind by the departing tourists, by the unsettling knowledge that the best—the most lucrative—part of the year had already past, that whatever ground had been lost would most likely not be made up in the next eleven months.

The weeks that follow the exodus of Three Kings' Day is known among Anguillans as "the lull of January"—a period during which the local population can catch their breath, regroup for the restart of the season, and indulge, however briefly, in the luxuries made affordable by the exertions of a hectic fortnight. The lull of January is by no means as dramatic as the collapse of September or as long as the break of the summer, but it is a pause alright—a pause during which the occupancy of hotels and restaurants is substantially reduced, a pause during which the stock in shops and the energy of workers are replenished to last for the rest of the season.

All predictions to the contrary, Dragon Wings managed to

negotiate the month of December and the peak of the high season with reasonable success. Despite glitches, shortcomings, and
organizational misjudgments, Dragon Wings had shown more
promise during its first few weeks of life than anyone could rightfully have expected. However, instead of using the lull of January
to examine the cause of the numerous drawbacks that had arisen
during the first month of operation, instead of making use of the
temporary ease in the organizational demands to envision means
of preventing similar operational inconveniences in the future,
the board of directors of Dragon Wings opted to implement a
dangerous strategy of expansion and to pursue the bidding for the
thirty-seat Short 330s being liquidated by Air Tampa.

So, the lull of January came and, before long, it went, and
while the resolve of the board of directors meant that the entire
team focused its activity almost exclusively on the expansion of an
airline that was yet to prove its mettle, while SamB spent most of
his days fulfilling the demands of a busy schedule and elucidating
a productive plan that would take the Wings into the realms of
the French Antilles, while Sheila rediscovered the origins of her
name and swayed toward the Rawlingsons as she joined heads
with Uncle Glen to work out the best approach to persuade the
Indigenous Bank of Anguilla to lend their support to the ambitious strategy of expansion advanced by SamB and embraced by
the rest of the airline's board of directors (bar Dragon), while
Nathaniel was absorbed in the intricacies of contacting the administrators of the now-defunct Air Tampa, of making clear to
them not only Dragon Wings's interest in the 330s but also the
urgency of such interest, of deploying his skills as negotiator and
of making them work their magic, Dragon was left on his own to
deal with the demands of the daily operation of the airline.

But because Dragon Jones was the only member of the board
of directors who had voted against the adoption of such strategy,
and because he remained firm in his conviction that the timing

for such action was ill conceived, there was a tendency within the high command of the airline to disregard his concerns for the efficiency and viability of the operation as disproportionate.

Thus, when Dragon Jones pointed out that the 40 percent subsidy promised by the government of Anguilla stipulated only flights that included Anguilla as origin or destination, *which, given our extensive schedule, equates to roughly 70 percent of our flights, so the real extent of the subsidy comes to no more than 28 percent of our total passenger miles,* the only reaction he could get from his partners was a general acknowledgment that the airline could clearly not survive exclusively on the revenue derived from the government's subsidy—but that was not the idea in the first place. *The subsidy has always been conceived as an insurance policy to contribute to the running costs of the airline.* Similarly, when Dragon proposed to choose a quiet spell during the lull of January to bring together for a day the supervisors from each of the five islands where Dragon Wings conducted business in order for them to meet each other, raise issues, propose solutions, and discuss methods of coordination, the idea was commended for its positive intention but deemed uneconomical, premature, unproductive, and ultimately unnecessary.

Once the ease on the organizational requirements of the airline's operation was lifted by the restart of the season, by the proximity of Mardi Gras, by the flocking return of expectant travelers, it became evident that the wasted time would be costly. Little had been done during the lull of January to optimize or even improve Dragon Wings's improvised operation, but because little went wrong during the calm weeks that followed the peak of the high season, the limitations of the setup remained disguised and the previous complications were dismissed either as elements inherent to the nature of the business or as temporary hiccups to be expected from any new venture. Inevitably, then, as soon as the busy schedule operated by Dragon Wings was again pushed to the limit by high occupancy levels, by equally high expectations, the lessons that should have been processed during the lull of January crept up again and proved to be unlearned.

Consequently, February was a difficult month to cope with, and by the time March had come and gone the enterprise had become a nightmare. But because everyone was too busy day-dreaming about an ambitious strategy of expansion that would see Dragon Wings emerge as the strongest airline in the Leeward Islands, no one actually realized that the initial sympathy extended toward the company was progressively eroding, as the company's reputation slipped well below that of their most disreputable competitors, as the cheap prices offered by the airline were equated with the worst service imaginable. In fact, no one even listened to Dragon as he announced from his alienated corner the weekly list of cancellations, delays, and disruptions that grew on his desk like moss.

Dragon sat in silent amusement some weeks later when the collective eyes of his partners were forced open by the largest organizational meltdown conceivable: a collapse in the server made the web page where bookings were stored inaccessible. It had not yet occurred to anyone to develop an internal network to share information and no manual record was ever kept in any of the offices of Dragon Wings. The consequences were disastrous: for five hours that day, staff in the different airports where Dragon Wings was supposed to fly were unable to reach records of any reservations; no data was found anywhere specifying the amount of passengers booked on any of the flights; some passengers brought printouts of their confirmation page, others arrived with confirmation codes, but others still came along with nothing more than a passport and a destination. Delays were such that the late flight to Antigua had to be canceled for fear that it would not be able to get back to Anguilla during daylight hours; bags were sent to all corners of the Leeward Islands; passengers with connections to Europe had to be flown in a separate charter at Dragon Wings's expense. It was later discovered that two passengers had taken advantage of the situation to hitch a free ride, while another was left behind despite having checked in himself and his bag two hours early. Dragon Wings had hit its lowest point yet.

V

F riday night and I'm not scheduled to fly tomorrow. What a delight. To think that it has come to the point where I'm actually excited about the prospect of a night out at The Velvet. Go figure. But after living in this desert for seven months, you have to take whatever you can get. As my uncle used to say, in times of war any hole will make a trench. Although if I'm honest, I have wasted chances to get inside a couple of girls' pants in the last few weeks. But that other girl has really gotten into my head. Who would have guessed? Then again, she isn't just any girl. She is exuberant and delicate and yet she can't disguise her lustful nature. I hope she shows up at The Velvet tonight. I *really* hope she turns up at The Velvet tonight. But if she doesn't, I won't miss another opportunity to get laid. Tonight, I'm on the hunt. Tonight, I'll take home anything I can pick up—and I *will* pick up something. But how I wish she'd come to The Velvet tonight, how I wish it to be her whom I take home tonight.

I have seen her here twice already. Last time she was with that lame kid, the son of the former chief minister. He had his hands all over her pretty little body. I made certain she saw me but I pretended I hadn't seen her. I've got one on you, but you don't know I do. I won't do the same tonight, though. If she shows up tonight, I'll go up to her and take my chances. I don't care about Nathaniel. I don't care about Dragon or the

On the Way Back

Wings. I'll just go up to her and see what happens. How that girl has gotten so far inside my head, I do not know. But all I do is think of her, and all I think of is her pretty little body wrapped in mine, her svelte figure beneath mine, her perfect legs spread wide, allowing my passage, relinquishing to me. There is a savage instinct in Sheila Rawlingson. An instinct that I'm sure Nathaniel Jones has been neglecting—if he has been able to find it at all, that is. This girl doesn't want to sit on the board of directors of an airline. She is young and beautiful and lustful. She wants to have fun. She wants to savor what it's like to be a woman. She wants a real man to make her feel fulfilled, and comfortable, and pleased. I'll show her what it's like to be with a real man, I'll show her what kind of a man I can be for her if she shows up tonight.

The Velvet is such a dingy place, just a small wooden shack, a coat of white paint chipping from the corners, and a few of the planks rotting from the sea water. Every time I come here I get more surprised how much fun you can have in such a terrible venue. By the looks of it, you wouldn't think you could enjoy a single minute in this barrack. And yet, life in Anguilla is boosted with a dose of excitement every Friday night, the only night of the week when The Velvet is buzzing. There is an element of uncertainty to Friday nights: you never know what's going to happen, you never know who's going to show up or where it's all going to end.

There she is, dancing away, quietly, gently, almost erotically, at the opposite corner of the bar. This is my chance, I've got to make my move. *How long have you been here?* Sheila looks surprised to see me—but she doesn't look upset. Two kisses, a hug, our greetings, and *Let's have a drink.* I've got a feeling this might end up being easier than I thought.

I love dancing. Is de way I drain de frustration of de week.

Frustration—I like to hear her acknowledging the fact that

she is frustrated. *I love dancing too. It's in our nature, you know. You Caribbean, me Latino: we have so much in common, like dancing.* I say this as I smile, wink at her, and shift my feet to the rhythm of the soca.

She doesn't know how to interpret my words, she doesn't know what to do. She's sipping coyly from her daiquiri, moving very softly, almost as if she isn't dancing at all. *I don' know how Nathe does it, you know. Dragon have he drinking, I have me dancing, SamB have de sky, flying for hours no end. But Nathaniel seem to have nuttin' to help he escape.* If you are not enough for him to escape, darling, what that man needs cannot be found on this earth.

But the word *escape*, paired with the word *frustration*, tells me a lot more than she thinks. *Dragon Wings, Nathaniel,* and *escape*, all in the same sentence: looks like someone needs a chat. But it's too loud in here, and talking simply makes no sense, and Sheila likes dancing, so I grab her by her tiny waist and I pull her to an area where there's a little bit more space, and I prompt her to dance that millenary island dance, and even though I can sense the restraint in her hips as she sways them from left to right, and even though her attitude is distant, and her motions conservative, and her butt still nowhere near me, I enjoy the sense of intimacy that springs from our legs, our bodies, our sweat flowing to the same rhythm. Let's stay like this a little longer, let's just stay like this. I will move onto the next stage soon, I will take her outside, ask her a few questions, have a drink with her sitting on the sand, but for the time being let's just dance.

Friday nights at The Velvet are slow burners. The action generally smolders for hours before catching flame sometime in the small hours of Saturday morning. The crowd has begun to grow. The unsuitably slippery, white tile floor has become sticky, the red velvet wallpaper is drenched in sweat, the room

is covered in smoke. *Let's go outside.* A walk, a drink, barbecue ribs, and suddenly, *Dis week goan was so horrible. I never
t'ought t'ings could be so bad.* Sheila's still thinking of work, of
course. I guess she's been affected by the debacle of Tuesday
in a way that I haven't.

*There's nothing we can do about it now, Sheila—don't
punish yourself for it.* Her wide black eyes search mine for the
meaning of my words. I need to sound honest now, I need to
sound concerned. *All we can do is work harder in the future to
try to keep things like this from happening again.*

The black eyes go misty and I know my face is genuine
enough to convince her. *I ain' know how long I kyan keep goan
on like dis, Art. I ain' know how much longer I kyan resist.* Now,
if ever there was an appropriate moment to move closer to
your prey, this is it.

What are you talking about, Sheila? My voice comes out
soft, my left hand wraps the right side of her face, a cloud of
concern covers my expression, and I pull her caringly toward
my shoulder. *You're just stressed after a tough week, that's
all. But things will be better once we open our new routes.*
For seven spectacular seconds, Sheila rests her face on my
shoulders, her left hand on my chest, her right arm around my
back, and I can feel her heartbeat through the firm softness of
her bosom.

I hate Nathaniel. This is turning into a promising night. *I
hate he 'coz he so stubborn, he goan ruin everyt'ing else. He
insist he wan' make true dis fantasy he have, an' now all goan
to hell.* Sheila is opening up. My reaction at this point is crucial.
Too much silence, and she'll think I don't care; too little, and
she'll think I'm not listening; sympathy toward Nathe will make
me look like I'm taking his side; antagonism toward him would
expose my intentions too early.

Why do you say it like it's all finished? Is this not worth fight-

ing for? Are you not in love? Sheila's startled by my question. Have I gone too far? I might have spoiled it all.

She pushes me away slightly. We're sitting on the sand, just a fraction farther apart than we were a minute ago, but Sheila has changed her attitude: she looks stronger than just now, less helpless; her head turns slowly, hesitantly, in my direction; her eyes are no longer misty, but overflowing with determination. *No.*

She has dropped any guise of pretense. I could make my move this very moment but she might misconstrue my intentions— she might think I just want to take advantage. Be patient, Arturo. Be patient. She's mad at someone else, not you—don't let her turn you into the scapegoat of her anger. I lift her up from the sand and, *Let's go back inside.* Courting is an art, like war: move too quickly and you become overexposed, move too late and you become predictable. By the time I get you, Sheila, you'll be as desperate for me as I am for you right now. When the time comes to make my move your desire will be stronger than your anger, than your fear, than your shame. But not yet. For the time being let me just wrap my arm around you and shield you from the crowd as we walk back into The Velvet.

The room's still crowded, the dance floor's still a nightmare, and it stinks more and more. But Sheila has forgotten all about moderation, and suddenly the ritual of her dancing becomes absorbing. Sheila is not thinking anymore, and I just love to be her pole. I get aroused by her moves and the presence of my hardened member between her cheeks encourages her to continue. This is too much. Asking for composure in this situation is simply asking too much. I lose control, my hands land on her perfect body, my hips shake to the rhythm of hers, our sweat blends into one, and we continue dancing until closing time. The dance floor of The Velvet: the place where fantasies come to life.

It's time to go. Sheila's nervous. The hour is late—just before the break of dawn—and Nathe will be wondering where she is. She's worried again, but our connection on the dance floor cannot be dismissed so easily. I walk her to her car. *Sorry to spoil your day off wit' all my problems.*

Spoil. That's the word she's used: spoil. *You've made my night, She.* You've made my night and there is a lot more you—we—could do. But not tonight. We'll leave it like this tonight. I'll leave you thinking you owe me one. *Thanks for the dance.* And before she gets into the car her fleshy lips pay me back with a brief kiss. *I'm not off again until Wednesday—can I see you then?*

VI

The debacle of March lasted six full days. For one full week a constant state of emergency hovered over the premises of the Business Center, where the board of directors of Dragon Wings met to resolve the complications that emerged as a consequence of an organizational catastrophe. On the final day of the crisis, once the last lost bag had been traced in St. Kitts, flown to Antigua, entrusted to British Airways, and dispatched to its owner in England, Dragon Jones brought up the subject of expansion one more time. At this point, negotiations with the administrators of Air Tampa were far advanced and the application for further support from the Indigenous Bank of Anguilla had already been submitted to the bank. But the outlook of the general situation had changed dramatically with the list of extraordinary expenses that had resulted from a five-hour telecommunications failure, and the future looked ominous, charged with the negative publicity derived from a six-day organizational crisis, and given the circumstances, *I think we need to reconsider our position and seek viable alternatives to continue our progress in the establishment of Dragon Wings as a real force in the air carrier business in the Caribbean.*

The debacle of March planted second thoughts regarding the purchase of additional machinery in the mind of Nathaniel Jones. In fact, the debacle of March planted second thoughts regarding the adoption of an ambitious plan of expansion in the minds of most members of the board of directors. But by then Dragon

Wings's ambitious plan was well underway, and the only viable alternative was Dragon Jones's drab policy of consolidation. A fundamental change in the direction of the company could only be effected through secondment by two-thirds of the board in a vote, and at that stage Dragon was as unpopular a character as there could have been in Dragon Wings, but the magnitude of the six-day crisis meant that on the seventh day yet another extraordinary meeting was called to order, this time to reconsider the plans for the future of the organization.

The debacle of March presented Dragon Wings with a major problem and one simple solution, but on the seventh day of a crisis that lasted six, too many individual ambitions clashed, making it impossible for the board to agree on what was clearly the best decision for the airline. Nathaniel knew that the sensible thing to do was to favor the policy of consolidation proposed by Dragon Jones months earlier, but his relationship with his son had deteriorated to such lows since the day, many months back, when Dragon had told him he was not his marriage counselor, that he felt inclined to vote against it just because of who had proposed it. And Sheila Rawlingson had been drained of the last trace of enthusiasm she'd been able to muster for Dragon Wings by the application for the acquisition of Air Tampa's Short 330s, so the prospect of seeing the labor of the past two months put to waste filled her not so much with frustration or disappointment but rather with courage—courage to do exactly that: put it all to waste, not only the labor of the past two months but the rest of the time she had invested in the airline. And Glenallen Rawlingson had absolutely no interest in showing common sense, because his own personal agenda would be far better served if Dragon Wings continued its progress down the thoughtlessly rash route it had opted to follow, and *consistency is de key for success in business. We cannot convene every time we face a problem to double guess weselves an' change we plans. Samuel Bedingford was incorporated in dis airline for his expertise, judgment, an' knowledge of de market. We kyannot turn our backs away from his advice upon de first difficulty we encounter.* And SamB was never going to accept that he had been wrong all along in insisting to bid for Air Tampa's Shorts 330s, so despite the fact that the debacle of March planted serious doubts in each of the members of Dragon Wings's board of directors, the seventh day of a crisis that should have lasted only six saw little change in the direction of the fortunes of the airline.

And yet, somehow, Nathaniel Jones still looked confident, because Nathaniel Jones was aware that the meeting of the board of the Indigenous Bank of Anguilla would not take place for another week, and Nathaniel Jones was convinced that given the scope and magnitude of the debacle of March, the bank's board would be forced to reject Dragon Wings's application for operational support, and Nathaniel Jones suspected that despite Glenallen Rawlingson's connections—power—there was little he or anyone else could do presently to change the tide in favor of Dragon Wings. Indeed, Nathaniel Jones was so confident that the airline would ultimately be forced by circumstances to follow the conservative path of consolidation advocated by his son, despite his outward skepticism toward it, that he neglected the duties entailed by the implementation of an ambitious strategy of expansion over the following week and devised instead a marketing strategy aimed at redressing the damage caused by a five-hour telecommunications failure and a six-day organizational crisis.

Nathaniel Jones might have spent less time devising a marketing strategy that would never have be to deployed if he had known that, in addition to Glenallen Rawlingson, Bacchus Stewart was also contriving to ensure the success of Dragon Wings's application for operational support in order to raise the company's debt to near-fatal levels. Given the situation, the only thing Bacchus could think of that would be more damaging to the airline than allowing it to go ahead and spend as much money as it wanted

on planes was to grant a secured loan for Dragon Wings to purchase only one of the two Short 330s it was after. Thus, when the
news came that the Indigenous Bank of Anguilla had approved
the secured loan of US $400,000 for the purchase of one Short
330, it was greeted not with a daylong celebration but with a smug
snigger by SamB.

But the end of Dragon Wings was well within sight long before the approval of the acquisition of one of Air Tampa's Short
330, because even if the full extent of the consequences was not
to be discerned until Easter, it became immediately obvious that
the six-day organizational crisis suffered in the month of March
by the airline would have far-reaching repercussions.

Dragon Wings managed to limp through the month of March
and much of April at a pace comparable to that of the competition, producing decent levels of seat occupancy and performing
so consistently that at one point it almost looked as if the subsidy by
the government of Anguilla would become unnecessary. During
the month that followed the debacle of March it looked as if
Dragon Wings would hold its own, at least through the remaining
months of the high season. Except for the fact that the airline's
expenses increased weekly, and the need to assemble new teams
in prospective destinations burdened the partners, and negotiations with foreign governments consumed large chunks of time,
and the daily operation was still plagued by all sorts of delays and
inconveniences which should have been addressed long before.

Thus, by the time Anguilla was hit by the seasonal resurgence
that is Easter, Dragon Wings already faced another, entirely different crisis: financial distress. Dragon Wings entered the short
period of bonanza that in Anguilla is Easter with the imperative
task of making up the ground lost and strengthening the health
of the company's books in preparation for the long drought of
the summer. However, once the floodgates were opened for tourists to return to the Caribbean, it became evident that Dragon

Wings was not only not preferred above any other regional airline, but, in fact, a large portion of the visitors actively sought to avoid using it. The marketing strategy deployed by Nathaniel Jones to counterbalance the negative effect of the debacle of March had come too late to be effective, and, worse still, the setbacks that had hindered the operation since its insertion in the market were still there unsolved, so Dragon Wings found itself having lost all credibility, respect, sympathy, and, in the end, customers. Thus, the short period of bonanza that in Anguilla is Easter flew past Dragon Wings's record books without leaving an impression of any kind—April was gone, and the prospect of making up the ground lost vanished with it, and the Joneses simply had to learn the hard way the lesson that had made so many others feel miserable in the month of January: lost ground in the Caribbean is ground that cannot be made up. The company's financial situation was still precarious, and in front lay the barren summer months—May, June, July—before the next period of activity to which anyone could look forward: carnival in August.

Hence, when Deianira Walker broke the news to Nathaniel that Dragon Wings had been successful in its bid for Air Tampa's Short 330, his reaction was less jubilant than she expected. The actual acquisition of the aircraft meant that the efforts by the team to expand the operation had to become more urgent. It also meant more expenses, larger repayment installments to the Indigenous Bank of Anguilla, and additional costs. Nathaniel knew there was no way Dragon Wings would be able to cope with these added expenses. The time had come to declare financial distress and make use of the funds provided by the HTA.

Nathaniel Jones called for yet another extraordinary meeting of the board of directors of Dragon Wings to inform the rest of his partners of the details of the situation, making it clear from the start that *this is a matter of survival.*

This time there was no vote, just the objection of the ever-more-estranged Dragon. *We will run through that money in a matter of months. If we cannot make this business self-sufficient we might as well shut it down.*

Nathaniel's eyes lit up with anger at his son's suggestion. *We need to earn people's confidence, Dragon, and that takes time. It would help if you could run the operation smoothly at least for one week.*

Thus, the small office in the Business Center became the ring where father and son chose to vent the frustration, the rage, and the resentment that for months had eroded their relationship. Sheila Rawlingson watched in silence as the man she had once loved and the son she had grown to despise openly and viciously traded insults. SamB, on the other hand, seemed too immersed in his own world to care about anything that happened around him. Thus, Glenallen Rawlingson was the only member of the board of directors of Dragon Wings to react to Nathaniel Jones's announcement.

VII

Glenallen Rawlingson was the only member of the board of directors of Dragon Wings to react to Nathaniel Jones's announcement that the airline had reached the point of financial distress and required the liberation of the funds provided by the Hotel and Tourism Association to stay afloat. But Glenallen Rawlingson's reaction was silent and long-winded. He demanded to see the books of the company, and went through them in detail, armed with patience, diligence, and more than just a pinch of malice. After a full week of fastidious examination, Glenallen Rawlingson added determination to his malicious scheme, and contacted his lawyer, Deianira Walker. *I need to talk to you as soon as possible. No, not over de phone—dis is a very serious matter. I wan' see you personally.* Deianira Walker canceled all the appointments she had scheduled for that afternoon, and asked Glenallen Rawlingson to *pass by my office at four.*

When Deianira Walker received a call from Glenallen Rawlingson at eight a.m. on a Monday morning, she was neither surprised nor alarmed. His attitude when he called was always severe, always urgent—even if nothing, really, was wrong. But Glenallen Rawlingson was more secretive with her that Monday morning than was usual, and he had insisted on making an appointment to meet her in person, to discuss the details of a very serious matter. Deianira Walker cleared up her afternoon for his sake, was already waiting when Glenallen Rawlingson, looking stern, severe, knocked on her door at four p.m. sharp. Deianira Walker could still not guess what could be so urgent but she knew immediately it would not be long before she found out. Glenallen Rawlingson did not waste any time greeting her: he took a seat, proceeded to make his case. *A situation has developed at Dragon Wings whereby we will need to declare financial distress to stay alive.*

Deianira Walker had been the adviser to the Joneses in their negotiation with the HTA for the half-million-dollar operational subsidy, so she was perfectly aware of what Glenallen Rawlingson was talking about. *I've inspected de company's financial records. Given de evidence I find in dem, I ain' de least bit surprised we face distress.*

His eyes gleamed with intent, and for a brief moment Deianira Walker was made to feel uncomfortable in her own office. *De books show glaring irregularities, obscure payments, unaut'orized transactions. Dis cannot continue. Dis kind of behavior cannot be condoned in Anguilla.*

Deianira Walker had been involved—or so she thought—in all transactions carried out to date by Dragon Wings; she had—or so she thought—an insider's perspective on all things related to the airline; Deianira Walker was aware—or so she thought—of all the factual details that were transcribed in numerical terms on the financial records. So Deianira Walker was left to listen with both attention and surprise as Glenallen Rawlingson mentioned the words *embezzlement, corruption, misappropriation of funds.* There was no room for misunderstanding in his delivery, he gave her no alternative: by the end of their meeting, late into the night, he had made it perfectly clear that *I wan' have everyt'ing Nathaniel Jones owns, even his oldest pair a shoes.*

Deianira Walker's tidy dreads dangled loosely over her stupefied semblance long after Glenallen Rawlingson shut the door of her office on his way out. She absentmindedly browsed the folder with documents, files, photocopies he had left behind for her to inspect. She identified the threat of extinction faced by the airline she had so decidedly helped to build. She recognized deals, transactions, procedures carried out in the past, looked at them from the outside with the greedy eye of a voracious solicitor. Over the course of the next five days Deianira Walker battled herself—her scruples—in an attempt to defend the interests of one client without hampering another's. It was a battle she was bound to lose. Despite the affectionate respect she had developed for Nathaniel Jones, despite the time and energy she had invested in Dragon Wings, despite her desire to see the project succeed, she could not escape the fact that Glenallen Rawlingson was Glenallen Rawlingson. So she compiled a portfolio with the details of the case, and kept the secret of the impending threat away from Nathaniel Jones, and by the time she was summoned by Glenallen Rawlingson she had already envisioned the strategy that would best satisfy his expectations, inflicting the least harm on Nathaniel and, most importantly, procuring her peace of mind.

We have a case here, Glen, I ain' goan say no to dat. We even have a strong case. But we also have a long, painful process to win dis case we have. Dis ain' goan be decided in weeks, you know. Dis might not even be decided in mont's. Dis case you bring me here, dis case will drain us all. Glenallen Rawlingson wanted to hear a lot less about the length of the process and a lot more about the state of Nathaniel Jones's oldest pair of shoes, but Deianira Walker had expected this reaction, continued to deploy the plan she had envisioned to make Glenallen Rawlingson understand that *if de airline matters at all, den we should reach an agreement before goan to court.* But however much the airline mattered, and, indeed, it did, Glenallen Rawlingson was far from satisfied with a course of action which concentrated only on the ownership of Dragon Wings. What Glenallen Rawlingson sought, what he really craved, could be more aptly described as payback, retaliation, restitution of personal, in fact, of familial pride. The discrepancy between Deianira Walker's strategy to achieve her client's expectations to the least detriment of Nathaniel Jones's integrity, and what Glenallen Rawlingson considered to be enough humiliation to satisfy his ego, was the basis of a long negotiation between the two in an attempt to forge the terms of an arrangement which, under the circumstances, Nathaniel Jones would be crazy not to accept.

The instincts which once upon a time, at the beginning of a hectic period of activity, had guided Nathaniel Jones to the doorstep of Deianira Walker's office had provided Dragon Wings with the best lawyer for which they could possibly have hoped. Mrs. Walker's services could not just be bought—they had to be earned. But something in Nathaniel Jones's appearance had struck her as extraordinary, and she had seen even at that early stage the lucrative promise in their collaboration, so she had decided to help Mr. Jones in his project. It was a decision that would procure Deianira Walker and her law firm an immensely profitable business. Deianira Walker personally set up the legal scaffolding that held Dragon Wings together. She completed the registration of the airline at the International Air Transport Association. She negotiated with Anguilla Insurances to devise a policy which would protect the airline effectively and efficiently. She liaised with the syndicates and drafted the first contracts for pilots, supervisors, and other personnel. Deianira Walker had been forced to hire a specialist in aeronautical law and two assistants to cope with the paperwork resulting from the airline's multiple negotiations. In other words, Deianira Walker had a vested interest in the survival of Dragon Wings, an important client for her boutique business toward which she felt attachment, if not indebtedness. This attachment, this unspoken bond of trust, extended to Nathaniel Jones, the white gentleman with the pale blue eyes who once upon a time had earned her services with his agreeable approach. So Deianira Walker kept Nathaniel Jones's interests clearly present in her mind while she negotiated with Glenallen Rawlingson the terms of the arrangement she would propose to the Joneses—despite the fact that they were as yet unacquainted with the latest developments.

Deianira Walker felt the emptiness associated with the ending of a love affair on that warm May afternoon when she went to Dragon Wings's office in the Business Center. She had spoken to Nathaniel Jones on the phone earlier that day, had explained that she needed to meet him urgently to discuss a serious matter. Nathaniel Jones had expected to meet his legal adviser. Instead, he received a visit from Glenallen Rawlingson's lawyer. Deianira Walker explained the situation in detail, felt her heart shrink as she saw Mr. Jones's semblance melt to the ground.

Mrs. Walker, I'm afraid I have nothing to say—you will need to speak to my attorney.

She was disarmed by even the most obvious of possible answers. *Mr. Jones, dere ain' nuttin' your attorney can do 'bout dis.*

Nathaniel ignored her as he walked toward his desk pointing his right index finger toward the door. Deianira left the papers on the nearest desk, made her way toward the exit. Before reaching the threshold she turned around, lifted her glasses from her nose, loaded her voice with uncharacteristic familiarity. *Nathaniel, I had no alternative. I couldn't warn you: it would have been unethical. De firm still on your side, you know, but I kyan't represent you no more. I will send all de details of de case to my partner, Hubertus Warren. He will be in touch soon.* There was a pause in her speech, a moment of lingering silence. Nathaniel did not raise his eyes. *Off de record, as a friend, I guarantee you dem be de best terms you will be able to negotiate. You'd have to be a madman not to take dem, an' I know you ain' dat. Farewell, Mr. Jones. An' good luck.*

VIII

Sheila Rawlingson-Jones came home so late the Friday night that followed the debacle of March that, in fact, it already was Saturday morning. Nathaniel Jones had been kept awake by lingering preoccupations, by thoughts of gloom, by the sort of financial and entrepreneurial worries that had crowded so many of his recent nights. Insomnia was no novelty for Nathaniel. He had not stayed up waiting for Sheila—he would have been up even had she lain by his side all night—but the delay in her arrival added anger, malice, jealousy to his already-fragile frame of mind.

Sheila Rawlingson-Jones came home so late the Friday night that followed the debacle of March that, in fact, she arrived with the break of dawn. She knew Nathaniel would be awake, so she removed all trace of guilt from her demeanor before she faced him. There was no greeting, just a spiteful grunt. *Where have you been?* Nathaniel regretted his words as soon as he uttered them. He had understood long before that the dynamics of a relationship with a woman half his age required certain concessions that would not be pertinent under other circumstances. One such concession involved tolerance and allowing each other enough space to act according to their respective ages. These were things Nathaniel Jones understood rationally, and wanted to put to practice, but sometimes, almost always, it was difficult to be reasonable when you were also jealous. So Nathaniel Jones met his wife with unscrupulous scrutiny at the start of the morning after the Friday night when he had been kept up by his worries and she by Arturo Sarmiento. *Dancing* was Sheila's plain and truthful answer, her skin covered in a coat of dried sweat, her eyes bloodshot, her clothes oozing the scents of the night, the smoke, her bodily odor, and the trace of the men with whom she had danced. None of that was any different, really, to most other Friday nights—the time when Sheila religiously sought relief in an environment which Nathaniel had come to avoid at The Velvet—except for the late hour. But that key difference in the handles of the clock tore through Nathaniel's defenses and made him want to know exactly what his wife had been up to. *Dancing? Till sunrise?* The question feigned a trace of interest which miserably failed to disguise the jealousy that prompted it.

Sheila knew there was no need to lie—the easiest way out would be telling Nathaniel the truth. But the truth was precisely what Sheila did not want him to know, because she had enjoyed Art's company in a way which she had not experienced with Nathaniel for months. So Sheila made up some story, invented some farfetched plot, mentioned some people she knew she could trust. She knew as soon as she spoke her words, as soon as she devised her lie, that what she had done that night, even what Nathaniel suspected she had done that night, would hurt him considerably less than the lack of honesty in her reply. She also discovered for the first time that she did not care. The silence that followed was so laden with emotions it became unbearable. Until *I'm your husband, Sheila.* Something was supposed to follow such statement, but Nathaniel cut his own flow midsentence, as if he had suddenly been made aware of the pointlessness of his assertion. Sheila walked away, toward the bedroom, without saying a word.

Once Sheila experienced in full the tension that threatened to tear down the home she had built with Nathaniel, the burden of everyday companionship with the same (old, white) man seemed heavier than ever. The domestic battle that ensued was as cold as it was palpable. Silence reigned at home, and the double bed that lodged their distant nights had never seemed as wide as now, when each made one side of it their own, opening a rift between them where no one was safe. Viewed with the specs of time and tainted by the largest domestic crisis the couple had endured in their relationship, the good old times seemed never to have been good enough to warrant this ordeal. And certainly compared to the natural ease with which things—simple things: conversation, a drink, a dance—had flowed with Art on Friday, the situation at home seemed excessively tortuous.

Sheila had not decided whether or not to meet Arturo on Wednesday before the contempt that invaded Nathaniel's den of love made her turn away from him to look for something, anything, to bring back some joy to her life. For the first time since Nathaniel's hundred-day siege, she found herself questioning the merits of her marriage. Up to that point the isolation and the condemnation that she had always known would be sparked by their union had been shared, had been endured by the two together. But now for the first time she saw in Nathaniel not an accomplice in her crime but the source of her heartache. The problem was emphasized when she added to it the fact that Nathaniel was the only solid element left in her life, because she had sacrificed everything else for it. Sheila felt more painfully than ever the breach caused by her decision to opt for the old white man who had seduced her with his experienced devotion ahead of the friends and family who had offered her an uncertain yet promising future on the island. Sheila Rawlingson-Jones had carved a moat around Nathaniel's den of love, and now that it had become her prison she was desperate to find a way, any way, out of it.

So Sheila met Arturo Sarmiento on Wednesday night, after dinner, for a drink that did not go down in a hurry, and though there was time for a second drink, that was as far as they would take it: a pleasant conversation and a nice time. Little—nothing, really—in Arturo Sarmiento's reckoning, but the world for Sheila Rawlingson, because when she arrived to the rendezvous she was aggrieved, stressed, desperate, but she was able to vent her anger, complain about work, bicker about her marriage with Arturo, her friend, and while he could tell immediately he would not take her home that night, he still held out hope for the future. For the first time in weeks, Sheila felt at ease.

I gotta go, nuh. When you next free?

Art's expression lit up with joy. *Monday afternoon. Meet you in Shoal Bay for ice cream.*

The weather was sublime that Monday afternoon, and Sheila was happy to see Arturo Sarmiento again, and this time he did not allow the conversation to dwell on Dragon Wings, and while the sun set on the sea just off the northern tip of the island, Art and She walked toward the western end of the bay, facing the orange sun, licking their ice creams, laughing away, knotted in a friendly embrace. *Listen, nothing in my contract says I can't meet you when I'm on the rota to fly the following day. What are you doing tomorrow?* Sheila's heart skipped one beat before filling with gladness. She knew she should decline but she didn't want to. She knew she was not giving her marriage much of a chance, but she felt she had already given her marriage enough. She didn't think it then, maybe she never consciously rationalized it this way, but Sheila felt she had already given Nathaniel everything she could.

She met Art every day for the following week. This was the period of courtship, the week during which the groundwork was laid in her heart, in his, for the betrayal that would ensue. Eight days later they still had exchanged no more than a brief kiss—late on a Friday night, which, in fact, had been a Saturday morning—but they had grown so close to each other that Sheila spent her days thinking of him, while he spent his nights dreaming of her.

Sheila Rawlingson-Jones was progressively but quickly estranged from her husband, from her business, from her own life. She had already given up all interest in Dragon Wings by the time Nathaniel and Dragon exchanged insults in the Business Center during an extraordinary meeting called after the debacle of March to reconsider the airline's ambitious plan of expansion, and she found no sympathy in her heart for Dragon when he garnered absolutely no support at all from the rest of Dragon Wings's board of directors in his efforts to steer the company in the direction of consolidation. If Sheila took no part in those discussions, if she revealed no emotion when Deianira Walker soon informed the company that its bid for Air Tampa's Short 330 had been successful, it was because she simply didn't feel like she was a part of any of that, she simply didn't care anymore. So, by the time the writing could be perfectly made out on Dragon Wings's wall, by the time Nathaniel Jones called for yet another extraordinary meeting of the board of directors to announce the extent to which the airline had come to be under financial pressure, Sheila no longer felt affected, because to all practical purposes she was no longer a Jones.

Then, one Friday evening, Sheila went to The Velvet much earlier than usually, found Arturo Sarmiento looking somewhat crazed or desperate, waiting for her. He noticed her immediately, came to greet her outside the club. Before she could say a word he led her toward his car. *Come with me.* Arturo Sarmiento turned the corner, pointed his car in the direction of his house, steering with his left hand while his right carved a rudimentary path from her knee upward, dug deep between Sheila's thighs, lifted her skirt, roused her urge. He almost choked her on the short walk from his driveway to his door. Once inside he lifted her strapless top hurriedly, almost urgently, and drove her back against a corner. She tried to make some room, to push him away, to bring back normality. He pinned her right wrist against the wall while he undid his pants with his right hand. Sheila was startled by his use

of force, by what she saw was an uncharacteristic display of brut-
ishness. Her wrist began to hurt, but before she could complain
his hand was already pulling her underpants aside, reaching her
rump, firmly holding her left buttock, digging his nails into her
before lifting her from the ground. She instinctively put her leg
around him as a violent thrust let him inside. His hand squeezed
her tight, his arm pulled her down, his every impulse shoved her
lower back against the wall, sending a shiver up her spine. She felt
him pulsate inside, growing larger, sturdier. She grabbed him by
the hair, pulled his head back. He caught her left nipple between
his teeth, and as she began to ride him he voiced his relief. His
right hand joined his left as he pulled her down one final, brutal
time. Just then he felt her grip around his waist tighten, her riding
get more arduous, her long nails drawing blood on his back, her
fleshy lips searching for his lobe, her perfect teeth digging inside
his neck.

Sheila never made it back to Nathaniel's home. She spent a
miserable week living with her brother Jamaal, devising a plan to
escape the island with Arturo Sarmiento. *Is somet'ing I gotta do before
we can go.* Sheila could not leave Anguilla for good without spending some time with her beloved grandpa. So she kept her ploy
from her family, and she begged for forgiveness, and she recognized her mistakes, and she accepted her guilt, and she returned
in shame to her parents' home where she spent six days distanced
from the world, talking only to the old man she had come to bid
farewell. On the seventh day she sat in her room through most of
the night, writing a letter in which she offered some explanations;
she asked for, if not forgiveness, at least understanding, and most
importantly she expressed her undying love for the most important
man in her life: her grandfather.

It would not be long before the remaining two Joneses had to
plan their own exit from Anguilla.

IX

The Caribbean is a subtle place. Everything is tenuous, delicate, fragile in the Caribbean. In fact, the Caribbean, as such, does not even exist: there is no homogenizing trait in the Caribbean. No feature is shared by the islands between Cuba and Trinidad. Or perhaps one is: the sea. The beautiful Caribbean Sea: as large as blue, as threatening as picturesque, generous and, there as you see it, unforgiving. People in the islands live by the sea; not only do they live close to the sea, but they are also dependent on it. The sea becomes a sort of power, an almost divine power which takes and provides, perhaps not consciously, perhaps not even willingly, but which takes and provides nonetheless. By sea arrive most provisions; the sea is the major source of food; the sea is the main basis of tourism, the largest industry in the region. Unwittingly, yet irreversibly, people in the islands are all children of the sea.

I wonder what it is that Nathe has to tell me. He sounded agitated over the phone. He must be feeling the pain of Sheila's betrayal, now that he can look at it with some perspective. Fourteen days since she left. Fourteen days without Sheila Rawlingson. Mind you, she left home long before that. Sheila Rawlingson, gone with my friend. What friend? I never could reestablish my friendship with Arturo Sarmiento. Something had changed. Something has changed. I wonder if it was me or him. I wonder why she left. The most beautiful woman in the world, and she seems unable to find happiness. The most beautiful woman in the world. An absolute storm. A hurricane.

Just like the sea, hurricanes are an essential part of life in the islands. Hurricanes in the Caribbean are not a living threat; they are not just a genuine possibility of disaster. They are, rather, an imminent certainty waiting to happen. Life in the islands is shaped by, and around, hurricanes. Business plans, construction methods, memory, even life expectancy are all shaped by an instinctive acceptance of loss that is produced by periodic devastation—a devastation that Anguilla has not experienced for years. Caribbean time varies from island to island, depending on the gap between one hurricane and the next. Centuries—millennia—have no place in the islands. For this generation of Anguillans, the latest reincarnation has lasted over a decade; because with every wave of destruction comes another resurrection. For the present generation of Anguillans, events are ordered around Hurricane Luis: in the year of our Lord 5 A(fter) L(uis) the island was hit by the first prophet of the new advent: Hurricane Lenny. For members of the older generation, chronological reference revolves around Hurricane Dona; if you live a few hundred miles northwest, replace Luis with Katrina; a few hundred miles south: Hugo.

I can see Nathaniel approaching in the distance. His face cannot mask the suffering of his heart. He has two drinks in his hands—his obligatory Guinness and, presumably, my usual rum-and-Coke. His walk is determined, if fatigued. I haven't seen much of Nathaniel in months, and only now do I become aware of how much he has aged since I got here. Nathaniel called me to talk about Dragon Wings casually, informally, just a father and a son chatting the way we haven't in ages. He greets me with a smile, goes straight to the point.

We have a problem. All we have had since we started this business is problems. The only moments of joy have come from overcoming problems which have been followed by even greater problems. *I received a visit from Deianira last night. She was representing Glenallen when she showed up. They're threatening to press all sorts of charges against us.* My initial confusion is only enhanced by Nathe's expression, which shows not so much concern as resignation. *Corruption, embezzlement, personal enrichment. Mainly concerning the loan from Jones Investments.* I know that, if anything, we might have misrepresented the company's obligations to Glenallen Rawlingson before he joined. *Glenallen claims that even if the loan was legit it should have been refinanced not repaid, certainly not without consulting with the board anyway.* Nathe's voice is still serene. While I get more incensed by the second, he sips from his bottle of Guinness with thirst and delight, without allowing the slightest trace of anxiety to filter into his speech. There is some talk of administrative negligence, excessive expenditure, and I know not what more. I am shocked both by the nonsense of all these allegations and by the composure Nathaniel shows while telling me this. He brings up more charges and deals that look dubious on paper. I have lost interest, mainly because I can tell where this is going. *Glenallen is dissecting arrangements like the one with Pinturas Borinquen and deliberately stripping them from their contexts.* A shade of grief dyes Nathe's eyes with sadness. *I think they might have us by the balls this time.* He sips the last drop of beer from his bottle, slams it heavily, loudly, but not violently on the wooden table. As he makes a tiny circle in the air with his right index finger to make the waitress aware that we need another round, it occurs to me that Nathe's words don't correspond with his attitude. He should be outraged, furious, like me. Instead, he seems hurt but calm—at peace, almost. I wonder if he is thinking of Sheila. I wonder if he is thinking of failure. But before I get the chance to ask him, he starts again. *They won't press charges if we agree to withdraw from the business immediately.* His eyes land on mine, as if looking for consolation rather than relief, but I have little to give, because what confronts us is too complex, too difficult, too sad to digest. No, not so much what confronts us but what must follow. We are innocent, but that will have absolutely no bearing on the matter—no court of law in Anguilla will put our interests ahead of Glenallen Rawlingson's, and dragging out the process for any significant period of time would run the airline to the ground. So financially we stand to win nothing at all from this case. More importantly, though, the real question emerging tacitly here, the real purpose of this conversation with Nathe, I suspect, is to determine whether there is a reason, any reason, why either of us should feel an inclination to stay in this godforsaken country fighting for Dragon Wings. Is there any point in being here, now that Sheila is gone? Is there any point at all in fighting till the end for something I'm not sure we even want anymore?

Nathe's beloved game of trust and intrigue has come down to this. I guess it's safe to assume that he—that we—have lost. Maybe that's where it all went wrong with Dragon Wings—maybe we let too many people in, too many opinions, too many personal interests. And now they want to force us out, to wrest control of the company from our hands. With Sheila gone, they can probably do that even if we went to trial and we won. *Maybe it's time we got on our way back, Nathe.* I don't know how long we have sat in silence but I can tell that all the while he has been entertaining similar thoughts, because as soon as he hears me saying this his eyes glow with something other than just the reflection of the fading sun.

There is no way back, Dragon—there is only a way forward. Nothing could—hang on a minute, let me try again: nothing *should* be allowed to disturb the serenity distilled by Nathe's words. I sit, placidly drinking my rum-and-Coke, staring into the west, where the distance hides the Virgin Islands from our sight, where the glow of the setting sun blinds the eye, while the silence that follows Nathe's words creeps into the scene and settles with the ease of harmony. I think of Linda. I think of Mum. I'm going to have to buy two very big presents. I'm filled with gladness at the thought of how it'll be once I get back home—the same kind of gladness, somehow, that I associate with memories of my time in Anguilla. I would confide this to Nathe but I recognize in his acquiescing eyes, in the understated smile on his face, the same peace of mind. There's still one last drop of rum to be had from the bottom of my plastic glass. I tilt it toward me as I throw my head backward. From the corner of my eye I spy the last orange cord of the waning sun tuck itself beneath the blue surface of the ocean and—instantaneous, evanescent, like the glimpse of a bolt of lightning you have almost missed, but not quite, almost seen but not either—the green flash of the stunning afterglow. At last.

MAY 1 7 2016

NEW BOOK

CPSIA information can be obtained at www.ICGtesting.com
Printed in the USA
LVOW07s1230100316

478581LV00011B/22/P